WHEELSTOC
AND
PLOUGHSHARES

WHEELSTOCKS AND PLOUGHSHARES

by

Thomas Hudson

TABB HOUSE

First published 1988
Tabb House, 7 Church Street, Padstow, Cornwall, PL28 8BG

ISBN 0 907018 63 7

Cover design from a watercolour sketch by Cicely Roscoe

Typeset in Great Britain by Quintrell & Company Limited, Wadebridge, Cornwall.
Printed and bound in Great Britain by A. Wheaton & Company Limited, Exeter, Devon.

CHAPTER ONE

I was exhausted. The weather was warm and I was struggling with two heavy bags. The overcoat I was wearing was a good winter weight and slightly too long for me. Sooner than carry it I continued to perspire inside it under the early April sun. It was one of those unusual Aprils when suddenly the winter has gone and warm sunshine fills the countryside to strengthen the peeping primrose and bring the tender scents of a new spring to the nostrils. I put the bags down in the middle of the road, took off my warm coat and flung myself down upon the cool green grass at the side of the road. I gazed up at the cloudless blue above me and felt the earth beneath bursting with springtime excitement. Some grasses, already tall and waving, tickled my face and busy insects tried to continue their tasks in spite of my sudden interruption. I could not help feeling glad. Every single thing seemed fresh and eager. I immediately forgot my exhaustion and without my coat I felt light and cool again. True, my arms still ached from the weight of the bags but I forgot that too, as I sat up to look around.

Nothing had come along that road since I set out along it from Remsditch. It was two and a half miles to Nether Oldston, I had been told. 'Seems more like twenty-two!' I thought. I pulled from my pocket the big watch that my father had given me the day before, when he told me it had belonged to my grandfather. It was one o'clock. I lay back in the grass and wondered what the future held. I was nearly thirty miles from home and this was the day that a certain Mr Hardwick had decided I could start as an apprentice with him, so here I was struggling towards his workshop at Nether Oldston. At sixteen I was already old to begin to train as a wheelwright but everyone including myself, until recently, had thought I would be a farmer, like my father and three brothers.

I liked farming and certainly when I left school to work on the farm full-time I was quite happy. However, after a year or two it became obvious that the farm could not provide us all with a living so I, being the youngest, began looking for something else. I had often spent time, after school and after work on the farm, in the company of Jimmy Townsend whose father was a wheelwright. Many hours I had passed, watching the men working on waggons and carts. Often I would hold something or give a general hand with odd jobs, sometimes drifting into the smithy next door to watch the sparks flying and the burning wood when an iron tyre was dropped into place on a wheel; then the hissing and steam clouds enveloping everyone when water was poured over it to shrink it tight onto the wood. I remembered, as I lay in the grass, how I had thought the wheel was breaking the first time I heard that creaking and cracking as the iron ring contracted violently round it, pulling tight every spoke and fellow on to the nave. Those hours had led to this, and now here I was setting out to learn the trade from a similar craftsman nearly thirty miles away.

I thought of home and how I had left that morning after breakfast. My thoughts were therefore far away when suddenly I was aware of a horse approaching along the road, and I heard a girl's voice.

"Quiet boy, steady! What silly fool has left these things here in the middle of the road? Come on boy, come on!"

I sat up abruptly to see a young woman trying to lead a chestnut cob past my cases. At the sight of me shooting up from the grass the horse reared, lifting the girl off the road. She hung on, and managed to hold him, his head high and his eyes rolling with terror, while I crouched in the grass looking, no doubt, like a white faced demon to the unhappy creature, who would have shot away if the girl had not hung on tightly.

"What on earth are you doing?" she screamed at me. "Stand up and let him see you!"

"I'm so sorry!" I gasped. "I was just having a rest."

"What a stupid place to leave your bags!" she answered angrily. "Who in their right mind would leave anything in the middle of the highway like that and then hide in the grass?"

"I just put them down without thinking," I mumbled weakly.

"If you don't know what you are doing then you certainly ought to be certified insane!" she retorted.

"Can I help you remount?" I asked awkwardly.

"Where have you been, bright boy?" she asked sarcastically. "Would you like to sit on him at the moment?" I could still see the whites of the cob's eyes and he twisted away from me as I approached him.

"Move those bags away and hide yourself somewhere while I try to calm him down," she ordered crossly. I dragged the offending bags and coat to the opposite side of the road and obediently sat in the ditch.

"Good boy, there won't be any more horrid clowns leaping out at us!" I waited until she had disappeared before I crawled out of the ditch to sit on my cases.

'A good beginning!' I thought, and hoped she did not live in Nether Oldston. I put my coat on again and continued on my way. The loud crunching of my boots on the road in the quiet of the countryside made some lambs on the other side of a hedge run bleating to their mothers, who bleated in turn, looking as startled as their lambs. I trudged on, wondering what Mr Hardwick would be like and thinking that unless it was much further, I must surely meet him soon.

Presently I nooticed that a waggon had stopped a little further along the road and I could see a man on top of its load of wooden stakes. The man ignored me while he adjusted the load, which had slipped to one side. He threw one or two stakes onto the grass verge, and when I drew level I saw that he was breathing heavily as he pulled at the topmost ones, trying to heave them across the waggon.

"Can I help?" I called. The carter seemed not to hear and went on panting and straining at the stakes. I crossed the road and looked up at him enquiringly.

"What do you want?" he asked.

"Can I help?"

"No. I can manage."

"Let me pass these up to you."

"I can manage. I've nearly done." The man went on moving the top stakes as I stood watching. After a few more minutes he stopped, asking again, "What do you want?"

"Nothing," I replied.

"Get along with you then!"

I could see he was ready for the stakes on the ground so I lifted one and handed it to him.

"I said get along with you!"

"I'll just hand these up to you," I said, and the man,

disgruntled, took it without a word and laid it on top of the load. The stakes were rounded in section and as he continued to build them higher it became more difficult for him to remain standing on top of them. I took off my coat once more and put it on the cases. As I handed up the next stake the man had to lean down to reach it and in so doing he slipped slightly. As he grabbed at the stakes to save himself he dislodged another one, causing seven or eight more to roll over and crash onto him, knocking him sideways and trapping one of his legs. He hung precariously over the side of the load, cursing loudly. I climbed up quickly, calling to him to hold on. I heaved at the top stakes and threw them back onto the grass below. There was a danger of more rolling across to the place where the man's leg was held but eventually I managed to remove enough of them to free him. As I pulled the stakes away I noticed a heavy wooden case under them and thought that that, no doubt, was the reason for the load not having settled properly. I did not allude to it as the man lowered himself to the ground and stood rubbing his bruised and grazed leg.

"If you hadn't interfered that wouldn't have happened!" he shouted angrily as I jumped down to see if he was all right.

"I'm sorry. Is your leg damaged?"

"'Course it's damaged! Look at it!" he shouted, rolling up his torn trouser leg to expose the grazed area. "You get off with you now. You've done enough damage. I'll be all right in a minute and I'll manage myself!"

I stood looking at him. "Let me load it for you while you have a rest for minute."

"What, you?" said the carter, "You're only a boy!" then as I moved towards the load, "Keep off that load! I'll do it meself!"

I shrugged my shoulders. The man stood looking up at the waggon, then said suddenly "All right, I'll get back up there and you hand them up to me, then."

This time the load was put right and at last the ropes were drawn tightly round it. The man climbed up on the front saying "I'll bid you good-day"; then calling to his horses he drove off in the direction of Remsditch.

I watched the waggon disappearing and, although through my exertion I was feeling even warmer, I replaced my coat before trudging on with my cases towards the village.

I passed a turning signposted to Lonestock and then round the next bend the village of Nether Oldston came into view. I could see the church tower and a cluster of houses. A farmhouse lay to the left of the road and geese were cackling in a nearby orchard, making me think of my mother who would be feeding the geese at home. Just then, as I approached an open gateway to the right, a herd of cows began walking leisurely onto the road, turning towards the village. I put down the cases and waited until they had all left the field, nodding to the man who followed them and who had been shouting at them to "Git on!" as each one hesitated to pass me. The man nodded back and would have walked on behind the cows without further talk had I not strode after him and asked him if Mr Hardwick's premises would be hard to find.

"This road'll take yer past it," he said, poking with his stick at a cow that had stopped to snatch a mouthful of grass from the roadside.

"Warm today," I commented, unable to think of anything else to say.

"Ah, 'tis fer them a wearin' overcoats," replied the cowman. That concluded our conversation and we continued along behind the cows with the man tapping his stick on the road and calling "Git on," at regular intervals until they turned into a farm lane leaving me to continue into the village alone.

The pathway widened on one side. I passed a blacksmith's and recognised the familiar tang of burning hoof coming from its darkened doorway; then immediately next to it, above a wooden building with large open doors, I read the painted sign, 'A. Hardwick, Wheelwright, Carpenter and Undertaker'. The first thought that struck me was how very quiet it was. I stepped through the doorway and as I thankfully put down the cases, I blinked hard to adjust my eyes to the gloom inside after the bright sunlight.

"E'll be back in a minute," said a voice from somewhere in the far recesses of the interior. I looked in the direction it came from, where I could just make out two figures, one, bending over a bench, obviously intent on something, the other holding a frame of some kind. They said nothing more to me, but went on with their work, one doing some intricate 'working out', the other giving his opinion in a low voice while holding the frame at various angles to the job on the bench. As they continued to murmur inaudibly to each other I took off my overcoat and sat on the cases to await the return of whoever would be 'back in a minute'.

The workshop floor was strewn with shavings, and five benches stood at the end where the two men were. Tools lay upon each bench with various pieces of timber. Large, strong-looking wooden vices were fixed to some benches and a long delicately curved piece of timber was held in one of them. The doors where I had entered were at about the centre of the front wall. Looking to the other end of the shop, I could see a large farm waggon with its back axle propped up on a heavy trestle. Nearer to me stood a cart. The whole workshop seemed crowded with pieces of timber, shavings, benches, and parts of waggons. Here and there, as if filling a tiny wall space, stood a cart wheel. One was obviously new, with no paint on it yet. Between the benches and various racks holding timber, cramps and jigs, were cupboards and toolboxes. Everywhere was the comfortable smell of a woodworking shop which such substances as freshly-sawn timber, turpentine, putty, shellac, methylated spirit, resin, linseed oil, and hot scotch glue had combined to produce.

After a few minutes of taking in the situation I stood up and walked across to a small stable-type door at the back of the shop. As only the bottom half was closed, I could see out into a small yard.

"Gettin' a few bullocks back in. 'E won't be long now," came the same voice from where the men were and I nodded towards them.

The yard outside contained buildings and a few brown leghorn hens strutting about uttering the contented crooning and clucking they make when undisturbed on a warm sunny afternoon. From a window in the far corner of the shop beyond the wheel-less waggon, I looked out onto a field, rather muddy, but becoming quite green as it sloped away down to some ash trees. A willow grew in the corner bordering a stream that ran along the bottom. I was just in time to see a middle-aged cart-horse trotting with interest towards a gate by the road where she stopped, with ears forward, observing what I could just make out to be a bullock going past at some speed. This was followed by another bullock; then suddenly the clatter of hooves sounded very loud and close, as the beasts came noisily and clumsily through the open doors and into the workshop. As I turned from the window in amazement they skidded to a halt, breathing heavily. They were obviously frightened, and panicked to get out again. The two men from the other end of the shop moved quickly to turn them back and I did the same but one sliding, skidding creature sent my cases flying. My overcoat attached itself to a hoof for a minute when the terrified creature turned and scoured all over it.

A heavy wheel and some planks crashed to the ground as the bullocks rushed out to join a number of other steers that were now coming along the road. The two men in the shop went out to help turn the creatures back down the village as other men came puffing and running behind them. I tried to scrape the warm muck off my coat with a piece of wood and again stood my cases together. I was picking up the things that had fallen when a young man came into the workshop. He told me his name was Sammy Blofield. Mr Hardwick had sent him to take me to my lodgings.

"What's bin a goin' on?" he asked, looking round in surprise. I told him about the cattle coming in and he laughed.

"Hey, look at your coat!" he said, noticing the yellow-green stains where I had scraped away the cow muck. I looked at it ruefully as he held it up.

"Tell the gaffer!" he said. "'Tis 'is fault! You tell 'im, a very good coat ruined by them cattle of 'is." I said nothing. "Come on then. You be young Staughton bain't yer?"

"Yes," I said.

"Come on then, you can carry the coat and I'll take one of the bags. Mrs Pickvance's, that's where you be goin' to stay. Better not let 'er see that coat with cowshit on it. She won't 'ave that in 'er 'ouse!"

We set off along the village past the church on the left.

"What d'yer want a come 'ere for?" asked Sammy.

"I've come to learn the trade," I replied.

"Ah, maybe. And no doubt you will in time. 'E's a good man at the trade but 'e is a bit of a sod at times. I was 'prenticed to 'im 'til last year, but now I'm a workin' there. You'll 'ave t'do all the odd jobs and look after the cattle and everything else y'can think of. Still, you'll git used to it, like I did, I suppose."

"How many men are there?" I asked.

"Seven, including me, besides the guvnor. All old 'uns except me. I'm glad to see another young 'un. Fed up I gets some days with 'em all."

We passed one or two village shops in between houses and at last reached the green where Mrs Pickvance lived at Number Three. Sammy banged hard on the knocker and the door opened before the noise had died away.

"Now, young Sammy, that's enough of that banging. Always were a noisy beggar. Is this Abraham Staughton then?" Mrs Pickvance stood glowering at Sammy and then looked at me.

"Good afternoon, ma'am," I said.

"Come in, young man. You wait here in the kitchen, Sammy, while I show him his room," she said, in a discouraging voice, leading the way up a narrow straight staircase with a thin carpet on it.

It was when Mrs Pickvance was half way up the stairs that I met Eva, her dog, who seemed to appear from nowhere, but in fact had been let in from the garden by Sammy. She shot up the stairs, squeezing past me and my cases, knocking Mrs Pickvance sideways and nearly backwards on top of me. I let go of one case to save her and it slid and bumped to the bottom of the stairs. Sammy came out of the kitchen to see what had happened, trying to hide a grin while Mrs Pickvance shouted at Eva "Go down at once!"

Eva stood at the top of the stairs, barking with excitement and wagging her tail furiously. I went back for my case and Sammy disappeared into the kitchen again before Mrs Pickvance could enquire how Eva had got in from the garden. Somewhat flustered, the lady continued to the top of the stairs and stood ordering Eva down into the kitchen.

By the time I reached the top with the two cases, Eva had not moved. She had stopped barking and sat with a grin on her face, wagging her tail steadily just as if no one was shouting very close to her ear to "Go down at once!" Seeing no notice was being taken of her commandment, Mrs Pickvance gathered the dog in her arms.

"Wait here young man!" she ordered as she marched downstairs. I could hear her admonishing Sammy in the kitchen before shutting the door firmly on Eva and joining me at the top of the stairs again.

She led the way into a pleasant bedroom with a high brass bedstead. There was also a washstand, a chest of drawers and a small wardrobe. Beside the bed stood a small cupboard which Mrs Pickvance opened to reveal a chamber pot.

"Only for emergencies!" she said firmly. "The privy is in the garden. Nice straight path to it. I want the room kept tidy and no dirty boots in it. You can wash in the sink downstairs. I shall want water carrying in from the pump each morning. I'll have a meal ready for you this evening when you comes in."

After she had finished saying this she looked hard at me and softened her voice slightly. "You look tired, lad. It's them big cases. How far have you carried them?"

"From Remsditch," I said.

"I'll make a pot of tea," she decided, and set off to the kitchen again.

I looked round at the room that was to be my base. It was clean, and the bed had white starched sheets and a patchwork quilt. I walked across to the window and looked out over a field to a farmhouse. My window was in the end wall of a row of three houses. If I looked to the left I could see the road winding round the green to where a pub called the Barley Mow stood.

I turned and went downstairs, to a great welcome from Eva. Mrs Pickvance poured out tea for Sammy and me, and we sat at the scrubbed pine table sipping the scalding liquid. Suddenly I noticed the smell from my overcoat which was folded to conceal the stains, and hung over a chair near enough the fire to be getting quite warm. Sammy's eyes met mine. I could see Mrs Pickvance looking questioningly around. She pulled Eva to her and sniffed hard.

"There's a strange smell coming from somewhere!" she suddenly said, walking round Sammy and then round me, sniffing hard all the time. "It's that coat!" she announced triumphantly, seizing the garment and unfolding it.

"Mercy me!" she said, "Mercy me indeed!" Sammy kept his eyes glued to his teacup. I began to try to explain.

"Take it out to the scullery," she said, holding it at arm's length. "It cannot come in here! Fancy bringing it in like that! Disgusting!" I took the coat and put it in the scullery.

Sammy and I finished our tea and left again for the workshop. Sammy was silent until we were out of earshot but when at last we were, just past the village store, he sank onto the grass and shook with uncontrollable laughter. I regarded him for some moments, then leaning against the shop wall I joined in with him.

"Did you see her face when she unfolded it?" he at last managed to ask. We eventually pulled ourselves together and continued back to Hardwick's shop where normal working was in progress.

Mr Hardwick introduced himself, and led me through the shop to his small office. As I passed I was conscious of the men watching me with interest, and although they did not seem to stop working, I knew their eyes were following me until I had disappeared into the office.

"Sit yourself down, lad," said Mr Hardwick, dropping himself into a large dusty double-bow Windsor chair behind a desk completely hidden by papers, with one or two chisels and pencils sticking out from the heap and some string with a long, slightly twisted bar of black iron on top.

He looked hard at me for a few minutes during which time I thought to myself how very different he was from how I had pictured him. Much smaller he was, and altogether more intense. He had very piercing blue eyes with exactly the same nose that I had seen before, strangely enough, on a carpenter and joiner at home. He wore a rather battered and very dusty trilby hat, which he now removed. Then, after slapping it against his knee and sending up a cloud of dust which caused him to sneeze and blow his nose loudly, he placed the hat carefully on the heap on top of his desk.

"Now then young Staughton; Abraham is it not? You will soon find your way around here. The men are mostly helpful. I'll put you with Jes in a little while; he'll see you're all right. Have you done much with wood?"

Having sat down, I realised how tired I was. The day had already been a long one, with its early start from home, seemingly in another world. I could have dozed off there and then, but I struggled to answer Mr Hardwick's question. "Er, not a lot Sir, although I've often done repairs on the farm at home and I did a little work on the waggons there."

"Your father has assured me you have a bent for it, and I'm taking you on relying on this, because you'll need it here on this work. We only produce the best here. I've a good reputation. Unless I was sure you had a bent for it and that you were inclined to work hard, I would not have agreed to set you on here. I warn you, unless I'm satisfied at the end of the month, there'll be no articles signed and off you'll have to go."

"I've always enjoyed working with wood, Sir," I said, anxiously visualizing the scene at the end of the month, unless he was assured of my interest. "I've collected a few tools and brought them with me."

"Good," he said, "you'll need them in time. You'll have to help with a the general livestock, of course. Your father will have told you that I keep a bit of stock I expect. But come and let us find you an apron; then you can get started with Jes." His hat slid from the pile of papers to the floor on my side of the desk. He began rummaging into the papers which in turn started sliding off on all sides. I picked up the hat and handed it to him.

"Ah good!" he said. "Keep your eyes open and remember everything you see. That's the way to learn a trade. You'll find later on when you've got some skill, the things you've seen before will come back to you and surprise you." He put the hat back on his head and led the way to the workshop. As I followed him between the benches the men watched carefully. As I met the eyes of each one they mostly nodded, some looking away quickly to peer intently at their work.

Pointing to a bench Mr Hardwick said "You can start here, lad. There's a new apron in the cupboard. This is Jes," he went on, nodding towards the man on the next bench. "He'll put you right for a bit. You'll need to borrow a few tools from me for a start, until you get your own."

Jes was a thickset man with dark hair and bristling long grey brows. His drooping moustache was the same grey. His eyes were friendly and a half smile appeared as I held out my hand to him.

"Jes has started off more than one lad before you. He knows a thing or two about wood, does Jes," went on Mr Hardwick, while Jes in a self-conscious way brushed some shavings off his bench with his hand.

"Be here just before six in the morning and I'll show you the stock-feeding," said Mr Hardwick; then leaving me standing feeling quite useless by Jes's bench, he went off round the end of the wheel-less waggon.

Jes waited until my eyes returned to him, then nodded towards some pieces of timber stacked along the wall near the bench that I was to use. "Winder frames, that's what these be. You needs ter be able ter plane straight if you are goin' ter be much good," he said, as though talking to himself, for he was now looking at what he was doing and seemed oblivious to whether I was listening to what he was saying.

He took up his long heavy beech trying plane and pushed it effortlessly along the timber that lay on top of the bench. As the clean, curled shaving shot from the plane's mouth with a low whistle and dropped down on to the pile below, he said "Ask the guvnor fer a jack plane and a square. I've got a bit o' pencil as you can 'ave".

I went over to the cupboard and found myself an apron. It was new and stiff as a board with starch. I could hardly unfold it, and when at last I managed to get it on it stuck out awkwardly. It was difficult to walk in it without drawing attention to myself, so when I began to move in it the man nearest to me stroked his chin and keeping a very straight face said "Very smart."

I walked stiffly round the waggon to ask about the tools. Mr Hardwick found me a plane and square.

"Keep them for now lad, until you get your own," he said. "Use the box under your bench until you've made one for yourself."

On my return Jes took the plane and struck one smart hammer blow on the top of it, causing the cutting iron and wedge that held it in to jump out. He sharpened it on his oilstone and then set it with a few taps from the hammer, checking it by squinting along the plane's sole.

"Watch me," he said, and proceeded to send a steady stream of shavings to join the heap on the floor. "Try yerself now," he said, handing me the jack plane.

I had used a plane before at home and knew to some extent

what was required, but I realized that after Jes's polished performance I was going to appear somewhat lacking. I was ready to make an excuse before even starting, but Jes had returned to his own place and was now continuing his work.

"Take it steady and try it fer flat!" he called without looking up. "Keep a-goin'!"

I kept 'a-goin''. The late afternoon sun had warmed the workshop roof and I felt the trickle of sweat on my back as I struggled to make my irregular shavings from the white, clean pine. How strongly it smelt as each push of the plane opened a fresh layer of its scented resin! Out of the corner of my eye I could see Jes still steadily planing and squaring his work. He would take a sawn piece from the pile, look at it, put it on the bench against the stop and place the plane on one end. After that, just a little push sent it sliding to the other end, producing another long shaving. After about four such strokes he marked the surface with a quick pencil line. This indicated the 'face side'. The wood was then turned and another side, adjacent to the first, was prepared in the same way and also marked. I noticed how occasionally Jes would rub a piece of candle-wax on the sole of his plane and I asked him if I might use it. He produced a similar piece from the pocket of his long apron and I rubbed it under my plane. When I tried it again I almost lost my balance, as the waxed tool slid with amazing ease across the wood. I can remember clearly, even now, all these years afterwards, how excited I felt that day in this simple discovery, and although it did not solve anything with regard to planing true, it certainly made my planing more enjoyable.

When the church clock struck six Jes and the other men put their tools away into boxes, swept the benches down, and then collected their jackets and sandwich tins. While I was clearing my bench Jes told me where to find a broom and showed me where the shavings went into a sack in the corner. The men called goodnight to the guvnor and the workshop was left empty and quiet, except for Mr Hardwick who was still working on his bench at the far end, and the occasional tap of my broom on the leg of a bench as I swept round the shop.

When the shavings were all in the sack Mr Hardwick put on his jacket, collected a bag from his office and said "We had better be off for tea; I'll just get some eggs."

He disappeared through the back door and I waited, leaning against one of the benches. The main doors at the front had been closed by one of the men and an orange sun streamed in through the back windows and across the quiet benches. The workshop roof creaked occasionally from the warmth earlier in the day and dust settled slowly over everything. A blackbird sang contentedly from the yard at the back and the brown leghorns continued their crooning and clucking, later than usual, in the April evening sunshine. I could hear, not far away, the mournful lowing of a heifer calling for her calf.

I walked with Mr Hardwick along the village as far as his house, passing some early blossom on trees in a cottage garden. We saw the heifer, who was looking over a gate and gave an extra bellow of disappointment at the sight of us instead of her departed calf. Mr Hardwick reminded me of the time for the morning and I continued towards Number Three, The Green, and Mrs Pickvance.

CHAPTER TWO

Mrs Pickvance was, as I can see when I look back, one of my greatest blessings. She was a treasure whom in those days I did not value greatly, which of course was not unusual for the age I was then, when one is far more aware of the reins and whip than the fodder and stable.

Eva welcomed me on that first evening as though I had always lived there and as if her greatest friend had returned at last. I managed to get past her and into the kitchen where Mrs Pickvance had prepared a hot stew and set it ready on the table.

"Get down, Eva!" she shouted, every time she turned round to find Eva with her front paws on my lap.

The stew was good. When Mrs Pickvance sat down Eva gave up and lay down in her basket watching us both.

"I've cleaned up your coat," Mrs Pickvance announced suddenly.

"Oh, er, thank you very much," I said, "I did not mean you to do it."

"I should think not indeed!" Her voice was sharp. "And don't bring anything like that here again. I know the sort of mess there would be if you had cleaned it in my house so I decided to do it rather than suffer that!" she said fiercely.

"Tuesdays, Thursdays and Fridays I help up at 'the house'," she announced next as she filled up my second cup of tea. "I'll give you a key in case you want to get in, and Wednesday I go to Remsditch. See you don't let Eva out if you comes in."

She asked me about home, and told me how she had become a widow three years ago. "Now you'd better get your things sorted out in your room," she said, and showed me where the kindling wood was kept for boiling the kettle in the morning when I got up. "Let Eva out in the garden to do her business then call her back in before you go. Jes will give you a few bits of kindling for tomorrow night. Ask him if he forgets."

I went upstairs and stood looking out of the open window across the green to the Barley Mow. The spring day was at its close and the light had almost gone. Birds were twittering in a nearby fruit-tree. In the evening air was the promise of summer. Sounds came clearly to me from the waiting village. Someone was feeding pigs in a nearby barn and I could hear the clank of buckets and the impatient grunt of the pigs with an occasional loud squeal as the feeding pail being lowered to the trough caught an over-anxious snout with a rough push. I was tired. It had been a long day.

The smoke from a neighbour's bonfire drifted thinly across to the window and somewhere a woman's voice was calling "Jimmy!" I fixed the window and sat on the bed. I would need to be up at five fifteen. I did not mind that as I was used to it at home. My father had expected me or one of my brothers to have the cows in ready for milking by six. I thought back to home where I had been only that same morning. I thought of how I had left on the carrier's cart. My mother had wept and my father and brothers had held their faces unusually rigid as they had wrung my hand before I climbed aboard.

"God bless you, lad!" my father had called, as the cart wheels started to turn and clatter with the horses' hooves.

I looked across at the packet of sandwiches which I had taken from my pocket and placed on the chest of drawers. I had been unable to eat them on my way because I kept remembering how my mother had hugged me and how I had needed to keep blowing my nose. I'd watched all my family waving as the cart turned the first corner, and now as I lay back on the strange bed, a great impulse to go home swept over me, and a lump came to my throat. In the gathering darkness, before I had been away for one night, I felt utterly homesick. The lonely heifer called again to her missing calf, and I fell asleep, fully clothed.

When I awoke it was dark. I wondered where I was and for a moment the faint outline of the window shape puzzled me. I suddenly remembered, groped about in the dark, undressed, climbed into bed and again fell asleep.

The next morning I reached the workshop a few minutes before Mr Hardwick arrived. I could hear noises in the blacksmith's shop next door, and then Mr Hardwick went round the back to grope inside before opening the big front doors to let in the early morning light.

"You'll find corn in the bin in the corner shed. Give the hens five handfuls and fill their water up." I went into the yard at the back and let the hens out. I threw down the corn for them and then, while they pecked at it, opened the gate leading into the field. It was now light enough to be able to see quite clearly and I found a heavy mare waiting outside.

"The hay is in the corner shed. Give her a good armful," came the voice of Mr Hardwick. I fed the mare and spoke quietly to her. She pulled at the hay through the bars of the hayrack as I patted her neck. Mr Hardwick came out to show me where the pump was in the yard, telling me to leave always a little water in the bucker for priming it next time as the pump was worn and unless water was poured into the top of it before pumping, it failed to work. I learned where the nest-boxes were and we collected the eggs.

At six thirty the men arrived and there was an exchange of "Mornin'"s accompanied by nods of the head in different directions. Within two minutes of arriving aprons were on and the sounds of wood being worked filled the poorly-lit workshop. A man called Horace was slower-moving than the others and had to stop for a fit of harsh coughing every few minutes until he had settled down.

Mr Hardwick was in his office so I asked Jes if I should carry on planing.

"That's it lad, there's plenty of 'em to do, but just dust over the winders afore you starts so we can see. The duster is down there in the corner." I dusted the previous day's dust off the windows to enable every little bit of available light to enter. Then I continued my labours, working at the same bench as the day before.

The morning passed with much planing. We stopped at nine thirty for a few minutes while the men brought out bread and cheese and took swigs of cold tea from bottles.

During the next months I learned to put a keen edge on the plane iron and how to judge accurately to a point where inaccuracy was no longer a constant fear. In fact, by the end of the first day, the plane seemed to go along almost on its own. I remarked on this to Jes who just smiled and nodded as he rubbed a little more wax under his own plane.

At twelve thirty I was shown how to put the big iron kettle on the fire which burnt in a brick hearth at the end of the shop. It was my job to make tea and pour it into the enamel mugs ready for one o'clock, when we stopped for three quarters of an hour. I then joined the four men at my end of the shop where there was an old bench seat. We all sat along it, opening food tins and washing the dry contents down with the tea. There was not much talk between the men except to discuss weather, crops, or village gossip.

On that first morning, while I sat with them, Sammy leaned across to me and asked "What do yer think to it then, boy?" and I, assuming him to mean the work or the shop, answered:

"All right."

"Can 'e plane straight yet, Jes?" he asked, and Jes, whose mouth was crammed with bread, nodded and went on eating.

"There's all them wheelstocks ter be fetched and stacked this week ain't there, Jes? When's he a'gettin' em?" Sammy went on.

"Termorrer," answered Jes, between swallowing one large mouthful and starting another of similar size.

"I dunno as how he'll git them winders done to time if I goes. Mebbe he'll send the boy." Sammy looked at me. "Can you drive 'orse and cart, boy?"

"Yes," I said, "I've done plenty of that at home."

Jes took another gulp of tea and said "What did yer say yer name was? Abraham is it?" Then, as if he had given the matter much thought, "Well, we better call yer Abey then as it don't take so long and you ain't old enough to be called Abe." After this decision, having finished eating, the four men leaned back against the wall, closed their eyes and appeared to doze.

I stood up and wandered quietly to the other end of the shop where the rest of the men were having their dinner. There were four men who worked as wheelwrights, making and repairing waggons and carts. Sometimes the carpenters from the other end were called upon to help work on such things as cart raves or floor boarding during busy times, but mostly they kept to their separate work. Two of them, George Groom, brother of Albert, who worked down near my bench, and Ben Steel, sat on trestles leaning against the wall, eating their refreshment. The other two, Ben James and Harry Teemer, went home for dinner. George and Ben were talking in low voices and nodded to me as I walked round the big waggon. Conversation seemed impossible so I wandered out to the yard behind the workshop and leant on the gate to the back field, where I watched the mare grazing down in the bottom corner.

It was another glorious spring day and the sun was warm. Blue sky stretched for miles and the blackbird sang from the workshop roof as though it had never before seen such a day. Primroses were growing along the back of the barn near a heap of stones and every blade of grass was swelling and trying to be taller then the next one. After a few moments I went out into the field and strolled down to the stream. It ran clear and sparkling over stones while the bright sunlight split into spectrum colours through the moving water. As I stood looking, my thoughts wandered, and I began to wonder what my brothers were doing. It seemed unbelievable that only yesterday morning I had been with them. I felt as though I had stepped into another world where no one would ever know me. These thoughts were suddenly interrupted by a feeling that someone was behind me, and on turning I found the mare standing close, twitching her nostrils apprehensively, curiosity and perhaps the hope of a titbit overcoming her caution. I spoke quietly to her and then after a few minutes of rubbing her nose, walked back towards the workshop. Horace was looking over the gate when I reached it and stood back to let me through. He grunted and nodded almost imperceptibly. I felt unable to say anything to him and he settled back on the gate drawing hard on his pipe, which seemed to have gone out.

During the afternoon Jes and I finished the preliminary planing and after gauging and more planing the timber was brought to width and thickness. Mr Hardwick discussed window sizes with Jes and moulding planes were brought out and used by Jes while I finished off the thicknessing and cleared up round him. I watched with interest as Jes used the various plane shapes to produce the right mouldings for the frames. Occasionally when a cutting iron needed touching up the old man would rub the edges with small and differently shaped pieces of stone, which he kept rolled up in a piece of rag in a tin marked 'Player's Navy Cut'. Sometimes he used oil on the stone and sometimes spittle.

After setting out lengths, mortices and tenons were marked with a rosewood mortice gauge and then the shoulder lines were knifed. While Jes sawed the tenons I started chopping out the first mortices, after being shown how to hold and use the heavy mortice chisel in one hand and the beechwood mallet in the other. Jes finished the tenons and chopped out four mortices perfectly while I laboured with aching wrists to produce one, sometimes a questionable one. However, towards the end of the week when I was beginning to doubt the wisdom of taking to such a trade, Mr Hardwick mentioned the trip with the cart to collect the wheelstocks, or hubs as they were sometimes known.

"It's about five miles," he said. "Man called Hawtin. You'll manage the mare all right. You've done plenty of that at home, and I can't spare time tomorrow nor any of the men. She's a quiet old girl. You had best get off first thing in the morning as soon as you have finished feeding the stock."

The next morning, as soon as the bright spring sunshine streaked long across the frosty grass, I led the mare, whose name I discovered was Magnolia, to the stable door and harnessed her. The supple leather of the harness, black with age and saddle soap, wrapped and fitted firmly round the great mare, and the buckles and pins shone and jingled in the sun. She champed on the cold bit as her tongue worked hard to warm it.

Mr Hardwick came out to give me directions for finding the yard where I was to collect the stocks. He added that I was to stack them carefully and not too high. "Take some rope with you, lad; there'll be plenty in the harness room," he told me.

I backed Magnolia into the shafts and made ready. The long reins I hooked back to lead her to the road gate. Outside, I caught up the reins and after climbing up behind her, gave them a twitch. A snort from Magnolia and we were off, the empty cart moving noisily down the road from the village sending an occasional stone flying from the iron-bound wheels.

I drew deep breaths of the early spring morning. The air was crisp. The clopping of hooves and rumble of wheels warned creatures ahead in burrows and fields and ditches of our approach. From my high position on the footboard I could see Magnolia's powerful shoulders rippling, her strong greying mane flowing out behind her arched neck. She gave a snort and blew down her nostrils from time to time, either to dissuade a flying insect or perhaps to savour the fine country air.

We passed a man driving a sow along with a stick. I had noticed most of the pigs in the village were of the Large Black variety, whereas back home the Sandy Oxfordshire type was more popular. Magnolia eyed the sow warily and I spoke quietly to her until we had passed it and her blinkers shielded her from the sight of the creature. Horses are sometimes nervous of pigs. As we continued I whistled and spoke to Magnolia whose ears were never still as they pricked first in one direction and then in another, to catch every sound above the noisy cartwheels. We turned off from the road that led to Remsditch and passed through a hamlet where a woman was leading a cow with a halter and carrying a bucket of milk. Further along a tramp was boiling an egg on a smoky wood fire. He nodded as we passed. We continued more slowly up quite a steep hill and after about five miles entered Lonestock.

The yard was easy to find and we turned into it.

"Mornin'!" shouted a man from beneath a hovel. He was shovelling old, damp sawdust into sacks. "The gaffer be at breakfast."

I climbed down and dropped the reins. Magnolia relaxed, blowing down her nose and resting one leg. "How long will he be?"

"Half an hour," came the answer, in between shovelfuls of sawdust. "Come fer they stocks 'ave yer?" he asked, nodding in the direction of a timber building.

"Yes," I answered; "do you know which they are?"

"Waal, I does, but yer better see 'im fust. 'Ere, 'old this bag." He pushed the sack towards me and I held it open while he shovelled the damp sawdust into it. "Come from Nether Oldston do yer?" he asked, as he put the last shovelful into the sack. "Put it over by the wall there." He went on "There's another empty one there, look."

I dragged the full sack across to the wall and picked up the empty one. "Yes," I said, slightly out of breath from moving the heavy sack, "well, that is, I'm living there now."

"What, 'prentice to old Albert be yer? Mind 'ee don't work yer too 'ard."

We filled half a dozen sacks and then the man put down the shovel. "That'll do. That's more an I'd a done on me own," he said, drawing out a small pipe from his pocket and pressing down whatever was in the bowl. He drew hard on it as he held a lighted match to it. Blue smoke completely enveloped him for a moment or two then drifted out of the shed and up over the roof. It occurred to me that anyone outside might well fear that the place was on fire.

"What do you do here?" I asked him.

"What do we do 'ere?" he repeated, removing the pipe from his mouth and staring into it as if he could not believe it had gone out after such an impressive start. "Waal, anything as there is to do. That is, to do with sawing and hammering. Not a lot of skill yer might say, but very good at making noise and mess."

I could see various piles of stakes and posts, rails and planks stacked in different heaps. The yard was untidy, with weeds, deriving nourishment from rotting sawdust and rainwater, growing in most places.

"Ee'll be out any minute," the man said, nodding towards the house. As he spoke there came the bang of a door across the yard and a man came round the end of the wooden building.

"Good morning," he called, then looking again he said, "Oh it's you, is it? You're with Albert Hardwick are you?" I recognised him then as the man I had helped with the load of stakes along the road when I had first been on my way to Nether Oldston.

"Right, these blocks are yours."

Mr Hawtin led the way round to the back of the building and into a smaller yard where calves were pulling hay from a rack. "Those in the corner, look. If you stack them carefully you will get them on. Bring your cart round while I hold the gate to keep the calves in."

I led the mare round and he closed the gate behind us. After calling to be sure to close the gate again when we left, he disappeared into the big wooden building, whence shortly afterwards came the sounds of sawing. I backed the cart as close as I could to the stack of stocks and let down the tailboard. It was still early and the air was crisp, enough to make a little exercise like loading the cart quite acceptable.

One by one I began lifting the heavy unseasoned elm blocks onto the cart. When I had lifted a few I climbed up to stack them carefully to the front. Before many had been put into position however, the calves, of which there were six, all of them born the previous spring, losing interest in their dusty hay, gathered round my loading operation to see what was going on. They pushed closer, eventually managing to get in the way of the carrying of every block. I found a stick to drive them away but no sooner had I loaded one more block than they were back. Pushing between these stolid creatures whilst carrying a heavy block of wet elm did not become better with practice, but no matter what I tried nothing kept them away. At last I sat in desperation up on the cart on the last block I had managed to stack. The cussed calves waited happily for me beneath, pushing gently all round the cart and licking at the grease round the axle and chain pins.

It was then that a voice, shrill and excited, called out, "Are you frightened of those poor little creatures?"

I looked across the yard to a door in the corner, near the hay rack, and saw a small girl of about eight standing smiling at me and pointing at the calves. "No," I called back, "of course not, but they're being nosey and making it difficult to load the cart."

She laughed and said, "Come on down if you're not scared! Come on down," she repeated. "I'll soon move them."

I climbed down and stood facing the child, who told me her name was Jenny.

"What have you got to do?" she asked.

I explained, and handed her the stick. She flicked it and the cattle moved quickly away. The rest of the loading was done without hindrance apart from the occasional question about where I had come from, the name of the mare, how old I thought she was and so on. It was quite hard work having to climb up and down upon the cart to stack every one of the heavy blocks. At last it was done, the tailboard put up and the pins dropped in, and the rope tied tightly and securely round the load.

"Now, if you will keep them back for just one moment more, while I take the cart through the gate, I will be very grateful to you, Jenny," I said.

"Hurry up then, or my sister Maisie will come out after us. I'm not supposed to be out here in this messy old yard."

As I led Magnolia round to the gate another figure appeared through the door and beckoned to Jenny to go in. She shook her head and pointed to me; I could not hear what was being said for the noise of the cart turning. I called out a thank you to Jenny and waved to her as I closed the gate behind the cart.

The older girl was descending upon her as Jenny pointed to her and shouted "This is my sister. She is very cross and not as nice as she looks!" She was then marched quickly back to the doorway by her obviously embarrassed sister. The door banged and I was left staring over the gate for a moment before I returned to lead Magnolia onto the road, waving goodbye to my friend, the sawdust shoveller, as I went.

We started for home at a steady pace. As the spring sun climbed higher the morning became warm. When we reached the hill I stopped the mare and put the specially-kept stone ready on the near shaft, in case we had difficulty descending the hill when I would thrust it under the wheel. I led her slowly down and without event we continued on our way.

My thoughts drifted over my new life here at Nether Oldston and the people I was starting to live and work with. I watched the mare, already counted as one of my friends, toiling in the shafts as she threw her shoulders against the weight of the timber. As I watched her move slowly between the verges of new April grass I anticipated returning to the shop where I had begun to know the men and their ways. I already liked working with wood and was eager to become more skilled. I felt the sun on my back. The promise of the early year showed in field and hedgerow, in tree and sky. I found myself thinking of Jenny's sister's flushed face as she disappeared through the doorway in the yard. The pungent tang of the wet elm blocks came to my nostrils and I wondered how long it would be before they became wheel hubs bearing loads along lanes, and whether I would be as skilled as Jes by then.

CHAPTER THREE

As I settled in at Number Three, The Green, with Mrs Pickvance, I became Eva's main concern. She was also always very interested in getting out, and nothing Mrs Pickvance could think of had the slightest effect on her. Her ever-present inclination to get out of the house became directed, after my arrival in the household, to finding where I had gone each day. Often she would appear at the workshop with wagging tail and bright eyes, then when I had run all the way back with her to Number Three, more than once I found her again waiting for me when I arrived breathless, back at the workshop. Every evening she waited for my approaching footsteps, lying just inside the front door, with her nose on her front paws and ears cocked. When I departed she would stand with nose to the draught between door and frame emitting a dreadful wailing which, in the early morning, awakened Mrs Pickvance and brought a hurled shoe flying down the stairs. At this the unhappy creature would take herself back to her basket in the kitchen to ponder further on her chances of getting out.

By the end of May I had become accepted as part of the workshop staff. My routine was expected and my help looked for. Mostly the men worked freely with me and called when they needed a hand with a long length of boarding or a heavy piece of timber. Planing and chopping mortices, holding timber, passing this or that, fetching something from the store and sweeping or tidying up as well as tending the livestock occupied most of my days. I watched, listened, used the tools whenever I got the chance, and every so often would take the mare to carry or fetch something. Conversation in the shop was very limited and I was generally expected only to speak if spoken to. The men did not talk a great deal to each other whilst working unless it was to discuss some problem with a job in hand, for mostly the work was strenuous or noisy, which discouraged talking.

Apart from Horace, who mostly ignored me, I seemed to get on well with the men, especially Jes with whom I spent much time during those first few months. We ate our meals outside during warm weather, unless it rained. New items of local gossip were exchanged and occasionally Harry Teemer from the waggon end would get onto politics with Ben Steel or Ben James, when voices would become raised. Sometimes their endless arguments continued back in the shop until Mr Hardwick told them he couldn't hear their hammering for their talking.

Mr Hardwick had purchased two in-calf heifers to put in his field with Magnolia so one morning Jes, Sammy, and I were instructed to fetch them from the farm at the far end of the village. Straight after dinner we set off and our heavy hobnailed boots clattered along the roadway, disturbing the otherwise deserted village slumbering in the warm noonday sun. Ruff, the cobbler's big mongrel, gave a tired, woolly bark as we passed his house, not bothering to get up from under the shade of an old walnut tree. Miss Betts' black and white terrier, already alerted by Ruff, jumped excitedly up and down behind her white painted gate as we passed, barking as if she would tear us apart if only the gate had not been there.

"Vicious little sod!" said Sammy, scraping the stick he was carrying along the ground in front of the gate and almost causing the furious bitch to burst with hysterics.

Crosswood Farm was preparing for haymaking. In fact the men had already started in with their scythes to cut round the edge of the field behind the farmhouse, ready for the new horse-drawn mower that Albert Lane had just that year bought and was waiting eagerly to try out. He was at that very moment oiling the cutter sections and trying out the big handle that raised and lowered the cutter bar. The two horses, harnessed and waiting for the men to finish round the field with their scythes, were being held firmly by young Jim Lane, who was speaking gently to them. They were still nervous of the new, bright red machine behind them, with its yellow wheels, its smell of paint and its clattering, chattering noise when they moved forward.

"There 'e is!" said Jes, "Over by that new mower of 'is. – 'Ow do Mr Lane," he called, as we approached him. "Made a start then?"

Albert Lane looked up from the mower. "Hullo Jes! Oh ah, we be a cuttin' in the back field and if this weather 'olds it'll be ready fer turnin' tomorrer this time."

"Well, the wind's in the right quarter. You let me know

when you wants us," said Jes, for he and Sammy helped in the evenings with the hay work after they had finished in the workshop.

"Right," said the farmer, "shouldn't be long now. They heifers be over in that box aside the 'arness room. They're quiet, but mind 'ow they comes out, the muck's 'igh in there."

Sammy opened the door of the loose box while Jes and I stood to turn the heifers towards the road and Mr Lane waited in the road to turn them towards the village. Sammy went in and one at a time the heifers stepped daintily out from the high layers of winter muck. Sammy walked behind them while Jes and I went ahead to stand in gateways and lane turnings to keep the beasts on the right road. Miss Betts' terrier was silenced for a few seconds while one heifer sniffed inquisitively at her then snorted hard down her nostrils, causing the small angry creature to jump backwards in surprise. The barking was soon renewed and continued until we were out of sight. When we got back I opened the workshop field gate and the heifers were turned into the pasture, where Magnolia stood holding her head up high in surprise as if she were certain that there had been a mistake. We stood watching for a few moments, as men do when they turn cattle into a field, and saw the two newcomers go all round the boundaries kicking up their heels and snatching a mouthful of grass here and there as they went.

"That's that then," said Jes, as we returned to the work in the shop.

A few evenings later I went with Jes and Sammy to Crosswood Farm to help with the haymaking. I called in at the village stores on the way to see if Roderick Walker was coming. I had become friendly with Roderick lately. His grandmother kept the shop. To enter it was something of an ordeal for a young person, as to start with for the first few moments after going in, it was not possible for anyone to hear anything but the commotion caused by the movement of the shop door. Cards of patent medicines, sink plugs, discs for mending kettles, bootlaces, pens, pencils, and bottles of Sloane's backache cure swung violently in different directions. Until these had all come to rest again, together with the doorbell, which was fixed to a long supple spring giving the impression that perpetual motion had been discovered every time it was triggered, it was impossible for one's voice to be heard and so, for what seemed an age, one had to stand before the counter facing the fierce inquiring stare of Old Daisy. From opening to closing time she sat continually behind the heavy polished dark mahogany counter. The question of shoplifting did not occur even though much was displayed all round the shop. Even when it was busy with perhaps two or three customers at the counter all talking at once, if you picked anything up, even right at the back and apparently out of her line of vision, Old Daisy's voice would ring out, "Was there something, young man?" causing you to drop the item immediately.

Her name was Daisy Middleton and when I went to Nether Oldston she had been keeping the shop for over thirty years. Few people knew her surname and those who did would have had to stop and think if asked, for she was 'Old Daisy at the Shop' to everyone. I fixed my eyes on a ginger biscuit until the doorbell gave its final twitch, then asked if Roderick was there.

"Go through," she said, intending me to go through the long passage leading from the shop to the store area where stock and orders were dealt with by Roderick's father.

In the back store Herbert Walker was getting ready to go home and told me Roderick was "seeing to Chaucer". I found him outside harnessing the pony.

"Can't come tonight, Abey; I'm off up to Lonestock to take Arthur Bourton's stuff. I might come up later if I get back in time." He went on buckling up the harness and pulling the bellyband tighter as Chaucer tired of blowing himself out to stop the band reaching round him. I collected some tea for Mrs Pickvance while old Ben James, who had come in and been served while I was talking to Roderick, let himself out from the shop, having narrowly missed sending an open tin of mixed biscuits crashing to the floor when his dinner bag caught the sharp corner of the tin.

Albert Lane had turned his hay twice since we had fetched the two heifers and with the sure recipe for making good hay, hot sun and warm breeze, he was now ready to carry and stack it in his rickyard. After tea I took Eva with me on a long piece of string. She gave Mrs Pickvance a sidelong glance as we set off, half expecting, no doubt the usual shout to come back; her tail wagged uncertainly and her ears were laid back wondering if we would get away with it. When we turned into the road, however, her ears shot forward and her tail changed to 'full speed' as she fairly danced on the end of the string.

In the field behind the farm we found Jes, Sammy, George and Albert Groom and Harry Teemer, all from Hardwick's, with another half dozen men from the village as well as the regular farm men. Farmer Lane gave orders, then within minutes men with wide wooden rakes were drawing the hay into rows. Soon after two waggons, with village boys at the horse's heads, were led slowly between the rows. One man on either side pitched the hay to a third who rode on the waggon, loading.

When the first load was ready it was hauled to the rickyard, rolling and pitching through deep rutted gateways of mud now baked rock hard in the hot sun. The waggon, almost completely hidden by the huge tousled hay load, creaked and groaned as chains and rings clanked from straining and steadying horses, sweat from their fringed brows trickling to their soft-cornered, bit-trembling mouths.

The bottom of the rick had been prepared during the day from faggots, branches, and straw to keep out wet and damp. Harry Teemer always built the ricks and had already taken up his position with Farmer Lane who would 'feed' him when the first load arrived. It was nine o'clock before dew came up and we stopped work, leaving the two waggons loaded and a canvas sheet over the centre of the rick. We all went to the farmhouse for cider, cheese, and homemade pickle. We mostly sat round outside in the yard where the long shadows were climbing up over the warm walls of pigsties and lean-to sheds, leaving masses of ivy dark and mysterious where it grew persistently.

As we eased the dusty dryness from our tired selves, Sally Pullen, one of the blacksmith's daughters, who was helping Mrs Lane to keep the supply of cider flowing, kept smiling at me. Presently she asked if Eva was Mrs Pickvance's dog. When I answered she smiled again, and as my mug was full of cider she said she would wait until I had drunk some. I told her

I had had plenty and must be getting home or Mrs Pickvance would be wondering where I was. The day had been a long hard one. The late warm evening drifted and mellowed softly as the moon rose and the cider settled me further back between the empty hen-coop and piles of sacks upon which I was sitting. Sally poured out more cider, which slopped over the sides of my sloping mug, and moved closer to me. I heard myself saying I was just going and in the distance I heard the men saying goodnight. In the dark shadows I smiled and dropped what was left of the cider over Eva who jumped up and shook it over Sally and me.

"Never mind," breathed Sally in my ear. Eva shook herself again and snuggled up close to me on one side while Sally cuddled close on the other. Silence settled round the yard and before the lights went out in the farmhouse I had fallen fast asleep.

I awoke slowly and as I struggled to grasp my situation I became aware of Sally shaking me and whispering loudly in my ear. "Abey! Abey! Come on, sit up, it's ever so late! Come on! You've been asleep. There's no one here only you and me! Abey, come on!"

I sat up. My heart sank as I began to remember the events leading up to my predicament. The moon had moved considerably and a cooler breeze had sprung up. I felt anxiously for Eva but she was still happily curled up next to me. "For pity's sake, Sally! What the blazes am I doing here?!"

I jumped up. Eva shot from the pile of sacks at the same instant, no doubt wondering what on earth was happening now. One of my shaky legs became caught in the piece of string tied to Eva's collar and down I crashed, grazing my arm and bruising my knee. I lay for a moment while Eva licked my agonised face and Sally, very concerned, helped me up again.

"Come on, we must get home," I gasped. I pulled out Grandfather's watch, and was just able to make out the time by the bright yellow moon. Three o'clock. I pictured Mrs Pickvance waiting. What on earth was I going to say? 'She'll probably throw me out,' I thought.

"I don't know what my Dad will do," Sally was saying. "He'll be furious!" My head ached and I felt dreadful from the overdose of cider; my knee ached and my arm was sore.

"How will you get in?" I asked her.

"Oh, the back door's always open. I'll creep in. Perhaps they'll be asleep. They might even think I'm staying the night with the Lanes."

We hurried through the silent village. I went round the back of the blacksmith's with Sally and watched her go quietly in at the back door. I whispered to Eva "Come on!" as I half ran back towards the green, using the grass verges where possible to silence my heavy boots, as the moon sank out of sight behind the church.

When we arrived at Number Three, I picked Eva up and holding her in one arm endeavoured to unlock the front door with my free hand. The door opened silently. I crept into the hall and took off my boots while still holding onto Eva.

Only one stair creaked as I stole up to my room, but as I turned to close the door there came a cross voice from the next room. "I don't know where you have been Abraham Staughton, but I do know no person comes into my house at this time in the morning without an explanation!"

"Sorry, Mrs Pickvance," I said.

"Sorry indeed?!" she snorted. "There'll be more about this tomorrow!"

I pictured her sitting up in the dark with the cotton scarf that she always wore in bed to protect her rag curlers tied round her head. I closed my door, ready at last to drop into bed.

"Go down and give Eva her supper!" came the voice again.

I took Eva downstairs, where her bowl of food awaited her. She quickly ate it and I let her out into the garden where I could see the first signs of sunrise. Eva settled into her basket in the kitchen and when I returned to bed I heard her whimper as I closed my door. Then Mrs Pickvance shouted "Be quiet Eva!" after which, silence reigned.

CHAPTER FOUR

Two hours later I was at the workshop. Surprisingly enough I felt little the worse for my night before. While I was letting out the hens Mr Hardwick came to tell me to get as much done as I could to some ladder rounds I was making, and then when Harry and the others were ready to start haymaking I was to go with them to Crosswood. This would not be before the dew, which was heavy that morning, had gone. It might not be before ten o'clock.

"Hens are all doing well this time, Abey," went on Mr Hardwick, "so are the cattle for that matter." He stuck his thumbs in the sides of his waistcoat and nodded slowly, watching the brown leghorns stepping jerkily, one at a time, out into the sunlight through their little wooden door, ready for another day of strutting, scratching, pecking, and crooning round the yard buildings.

"When the two heifers calve down this autumn I'm thinking of getting a couple of cows in milk to put with them, then starting a milk round in the village for a few folk." He said he thought Albert Lane would not mind too much as he had bought the heifers from him. The present milk supply came from Crosswood Farm.

I was not pleased with this news as I had my own idea of who would be doing the extra livestock work, and later on I complained to Jes about it. I was sitting astride the draw-horse, which was a wooden contraption made to hold a piece of wood at one end while being worked on with a drawknife at the other to taper and fashion it for a ladder round. Quite a simple thing it was, rather like a trestle with a pivoted frame, which you sat astride and pushed forward with your feet. The wood you were working on was gripped by the other end of the frame, while your hands were free to pull the drawknife towards you.

"I came here to be a wheelwright, not a cowman! I could have stayed at home if I wanted to be a stockman."

"Now, young Abey, don't you go a frettin' about that yet," said Jes. "Maybe you'll be gettin' a little dairymaid to help you out there in the dark evenings."

"I'm not joking about it, Jes, and I don't mind doing a bit of the farmwork, but if I've got to milk and then deliver round the village, I'm going to ask the boss what I came here for!"

"You wouldn't have to do all that by yerself, Abey! Now what about this sale I 'ears you're a goin' off to next week?"

"Well, Mr Hardwick's talking about me going over to see if I can get a few tools. I can't think why. It looks like I won't need them as much as a milking stool!" I added sarcastically.

A few days earlier Mr Hardwick had told me of a sale to be held in a neighbouring village the next week, which was offering, amongst other things, a collection of woodworking tools. He had suggested that he and I went along to see what there was, and if they were any good he was prepared to loan me enough cash to purchase some, my father having made this arrangement with him.

I continued working on the ladder rounds until Harry Teemer called that they were ready to go. It was quite usual for men to be sent to help at haymaking and harvest time when they could be spared. The men could not all go as waggon work and much else done at Hardwick's was directly connected with the farm work. Indeed, the ladder rounds that I was leaving to go haymaking for, were an order which would be required for the coming thatching of ricks.

The same five men were going who had helped the previous evening. They went on bicycles, except Jes, who could not ride one. I was going to ride on Sammy's crossbar, but as we were about to depart, Peter Brooks, the blacksmith's assistant came round.

"The boss wants to see you, Abey!" he said. I felt my heart sink. Peter obviously did not know what he wanted to see me about, but I certainly did.

"What, now?" I asked, trying to look unconcerned.

"Well, he did say to go round and fetch you."

I knew it was no good delaying things so told Sammy to go on without me, saying I would catch him up.

"Quite glad to come round here for a few minutes I am," said Peter, as we walked towards the forge. "The boss is in a bad mood this morning. He seems to be lookin' for trouble." I did not answer. As we entered the smithy I removed my hat as a sign of contrition. The shop was dark, with the fire glowing red.

Peter took a bicycle from the wall and went off up the village. Two Clydesdales, a mare and a cob, stood in the shop close together, tied to the same ring in the wall. They stood with their heads low, the cob's under the mare's neck. Shoeing was an ordinary thing for them. They were as unconcerned as they would have been in their own stable.

I stood for a moment while my eyes adjusted from the bright summer sunlight to the dark shop. I could see the rounded trousers of Abe Pullen as he bent over by the mare, holding a great feathered hoof between his leather-aproned knees. He finished pulling out the last two nails and threw the old worn shoe into the corner, where it chinked into a heap of old shoes. Dropping the pincers into his box, he put the hoof down, put his hands on his back then slowly straightened up. His face was red from the bending.

"What have you got to say for yourself then?" he said loudly.

"Nothing, Mr Pullen," I said.

"Nothing?" he roared. "You brings my gal Sally home at three in the morning then stands there saying 'nothing'! You better start thinking of something because I wants a reason, and a good one too!"

"I fell asleep up at Lane's farm last night, and so I believe, did Sally. When I woke up I walked back here with her."

"Fell asleep?" boomed the old smith, moving over slightly as the mare dropped a neat heap of warm, steaming dung close to where he was standing. "I've heard some feeble excuses in my time, young Staughton, but that takes a bit of beating!"

"It's quite true, Mr Pullen; I think it was the cider," I said.

"Heavy drinking, eh?"

"Not really, it was pretty heavy work," I answered.

Abe Pullen went over to the forge, raked up the embers and slowly operated the long bellows handle. It creaked and the fire responded immediately. "My father would have belted me," he said, thrusting a new shoe into the glowing fire with the long tongs he had picked up with his right hand. With his left he continued blowing. He raked the fire up over the shoe. "He'd a belted me coming in at that time, even if I'd not had a girl with me."

"I'm very sorry it happened," I said, "but really it was no

one's fault."

"Three o'clock in the morning is no time for a daughter of mine to be coming home, and I hold you responsible in the circumstances, young Staughton!" he said, taking the red shoe from the fire with the tongs and tapping it on the beak of the anvil with a hammer. He eyed it on both sides, tapped it again then tossed it into the trough of water at the end of the forge where it banged and continued to rumble.

"If it happens again I'll give you a good hiding and write to tell your father!" he said. I could see there was nothing more I could say to help the situation so I did not answer. "Do you understand that?" he asked, turning towards me with his hands on his leather-aproned hips.

"Yes Mr Pullen, it won't happen again."

"It better not. Now get off back to work you young varmint!" he said. I went out of the smithy and set off for Crosswood Farm.

The two waggon-loads from the previous evening had been unloaded when I arrived and Albert Lane had taken Harry's place building the rick. Harry climbed the ladder carrying his pitchfork, points down, then went all round poking and patting, moving a forkful here and pulling a forkful there, as if it had been getting out of hand without him. As the farmer moved over to make way for him he spat neatly into each hand before grasping his fork firmly, ready for business. I went with Jes to 'pitch on' one of the waggons while Sammy loaded. The hay was in perfect condition. The farm men had been round tedding out with their forks earlier to let the air through it. The horse pulling our waggon was an old hand at the work and needed no leading between the rows of hay. The commands of "Hup!" and "Woa!" started or stopped him as required, although he could inch forward at just the right pace for the picking up, which was better for the man on the load than starting and stopping continually.

The sun rose higher. It dazzled on the horse brasses and made the black horse leathers too hot to touch. Horses stood steaming and drenched with sweat, shaking their heads and swishing their tails in a never ceasing battle with the swarms of flies. Conversation was reduced to an occasional grunt or gasp as an extra large forkful of hay was pitched. Dry grass rained down on the pitchers and stuck to their brown, toiling bodies. Only a mouthful of pocket-warm, black tea from a bottle , kept saliva flowing.

At half past midday Mrs Lane brought out food and drink, while the men lay under the hedges and waggons out of the sun. Horses were taken for water and given a nosebag of rolled oats and maize, under a large and shady elm tree. There was no sign of Sally Pullen. After refreshment men and horses closed their eyes and dozed. At one o'clock big fob watches were drawn from waistcoat pockets and the time compared.

"Best get started," said someone. We began again and continued steadily until the field was cleared.

By the time darkness fell, the first rick had been topped off skillfully to roof shape, and the next was half way up. A young fresh horse called Jolly was put into the big iron horse rake and old Ben James, who had arrived late in the evening, rode it like a chariot up and down the cleared field to collect any remaining wisps of hay. The big black Shire cob stepped high and fast as old Ben bounced above the curved tines, high up on his long sprung seat with the slightly cooler evening air rushing past him.

I could hardly walk home after more cider and cheese fare but when at last I did, Mrs Pickvance lectured me on the evils of staying out too late. When I wearily tried to explain about the cider she changed to the evils of self-indulgence. Even after the refreshment at the farm I managed my supper with ease, for my work that day and my age provided me with a great appetite. I finished my meal, made a fuss of Eva, then wished Mrs Pickvance "Goodnight" before retreating to my room. Eva waited until Mrs Pickvance was not looking and silently followed me upstairs.

The church clock struck eleven thirty as I looked out of my bedroom window from which I could see right across to Crosswood Farm. The village was free of working noises but the night air was full of other sounds. The warm night was heavy with the scent of the honeysuckle just below my window, and when the faint breeze stirred the elms over the green I caught the perfume of night-scented stock from further away. A lamb bleated and crickets whirred away, down in the grass. As I watched, the moon rose higher and shone white on the stone of Froglies Bridge, which some folks said was haunted.

I was reluctant to get into bed although I was tired from my lack of sleep the previous night. I looked back over Crosswood Farm and wondered what had happened to Sally Pullen; I thought how only a few months ago I had never seen Nether Oldston or any of its inhabitants yet now I knew them all by sight and many of them to speak to. Bending to pat Eva, I wondered how my father's farmwork was progressing and resolved to write home tomorrow night.

Eva wriggled closer to my legs and I patted her again before turning to get ready for bed. The farm cider necessitated another visit to the privy in the garden before retiring but when I took the candle to go, Eva, not knowing I would return so quickly, insisted on going downstairs with me. Mrs Pickvance heard and called out to make sure Eva was shut in the kitchen before I went up to bed.

"I told you to wait quietly up there and that I would be back in a minute," I said to the dog, who regarded me reproachfully as I settled her into her basket in the kitchen. "Now you'll have to stay down here and you can't say I didn't warn you!" She howled mournfully when I closed the door and went upstairs without her until Mrs Pickvance's voice shouted, "Stop it, Eva!" after which there was silence.

CHAPTER FIVE

The sale, which included the tools I was interested in, comprised some articles of husbandry, a few pigs, and the contents of a small cottage. The well known firm of Jimkin, Spotter and Burr, auctioneers and valuers from Remsditch, were conducting the sale. They had sent Mr Hardwick a catalogue listing everything in detail. Viewing was on the day before the day of sale between ten and four o'clock. We were going to view, having decided that the description of the tools made them worth looking at.

Mr Hardwick had borrowed a pony and dogcart from the Pullens next door and after dinner we set off for the village of Apford, about six miles away. Being a small sale it did not attract a great number of people, but there was a steady stream during the hours for viewing.

Two auctioneer's porters had set out the various items in order of sale, and were now sticking lot numbers on everything with a big black pot of hot glue, smelling strongly of disinfectant. They completed this while we were there and then stood with solemn faces and long starched, white aprons eyeing every viewer and giving the impression of reluctance to answer questions. They called each other Seth and Charlie. Seth appeared to be much older than Charlie and also to be the senior in rank. They both came from Remsditch and according to Sammy, when I discussed it with him later, they held the view that all country folk were simple. They regarded the small country town of Remsditch as quite different. At intervals during the viewing Seth would call "Charlie!" in a very deep monotone: everyone within earshot looked up from what they were doing to witness another dozen or so catalogues transferred from the auctioneer's attaché case to the small table near Seth. The small ceremony completed, Charlie, after straightening up one or two items on the various tables, would take up his post again near the door.

We went straight to some trestle tables where the woodworking tools were set out. There was a good selection with obvious signs of having been well looked after. Chisels and gouges were rolled in green baize while the wooden planes and gauges were like satin to handle. There was a faint smell of spirits of turpentine and linseed oil about the whole array. Altogether the collection covered two and a half tables. Saw-teeth and clean oilstones spoke of a craftsman, which indeed their owner had been, until his passing in that very cottage six months before.

Albert Hardwick handled one or two moulding planes, looked along the saws and plucked at the back of each hand-saw, making the steel ring out like a bell.

"Best decide what you need, lad," he said; "it's all good stuff." I nodded. "Looks like there'll be plenty of folk after it," he went on, "judging by the interest here. Note down the numbers of the stuff you'll try for."

I already owned a few tools. I had a wooden smoother and some chisels. I hoped to get more chisels and gouges, but I most needed saws, a Jack plane and a jointer, although hammer, gauges, and marking out tools I needed as well. In actual fact I knew I could do with any of the tools on those trestle tables. I noted the lot numbers of the more important items and then we went quickly round the rest of the sale as Mr Hardwick needed to see as much as he could for the purpose of informing folks at home as to the condition of what was for sale.

We returned to the workshop and later that evening after the men had gone and I was sweeping up round the benches Mr Hardwick came out of his office to have a word with me. Hitching his corduroyed bottom up onto a bench, he took off his hat and to get rid of the dust struck it against his leg, sending up a cloud of sawdust from it. He sneezed loudly so laid his hat on the bench while he jumped off it to pull a handkerchief from his pocket. After blowing his nose and when the dust had settled again, he once more sat on the bench, by which time I was standing waiting with my dinner bag, ready to set off for my evening meal.

"Three pounds would be a lot of money to spend," he began, "but you won't need to buy 'em again, providing you look after them. You go to the sale tomorrow Abey, lad; Sammy will lend you his bike. Think carefully before you bids. See what you can get for about three pounds. Your father has said he will pay for them so I will give you the cash come morning. The saws were especially good, I thought; you might do worse than only get the handsaws. Get off on that bike as soon as you've done here in the morning."

I felt excited at the thought of going to the sale to bid, as I had never done so myself before.

"Good experience for you," nodded Mr Hardwick, picking up his hat again. He dusted it against the side of the bench quite forcibly and again the cloud of fine sawdust rose around him. Our conversation came to an end with more sneezing and I had reached the door and called "Goodnight" before the last nose-blowing had finished.

The day of the sale dawned with a heavy mist and dew over the fields and hedgerows. I was eager to get the stock fed and tended in good time. At this time of the year feeding was at its minimum for Magnolia and the heifers were out to grass and required nothing more. Sammy agreed to lend his bicycle on condition that if a mortice gauge went cheaply enough I would purchase it for him.

"Don't you get carried away Abey, lad!" warned Jes. "I sin many a man spend a sight more ner ee'd a got at auction sale." His voice lowered confidentially: "I mind old 'arry Teemer ere a payin' a darned sight more fer a bruz than ee could a bought a new one for, not so long back! Tell yer what though, young Abey, there's some feedin' buckets up there afore the tools; see what they makes and if you can get them fer next to nothin', I could do with a couple fer my old pig." I promised to keep an eye open for the buckets, then spent a little time doing work on the turning circle of a waggon with Ben James, who advised me quietly to look for a good oilstone if there was one to be had, for such a thing was a craftsman's treasure and not easily come by in the days when only natural stones were available.

At eight o'clock I put away my things and amidst a chorus of "good luck"s from the men set off on Sammy's bicycle with three sovereigns safely in my pocket. As I passed the green I saw Mrs Pickvance shaking the doormat. Eva was tied to the fence and barked loudly as I disappeared. I could see activity in the rickyard at Crosswood Farm, where hayloads were being unsheeted ready for unloading. The mist was rising and streaks of gold were beginning to filter through with the promise of another warm and sunny day. Being summer, the cows from Crosswood were turned out from milking individually as they were finished. They wandered out onto the green and the road where they poked about and stood cudding in the cool part of the day. One was rubbing her neck rhythmically on the gatepost by the farm and another was licking the axle grease underneath a wheelbarrow in the yard. They were dotted over the green and half way along Tiptoe Lane.

I could hear cowman Will Auger saying "Git on Biddy," and the clank of the chain as another unruffled member of the herd turned to make her leisurely way out to the elms on the green. There was no traffic. Perhaps a bicycle or an occasional cart might pick its way through the standing milkers until Will had finished, when he would appear with a wooden wheelbarrow and shovel. As he walked back to his cottage for breakfast he would drive the cattle along the lane picking up any muck they made on the way and calling, "Hi, Hi, Hi! Git on there my beauties!" and banging on the wheelbarrow with his shovel if one of them stopped to lick or rub on anything.

I pedalled on over Froglies Bridge where water tinkled over stones loudly enough for me to hear it as I passed. My mudguard rattled. Albert Lane's new red mower was cutting another field for hay and was already half finished. I could see the two horses stepping proudly together as the mist, still hanging low by the stream, was disappearing quickly over the higher fields. I passed nothing until I reached the main road, where there was more activity, obviously directed to the sale.

There was a different air about the sale premises from the day before and I could sense a much more business-like atmosphere as the two porters, Seth and Charlie, busied themselves arranging a few chairs in the small front garden where a table and chair had been placed on a raised platform of planks and trestles. As the weather was fine the sale was to be conducted outside. People were beginning to arrive and stood in ones and twos, talking. I walked round to the back to leave my bicycle, then strolled around looking again at what I had seen the day before.

There was about an hour before the sale was due to start so I used the time to check the lot numbers and find the buckets that Jes had been talking about. About ten minutes before the start more people arrived and before long it became difficult to move about. The area in front of the platform was full and people were forming some sort of order beyond the chairs. I had managed to get into a position not too near the front but where I thought I could be easily seen by the auctioneer if and when I wanted to bid.

A red-faced man with long sideburns and enormous checked waistcoat, which only just met at the front and was held by six overstrained buttons, climbed carefully up two wooden steps and sank breathlessly into the chair. Seth placed a glass of water on the table and when the auctioneer was settled he went inside the cottage and reappeared holding a brass coal-scuttle. This, as the catalogue showed, was lot number one.

Another important-looking man climbed onto the platform, smiling first at Mr Marty, the auctioneer with the straining buttons, and then at the gathered assembly. He clasped his hands, cleared his throat loudly to attract attention, then, still smiling, welcomed everyone to what he hoped and felt sure would be a profitable day for all concerned. He himself was Mr Spotter and after introducing his colleague he banged hard on the table with a wooden gavel, pronounced the sale open, and handed the gavel to Mr Marty. The auctioneer, having recovered from climbing the two steps up to the platform, pointed at the brass coal-scuttle, which Seth was still holding and now raised above his head, and asked for a starting bid.

"What am I bid? What am I bid? What am I bid for this fine brass coal-scuttle of considerable value, beauty and size?" rattled Mr Marty. I looked round at the crowd, wondering who amongst all these people was interested in the tools I wanted. My heart was beating fast as the first few items were knocked down quickly. People were still coming in to join the bidding and very soon the sale was well under way with first Seth and then Charlie carrying to the platform some article from the cottage, or if it was too big to carry, part of it. Among them came the buckets for Jes but they made a shilling each and were in poor condition so I did not bid.

Next came the articles of husbandry under which were sold items such as a wheelbarrow, cold-frames, a donkey-cart and a seed-fiddle. Then, at last, the tools came up.

"Very fine planes these are and in remarkable condition," Mr Marty was saying. He took a long draught of water, mopped his brow and his very red face with a white handkerchief, and then asked Mr Spotter in a loud voice if he had ever seen such a collection come under the hammer at one time.

"Never, sir!" replied the smiling Spotter. "And never likely to again. Such quality!" he added with a touch of awe, but just as loudly. I was excited and nervous.

As the long try plane was carried up to the table by Charlie I could feel my heart pounding so hard that I had to speak to myself severely for fear I might lose my ability to reason. This plane was a delight to behold and it was to remain on the table while all the other planes were sold.

"Now, gentlemen, what are you going to bid me for this first plane, this fine example of the tools of a craftsman? Come along now!" Mr Marty said, as Seth held up a small wooden smoothing plane that had never before known a world other that that amongst shavings on a quiet bench, yet now was the focal point of the gathered assembly.

"Thank you, sir, one shilling! - Two shillings, three shillings I'm bid - and sixpence? - I'll take sixpence - thank you, sir, three shillings and sixpence I'm bid - Sold!" The little wooden hammer came down, narrowly missing the glass of water, but no doubt denting the table top. The smoother was whisked away to be replaced by a similar plane. I was still thinking about the first one and how much it had made, when the second one was sold. I began to despair. I would never get anything, and I saw myself back at the shop saying I had bought nothing. Six chisels were being sold and without any previous thought I called out "Two shillings!" in a voice so loud that I startled myself. The hammer came down and the red-faced auctioneer was looking directly at me and asking my name. My face burned to match his as I called out my name and two more lots were sold while I recovered. Then I began to glow with pleasure and triumph. I felt emboldened with success and was ready for the next lot comprising mortice chisels, a cutting gauge, marking and mortice gauge. I bid steadily for them and after paying more than I intended, finally got them.

The long try plane was at last offered. It was lot number seventy-two. By that time I had acquired a good number of tools including two handsaws, a rip-saw and a cross-cut, and was now limited to ten shillings, which was all that was left of the three pounds. The bidding started at five shillings and at six shillings I raised my hand to add another six pence but it quickly went to seven, then on to eight shillings and was sold to a carpenter from Remsditch.

During the viewing I had looked at the carving tools. The previous owner had been something of a wood-carver and had collected a good selection. Mostly they were in green baize rollup bundles; there were three of these in fact. Two contained fifteen tools each and the other contained ten. Strangely the bidding was slow and the bundle of ten, the first to be sold, was being knocked down for six shillings when I, without any intention of buying carving tools, on the spur of the moment, raised my hand.

"Six and sixpence," I called.

"Thank you, sir!" said the now almost exhausted Mr Marty. His face has deepened to the hue of a beetroot and I remember, even at that moment, a feeling of surprise that the handkerchief with which he continuously mopped his neck was not stained like a napkin used to handle such a vegetable.

The hammer crashed down with a force indicative of Mr Marty's growing impatience to be finished, cutting short any possible further bidding and leaving me the possessor of ten carving tools in a neat green roll. The two remaining bundles made low prices but three and sixpence was all I had left.

At this point Mr Marty was helped out of his seat and down the steps by Seth and Charlie. He seemed to be almost in a state of collapse as they staggered, half carrying him, inside the cottage. Mr Spotter now stood again at the front of the little stage clasping his hands as before and smiling just as broadly.

"Thank you, thank you, gentlemen," he called out to the assembled bidders, who had now broken into earnest conversation amongst themselves. "Thank you, thank you!" he persisted. The smile weakened, he clasped his hands more tightly and still no one took any notice. He darted back to the table, grabbed the gavel which Mr Marty had abandoned, and furiously smote the table three times. The three loud cracks stopped everyone for a second and during that period of time his "Thank you, thank you, gentlemen!" was taken to indicate something more to follow. Attention was his again but although his smile was still there it lacked its initial enthusiasm.

"Now gentlemen, we are about to sell the pigs and this part of our sale will be conducted at the pigsties." He glanced at his pocket watch. "In ten minutes from now I propose to start the last part of . . ." His words were lost in the general murmuring and movement of the crowd as they turned away from him. The muscles of his face, unable to release the long-held smile, kept their shape while he gathered his papers and gavel and disappeared into the cottage.

I was anxious to collect my purchases but nothing was to be removed before the end of the sale and so I joined the crowd around the pigsties, where six half-fattened baconers were housed in two lots of three and one large sow was enclosed in a temporary pen. Apart from those people immediately round the pigs, few people could see them. I climbed up onto a small wall a little distance back where I could see some of the procedure. Mr Spotter, led by the two white-aproned porters, pushed through the crowd and climbed onto some scaffold boards, previously placed across the open brick sties. Both Seth and Charlie now carried sticks as props for their new roles in this, the finale of their performance.

Mr Spotter, no doubt refreshed by a tankard of beer in the privacy of the cottage, now pranced about on the scaffold boards. They were quite springy and at one point he tripped against the edge of one which caused him to move more cautiously as, no doubt, he envisaged the indignity of being hauled out from the company of the alarmed baconers below.

"Right, gentlemen! Six very desirable baconers we have here. You've all seen them and know what splendid stock we are this day offering you. This is your chance to take advantage of another profitable investment offered and conducted for your benefit by Jimkin, Spotter and Burr!" There was a slight pause while he spoke to Seth, then: "Lot one hundred and twenty, I am selling. What will you start me with?"

Each pig had a red number marked clearly on its back but all the same the two porters felt it necessary to prod continuously during the bidding the pigs that were being sold, with the result that the molested creatures ran about to seek refuge, finding it beneath the boarded area. As they disappeared beneath them one of the aproned men first knelt, then lay down, on the boards, endeavouring to poke out the pigs from underneath. The bidding was completed with all the pigs crouching beneath the boards, hidden from view, while both Seth and Charlie lay on each side of Mr Spotter trying to prod them out. The noise of the pigs beneath caused some difficulty in hearing the bidding but the six were eventually sold. Finally the sow in the pen was sold from the same position. As soon as Seth and Charlie stopped prodding them, the baconers became quiet again.

At the close of sale Mr Spotter hastened towards the cottage where he disappeared from view. I made my way round to join the queue outside the temporary office to pay for my acquisitions, then went to collect them from Charlie at the trestle tables. As I passed an open doorway I caught a glimpse of Mr Marty lying full length on a couch with a white handerkerchief over his face. I recognised him by the expanse of checked waistcoat, the buttons still holding manfully. Mr Spotter was leaning by a window with a tankard of ale in his hand.

Charlie handed me the tools in exchange for my receipt. He smelt faintly of pigs and his apron was by no means as white as it had been before.

'Quite a good assortment,' I thought, as I surveyed my collection. I had brought a haversack and some string with me and, after carrying them all back to my bicycle, I arranged my load carefully. I decided to let Sammy have the mortice gauge, although reluctantly, as it was a fine rosewood one and I still needed one myself. However, he had lent me his bicycle and I had agreed to try to get the gauge for him. I pushed the bike to the road, dodging between horses and traps and carts as people started for home, and rode off towards Nether Oldston wondering what Mr Hardwick would say about the carving tools.

CHAPTER SIX

On my return to the workshop, much interest was shown in my new acquisitions. Sammy was particularly pleased with the mortice gauge and said I could borrow the bike any time I liked. The remaining three shillings and sixpence were returned to Mr Hardwick who nodded in approval at all the purchases although he wondered, he said, about the need for the carving tools. They were a great pleasure for me, though, and I practised with them whenever I could.

The summer days passed quickly. I earned a little extra in the hayfields and again later with the harvest. Sally Pullen told me her father was very cross about the late night and cider. It was some time before she was allowed to go to the farm again.

By the time the bonfire on the green was lit for November the fifth, I felt I had become part of the village. Mr Hardwick had written to my father with a good report and Magnolia came whenever I called her. I visited home about every three months and although I felt the pangs of parting each time I left I was conscious that my interests and business were growing more and more in Nether Oldston.

One afternoon Sammy told me that a certain farmer was coming from a neighbouring village to collect a cart and that it was not ready for him. Apparently this particular farmer owed Mr Hardwick for the last three or four jobs that he had done.

"There'll be such a shemozzle," he sniggered. "The guvnor told him he'd do it as soon as he could, but old Jack Brant said he would be down for it at the end of the week. He's sure to come today or tomorrow." The cart he was talking about stood outside, one of its shafts broken.

"You wait, Abey; he'll be that mad when he sees it isn't done!" he went on.

The day passed and I had forgotten about the whole thing when suddenly, while I was outside feeding the stock, I heard a raised voice: "I told you I'd fetch it about now!"

"I'm afraid we haven't had a chance to do it yet," I heard Mr Hardwick reply.

"What am I supposed to do then, while you find time, Albert Hardwick?" shouted the farmer. I went back into the workshop. Jack Brant stood by Mr Hardwick's bench. He was tall and leaning forward in an intense way as he spoke.

"What else have you got on that's so pressing? You said as you'd have it done by today. Come on now, Albert, what's the hold up?"

"I never said that," went on Mr Hardwick quietly, continuing to spokeshave a long chamfer on the edge of a tailboard; "you'll have to leave it a bit longer, Jack."

"What's that supposed to mean?"

"Just what it says."

"Now look here, Albert, if you arn't goin' to do it quickly I shall take it somewhere else!" Mr Hardwick went on with his job. "Do you hear?" At that moment Ben Steel, who was working beneath a waggon close to them, started hammering loudly and the boss looked questioningly at Brant as if he thought he might have said something. Brant repeated "Do you hear what I said?" But the hammering started again after the first word.

"What's that?" asked Mr Hardwick. Brant looked towards the waggon impatiently.

"I said . . ." but each time he started he was drowned in the noise.

"Can't hear you, Jack!" said Mr Hardwick during a pause.

"I said, do you hear me!" shouted Brant, slightly red in the face.

"Yes, I can hear you now, Jack," said Mr Hardwick, turning over the tailboard. "What were you saying?" Before Brant could reply the noise from under the waggon began again.

"Tell him to stop that damn hammering!" roared Albert Brant.

"What for? We're already behind with the work," said Mr Hardwick. Brant shouted even louder but each time Albert Hardwick only looked up, raised his eyebrows and shrugged in a meaningless way. During pauses in the hammering a few words were exchanged but never enough to make much sense. After a time Mr Hardwick knelt down and disappeared underneath the waggon where he lay on his back working. Brant knelt down too and again tried to talk to him, but at last, getting no sensible reply, he stood up, looked round angrily, then muttering to himself strode towards the door.

"Tell him I'll be back for the cart!" he shouted to Harry Teemer as he left.

His cart stood outside for a number of weeks and when eventually it was done Brant sent a boy to collect it.

There were always small jobs to be attended to and such things as new handles for forks, spades, mauls, and pickaxes often occupied me and Sammy as well. Sammy did not seem to mind but I felt that the livestock and these small jobs took up too much of my time.

'No wonder it takes so long to become a wheelwright if you never get started!' I thought to myself more than once. With the shorter days I needed to start the outside work early because when the skies were heavy, the hens began roosting half way through the afternoon. There was much mucking out to do now, as during the cold weather the two heifers spent a lot of time inside. Mr Hardwick was still talking about getting some milkers and the heifers were due to calve very shortly. I wondered if I would ever learn much in the workshop and said as much to Jes one day while we were turning over the wheelstocks in the shed and inspecting them.

"Now Abey, me lad," answered Jes, straightening his back and putting his hands where it ached most, "I'll tell yer summat. Nobody learns his craft without living with it. You'll learn a sight more through being here and living with it than if you was ter be workin' with yer nose on that there bench from the word 'go'. You'll be a workin' there soon enough when you've learned the most important thing of all, and that is, 'What is needed'. In this'ere shop folks comes all the year round with their wood needs. We deals with every one whether it be fer a dog kennel, or a butter pat, or a waggon fer haymakin', or even a coffin box, like you've seed in theer often enough since you've bin 'ere. Now, when you've become what I calls a useful man with a hunderstandin' of what's needed from yer by the customer, and this 'ere shop, then you'll be on the way to callin' yerself a craftsman."

"But what about the skill and practice?" I insisted, watching a huge spider running for a dark crevice, as I lifted another elm stock.

"That's a comin' all the while. I can see you be a gettin' on all right, but you be like the rest — impatient! Same as all youngsters are: when you gets to my age you'll not remember anything else but being skilled. They reckons a 'prentice needs to breath sawdust fer three years afore there's enough wood in 'is 'ead to make 'im go on in the trade!" He added laughing, "Hullo, here's the gaffer a' comin'!"

Mr Hardwick came into the shed and poked a few stocks, holding one or two to his nose. "Not a bad lot these, Jes," he said, sniffing hard.

"Ah, they'll be all right in time, I reckon," Jes agreed. Turning to me, Mr Hardwick said he wanted me at the 'waggon end' next day to help George Groom and Ben Steel on the big waggon. I was to join them as soon as the livestock was seen to next morning.

"There you are lad, you'll be a wheelwright by termorrer night!" Jes said, after Mr Hardwick had departed. "But you're like one of these 'elm stocks: however good you be, you needs time in the right conditions to make you useable."

Next morning, after, as usual, managing to get out of the front door without Eva, I felt snowflakes settling softly on my face in the inky blackness. Only because I knew the road so well was I able to make my way to the workshop. I heard someone ahead of me and when he coughed knew it was Albert Hardwick.

"Morning, Mr Hardwick!" I called out.

"Mornin', Abey. Snowin' then," he said, coughing into the echoless, sound-dampened morning. "We're in for some bad weather." I nodded, although he could hardly see me.

We lit lamps in the bitterly cold workshop and I left him making up the iron stove while I went out to the yard.

"You'll be with George and Ben this morning, Abey," Mr Hardwick reminded me, as if I could have forgotten.

The two heifers were in at night now and were chained in their mangers. On these winter mornings Magnolia always stood so close to the door outside that I had a job opening it from the inside to let her in.

"Move over, you great stupid!" I would call to her, pushing the door against her. She never learned and every morning, unless I went round outside to lead her away from the door, I had to push her slowly away from inside as I opened it. The heifers were due to calve in two to three weeks and were now getting more concentrated food. Their udders were developing well and Mr Hardwick seemed pleased with them. Every time I fed them I made a point of handling their udders and teats so that they would be well used to it when the time came for milking.

As soon as the feeding was done I went to join the two men working on the waggon. The hens could not be fed until after sunrise, so during winter I had to return to this job later.

George Groom and Ben Steel were both about the same age and had worked for Albert Hardwick's father. I had often watched them. They always appeared to know exactly what to do. They never seemed to stop to scratch their heads over a problem, as Jes did occasionally and Sammy did most of the time, but this, I reasoned was because they had built waggons more or less continuously for so many years, whereas the carpenters at the other end of the workshop were often confronted with different and new things. George Groom was unlike his brother Albert as his hair was black while Albert's was slightly ginger. His moustache was of the toothbrush variety while George's was an enormous affair covering his mouth and reaching well across his cheeks. Heavily built, George moved slowly. If his voice had not been of a higher timbre than Ben Steel's, it would have been impossible to tell who spoke when they were close together, for Ben's moustache was, if anything, even larger than George's. Both of them talked without moving any part of their face which was not covered with hair. Ben was shorter than George and had the appearance of a prize-fighter which indeed he had been in a modest way during earlier years, when he had had a reputation at local fairs for prowess with his fists.

I had helped George and Ben before, on occasions, and of course I always liked the waggon work, which required the very best of timber, all specially selected and often earmarked years before when being sawn over the sawpit from a great tree bole. Albert Hardwick would watch the grain formation and the twist of the tree when it was opened by the sawyers. Such pieces as shafts, felloes, and other curved pieces where the grain needed to follow the shape for maximum strength, were set aside for seasoning and only after many years were they considered 'ready'.

I was fascinated by the different characteristics of the timbers available from the hedgerows and coppices around the village. There was the springy, tough strength of the ash when correctly selected and seasoned; 'frow' ash was brittle and snapped like a carrot so had to be avoided. The men in the shop did not like brown ash which was sometimes found near the heart of the tree although I always found it strong. Heart of oak could not be equalled for sheer strength; while elm, with its incredible interlocked and twisting grain, when grown in the English hedgerow, provided a material impossible to split and was ideal for the wheelstocks or hubs. In those days nothing had to stand more stress than a waggon wheel, destined to run for years on every sort of farm job. As the spokes turned in the wheel, pulling in every direction from load-weight and twist-force, as perhaps a pair of great Shires pulled hard at a load of mangolds, those wheels had to turn out of deep mud and stone ruts, to slide and crash into yet another set of ruts, and to jostle and bounce across mile after mile of wet or dry farm track.

The waggon that George and Ben had spent the last four months working on was now easily recognisable as such, and much other work that they had already done was simply waiting assembly, although it might take another two months to complete, depending on what interruptions they received in the way of waggon repairs and breakdowns. Waggon building was heavy work and most of my time was spent lifting or holding for one or the other of the men, but some of the shaping and cutting work came my way occasionally. I tried to make a mental note of all that was done.

Next to us Ben James and Harry Teemer were working on a nearly completed dung-cart. At one stage I spent some time with them, cutting and fitting the bottom boards which were now made from imported Norwegian deal. This made the work easier and cheaper than using the traditional elm.

"Won't last five minutes!" grumbled Ben James, as he stood with his hands on his hips surveying the creamy white new wood as I fitted it carefully.

"Ah well, Ben," I laughed, "we'll get the job of making a new bottom for it then!"

"Ah boy, 'taint nothin' to be a laughin' at. Time's fer doin' it proper; not fer wastin'. All the way from Norway that be a brought to take the place of somethin' better, which we already got. Can't see as 'ow it be cheaper!"

"Saves a lot of hard work, Ben."

"Huh, folks what be a frightened of 'ard work never ain't a cured be keepin 'em from it!" He turned away and began rubbing the cutting iron from a spokeshave on his old, worn, hollow oilstone. I looked across at Harry Teemer who was quite a few years younger than Ben.

"That's all right fer ole Ben," he said loudly; "he wouldn't be the poor sod sawin' out the old elm boards. He's a past that so it would be me or you, young Abey, put to that little task, and I fer one am glad to see that tripey 'orrible deal! And that don't make me a 'frit of 'ard work neither!" Old Ben went on rubbing on his oilstone and said no more.

It was twilight when I finished the bottom. Ben James gave me a nod, which meant he approved of how I had done it. I put my tools away and went to shut up the hens. The snow had not settled and had turned to icy rain.

A few days later, when I went to let the heifers, now named Teasel and Thistle, in for the night, only Teasel was waiting by the door. I called Thistle but I knew something must be wrong as they were always anxious to come inside to be fed. It was getting dark and a thick fog had settled during the afternoon. The one heifer pushed past me to bury her nose in the bucket of rolled oats, bran and bean-meal. I led Magnolia in to her hayrack and called Albert Hardwick who was sorting out accounts in his little office. We set off round the field in opposite directions, keeping to the boundaries. As the ground sloped away down to the stream, I stopped to listen. The fog hung thickly. My eyebrows felt heavy with it. Apart from the sound of the stream, all was silent. I groped on around the field until I met the boss.

"There's no sign of her yet," he said. There was a sharp dip down to the water of about eighteen inches. I said I would go down to grope along the water's edge. Mr Hardwick had brought a rope which he handed to me. I edged down to the muddy bank of the stream. My boots sank below the level of the stream, letting in the icy water. The mud sucked at each slow step as I moved along. Suddenly I came across her.

"Here she is!" I called, "She's lying here in the mud. Must have slipped." The stricken heifer made a scrambling with her front legs but seemed quite incapable of raising herself up onto her back legs.

"She's too heavy to get up in the mud," Mr Hardwick said. He had climbed down to look at her. We could only just see her now as the daylight had nearly gone.

"Stay with her, Abey. I'll get the mare and some help." He ran off into the fog. Silence settled round me and the distressed beast. I stood close to her head and spoke quietly to her. I wondered how long she might have been there in the icy mud and water. I could no longer feel my feet at all except for a dull pain where they were. She made no further effort to get up and, except for an occasional great sigh, she seemed to have become resigned to it all. I rubbed her neck in an effort to keep my hands warm and stop my teeth from chattering.

Within a few minutes Mr Hardwick was back with Jes and Sammy. He told me Horace was harnessing Magnolia and bringing her down. They had brought ropes, one of which they looped round the heifer's horns. We heard the mare coming and called out to guide Horace to us. The other end of the rope was fixed to Magnolia's collar. Horace led her very gently forward while the four of us, standing in the cold wet mud, pushed the poor fallen creature from behind. When she felt the firm pull from the rope, she made another scrambling, splashing effort. With her front legs up, the combined lifting of the four of us succeeded in getting her standing up. She swayed and staggered on trembling legs. Horace waited with Magnolia. We pressed hard against the heifer with our shoulders, keeping her up, while the mare began to pull steadily. Slowly the heavy animal staggered up the bank onto firmer ground. Albert Groom had joined us with a lantern, for it was now dark and the fog thick.

"Don't let her stop!" shouted Mr Hardwick. "Keep her going right up to the barn, then try to get her inside!" Slowly the little procession moved towards the barn, although the fog prevented anything but a general sense of direction guide us. The heifer moved better as we progressed. When almost there she walked without push or pull. Mr Hardwick slipped the rope from her and she walked straight in to the feed bucket which Teasel had long ago emptied. She was now halfway through Magnolia's hay.

"Greedy beggar!" said Mr Hardwick. "Give Thistle some more, Abey." As the rescued heifer ate her cereals she calmed down although her legs still quivered and she looked dreadful with the mud plastered all over her. She seemed to be recovering quite quickly.

"Couldn't have been there long," said Jes.

"No, very good thing," said Mr Hardwick. "We'll have to watch her, though, Abey." He turned to me. "She could very well have lost her calf; only another week afore she's due. Give her a clean down afore you comes in, then get yourself dry by the stove."

The men went in to get clean and dry, and I quickly rubbed the heifer down with sacking and straw.

"There you are, old girl," I murmured. When I had given her a thick bed of wheat straw and filled up Magnolia's hayrack, I hurried inside almost numb to the waist with cold and wet.

"Better get off home, Abey, and find some dry clothes," said Mr Hardwick, "I'll keep an eye on the heifer."

I ran all the way to Number Three where poor Mrs Pickvance threw up her hands in horror at the sight of me. She made me take everything off, there in the kitchen, wrapped me in a towel by the fire, then as I thawed out with a hot drink she boiled water in the copper outside. The tin bath was brought in and filled. After a hot bath and meal I was packed off to bed which had been warmed with a warming pan and contained a hot brick wrapped in a piece of flannel.

CHAPTER SEVEN

"Take Abey with you and see if you can move it. Most likely it will come off." Mr Hardwick was talking to Harry Teemer when I went into the shop from the yard next morning. The heifer, Teasel, had recovered remarkably from her previous evening's experience. She was still covered in dry mud but after feeding she went out into the field with Thistle. I had a little stiffness in my ankles but Mrs Pickvance's treatment seemed to have prevented anything else.

A waggon had broken down along the Lonestock road. It belonged to Seth Mottram at Trow's Farm.

"Get the cart, Abey," said Harry. I took Magnolia round and helped load up with wedges, hammers, ropes and other things we might need. It was just beginning to get light and snowflakes were again beginning to fall. I had my big coat on and some mittens which my mother had sent me, but it was bitterly cold. There was no wind and the snowflakes drifted slowly down.

"Put the sheet on, and I'll get my coat," said Harry. We set off. It was not far as the broken waggon stood just passed the turn to Lonestock. I could barely make out the name on the signpost. Maisie Hawtin flashed into my mind as I recalled my trip there to fetch the elm stocks. I wondered if she was still having difficulty with her younger sister.

"Overloaded by the look of it," said Harry, blowing onto his fingers. We pulled up alongside. The nearside back wheel had broken and about a quarter of the load of mangolds had spilled off and were still lying where they had fallen. "Get the jack out, Abey."

While Harry began to lift up the corner of the waggon with the jack I put chocks under the other wheels. The snow fell more thickly and made it difficult to see properly. From under the sheet on the cart I brought out hammers and wedges to remove the linchpin and ease the stock from the axle. Lack of grease made this difficult. The hammering was muffled by the thickening blanket of snow in the otherwise silent and deserted countryside.

Harry swore at the wheel, until at last it came off.

"Never bin greased since he had it!" he exclaimed with some

feeling, as he looked at the dry, rusty brown axle, shiny only where the revolving wheel had worn and burnished it. We built up blocks of oak under the waggon and removed the jack. Together we lifted the broken wheel into the cart with the tools. Magnolia, white with snow along her back and over the saddle, shook her head and snorted clouds of steam as we set off back to the workshop. The wheels of the waggon made two crisp lines all the way on the newly fallen snow.

Back in the shop we set to work on the broken wheel. The days were dark with the heavy snow clouds and even though we lit the lamps early it was difficult to see to work properly. When work was coming in or going out the icy blasts through the doorways brought the air in the shop down to the temperature outside. Even on days when the doors were kept closed and the iron stove was kept as hot as it would go, the workshop was bitterly cold. There was much coughing and stamping of feet. The water in the glue-pot froze at night and so did the pump in the yard. We had to take the cover off the well to let down buckets on a rope when we wanted water.

After another few days Teasel, having completely recovered from her distressing experience in the fog, produced a bull calf with no trouble at all. Not long after, just before we closed, Mr Hardwick brought Horace in to look at Thistle. He felt the deep hollows beside her tail, ran his hand round her bag and felt the milk veins.

"She'll calve before mornin' I reckon," he said quietly. I gave her a deep bed of straw before we went home.

"I'll look at her before I go to bed," said Mr Hardwick, and I agreed to go up and look again about midnight.

Mrs Pickvance sniffed and told me to make sure I locked the door when I let myself out. When I crept downstairs at midnight Eva made it plain that she was not expecting me to be leaving at that sort of time. I would have taken her with me for almost any other purpose, but a calving cow does not like to have a dog about. It had stopped snowing but a hard frost had made the previous day's snow hard and difficult to walk on. The moon was bright and as I looked across towards Lonestock I pictured Sedge Mottram's waggon and its load of mangolds standing frozen in the deserted snow. Again I thought of Maisie Hawtin, warm and snug in bed, whom I had only seen once across the yard, when she was calling crossly to her younger sister, so long ago now.

Mr Hardwick was there in the barn when I arrived and in the light of a hurricane lamp he was preparing to help the heifer who had already started.

"I'm glad you've come Abey," he said; "she's going to need some help. One of the calf's legs is turned back." He had rolled up his sleeves and with a bucket of cold water had started soaping his arm thoroughly. He pushed the leg that was just showing back inside, then by inserting his forearm endeavoured to straighten the one that was turned back. After a moment or two he looked at me; the shadows from the yellow lamplight were making strange shapes around us.

"The head's twisted as well." He tried for a few more minutes then said, "Run over and get Horace to come as quickly as he can!"

I ran to the cottage where Horace lived and knocked at the door. In the crisp frosty air with the moon now fully risen, the door-knocker sounded loud across the village. A dog barked next door and another one further away. Horace's wife put her head out of the bedroom window.

"What is it?" she asked. I told her and she disappeared inside. Shortly afterwards Horace's head appeared. "I'll be there, tell him," he said.

I went back to Mr Hardwick who was talking quietly to the heifer. She was lying on her side on the straw, her eyes big and frightened. She was straining hard and often now, to be rid of her progeny.

"Hold on now, old girl," he was saying, "don't you rush things. You'll be all right in a minute."

I added some dark brown disinfectant to a bucket of water and put the calving ropes in it. Within a few minutes Horace's cough could be heard coming along the village. He peeled off his jacket as he entered, soaped his arms and while Mr Hardwick held the heifer's tail to one side, he lay down beside the heifer and pushed back the twisted calf firmly. As he lay with his arm inside, up to his shoulder, he became more breathless and continued to cough slightly most of the time. After a moment or two of apprehension on his face, which was being studied anxiously by Mr Hardwick, he held his breath and made some supreme manipulation inside. As he relaxed he let out a long drawn breath that brought on a harsh fit of coughing. While he gasped for breath I handed him the ropes which he attached quickly to the unborn calf's front legs. The brown wet muzzle now appeared on top of the front legs; then, with an old piece of fork handle through the ropes we pulled steadily each time the heifer strained.

"Careful now!" said Horace, soaping all round the emerging calf, "Steady! - gently does it. All right my beauty, you'll be all right. Steady then - steady!"

After the shoulders appeared pulling was hardly necessary, and the calf slipped out onto the straw. Mr Hardwick pushed his fingers into its mucus-covered mouth and blew hard into it, but the exhausted creature lay quite still. Next he took a bucket of cold water and dashed it over the lifeless calf. It gave a great gasp and began breathing. We pulled it round to the heifer's head and she began to lick it.

"They'll be all right now," said Horace, drying his arms and putting on his jacket. Holding on to the wall he had another very hard coughing session, then sat for a few minutes on an upturned bucket.

"Make Horace some cocoa, Abey," said Mr Hardwick. "I brought a drop of milk with me."

Horace held up his hand and shook his head, unable to speak for a moment, then said, "No, I'll get back to bed. The Missus'll be up here, if I'm too long, to see where I be."

"Sit still, Horace," Mr Hardwick went on; "you'll have a drop of hot drink afore you go back. The night's cold. We don't want you laid up. It won't take Abey long."

I went into the workshop with a hurricane lamp and lit the oil-stove. The kettle, always kept full on the big iron stove, soon boiled. We sat round the stove with only the hurricane lamp while we drank the welcome hot cocoa. The two men spoke of days gone by. Other calvings were recalled and men long since gone were spoken of. I listened and drew closer in understanding to these two men who, as is often the case, were more relaxed out of the routine of daytime striving. Horace even leant across to me, once, to relate with a smile how Mr Hardwick's father had brought him home from Remsditch Mop Fair to calve a cow and how the cow had not calved until the following evening.

"I was at the fair with that Polly-what-was-her-name-girl, from up at the big house," he added to Mr Hardwick; "cross she was too, when I came away like that. Never spoke to me again!"

We took another look at the heifer before we left. She was standing again and the calf sucking underneath her on wobbling but quickly strengthening legs.

I walked back to Horace's cottage with him before going on to Number Three, but before we reached it he suddenly said to me in a low voice, "Give me a hand here a minute Abey," and led me alongside the house, then round into the back garden. "Don't breathe a word!" he whispered loudly. He was nearly choking, trying to stifle the persistent cough which the exertion and frosty air seemed to aggravate. He led the way along his garden path and slowly opened the door of the shed at the bottom to prevent the hinges squeaking.

"The're five bits o' walnut on the floor there. I want to get them up to the shop without anyone knowing. You'll have to feel where they are. You take one end and I'll take the other. We can manage two at once. It's my own stuff, lad, and it's quite legal, but I don't want it knowed about."

I felt for the ends of the boards. They were quite substantial pieces about two inches thick and six to seven foot long. Some were wider than others but averaging twelve inches across.

"If the missus hears us and calls out we'll have to leave it," Horace croaked. We carried the first two pieces up the village, over the frozen snow, and put them in the barn where the heifer was now suckling her new bull calf. Horace said no more because talking aggravated his cough, but as we entered the garden again he was seized with another fit that would not be stifled. As he waited to get his breath again we heard his wife calling from the bedroom window at the front.

"Is that you, Horace?"

"I'll go round," he said to me and disappeared, leaving me waiting in the garden. I heard the front door close and then silence followed. The church clock struck half past three. I walked round to the front and waited a little while but heard nothing more. The night was so cold that I decided it better to be doing something than standing about so I went quickly to the shed. By taking one board at a time I managed to get all of them up to the barn. I closed Horace's shed, thankful that I had not met the village policeman during the operation, then went home to bed.

Next morning while I was feeding the stock, Horace came out. Whether it was to see the new calf or to look at his walnut was difficult to say, but he came to the end of the stall where Magnolia was eating her hay to find me. "I didn't mean you to bring all that lot up here on your own, lad. Very good of you. I hoped we might get them up here between us, and not be noticed."

"What are you going to do with them?" I asked.

"We'll see, lad. I've had them boards for a good many years in that shed. True they took up a bit of room in there, but they're some good stuff.

"Are you going to use them up here, then?" I said, as I went round to the heifers.

"Well, not exactly," Horace said awkwardly. "You see it's the missus. She's bin on about them boards almost as long as I've 'ad 'em. She's asked young Hawtin to fetch 'em away, only I heard about it from Tapper Chalk as works there. She'll be 'oppin mad now when he arrives and they be gone!" He laughed quietly and started coughing. "Not a word about them lad, to anybody. I've mentioned it to Albert and he don't mind me keepin' them 'ere fer a bit. They won't hurt 'ere if we keep 'em flat. Good of you to bring 'em up 'ere like that, lad." He returned to the workshop, still coughing.

I went on feeding the stock and when I had finished Mr Hardwick came out to help me with the milking of the heifer that had calved the week before. I had handled her regularly before, so she was settling down to being milked quite well. After most of the milk had been taken her calf, which was now kept in a separate stall, was allowed to suck. The milk was now normal. The first milk, or bislings as we called it, was enjoyed by the men in the shop who had taken a little of it home each evening. I had taken some to Mrs Pickvance who used it to make a pudding. Mr Hardwick had arranged to supply one or two nearby folk regularly now, so the milk had to be cooled and put into jugs and cans left for the purpose. After a few days of bislings from Teasel her milk joined that of

Thistle, the milking being shared by Mr Hardwick, myself and a Mrs Green who nearly always helped at night.

Work continued on the waggon with George and Ben. The wheel for Mottram's waggon stood by the door, repaired and waiting for the frozen snow to thaw so that it could be re-fitted.

Two waggons were built in the shop that winter. I watched and noted their steady progress. The work in waggon building was satisfying although it was heavy; nearly every process was physically exhausting and tended to be mentally wearisome. The start was made by Mr Hardwick and the four men who worked at the waggon end. They would first set out the waggon on the floor of the shop to measurements known to all of them. The methods used, and the proportions of the waggons and carts that they made, had been established by wheelwrights of many generations. Information had been acquired by these men from their elders, and now in turn I began to absorb knowledge and understanding from my elders whose acquired skills were enriched by their own experience. No one said, "we do this" or "we do that," and no one explained why any particular thing was done, but over the months and years the ways and means of mastering ash, oak and elm were gradually absorbed. In this way a boy, later a man, would learn to feel intuitively, as much or even more than he could be said to know, the reasons for his methods.

For my first year I was mostly involved with helping at the wood end of the work shop as opposed to the waggon end, and under the watchful eye of Jes Beales I learned to handle the basic tools of my craft. However, the work of both ends was interwoven much more than in workshops of earlier times. Then, waggon making and carpentry had been kept distinctly apart, and the older men remembered when Mr Hardwick's father owned the wheelwright's business and had nothing to do with carpentry work. It was Albert Hardwick who joined the two together in the village, when the last carpenter had died and his business had been sold. The men in both shops opposed the idea originally but as more metal was used in the waggon-making and power was slowly introduced, it became accepted, although any reference to earlier days always brought a slow shaking of heads and expressions of regret from the older men. Often the work at one end overlapped the work of the other so I was able to see and occasionally give a hand with the waggon work, even while mainly occupied at the wood end.

CHAPTER EIGHT

It was shortly after Christmas, during my second year at Nether Oldston, when winter had deepened with a heavy fall of snow, and the men needed to blow hard on their fingers and keep stamping their feet in a desperate attempt to keep circulation going, that the door of the workshop burst open and, amidst a cloud of snow, the agitated figure of a middle-aged spinster from the village entered shouting, "Albert, come quickly!" She looked round, blinking hard to adjust her eyes to the dark after the brilliant whiteness of the snow outside, for the workshop was gloomy with closed doors and dusty, snow-covered windows. "Albert!" she shouted again, and looking round at the men demanded, "Where is he?"

Mr Hardwick came round from behind the waggon where he was working. "What's up, Betsy?" he asked.

"Oh Albert, my pantry roof has fallen in with the snow! What am I going to do? All my Christmas things are in there and all spoiled!"

"I'll get my coat," said Mr Hardwick, without further talk, and after beating the dust from his hat he accompanied her out through the little door, into the snow. The men looked at each other, smiling.

From beneath the waggon Ben Steel said, "Poor old Fitsy!" Betsy Harbottle had been known since her school days as 'Fitsy Bluebottle' and was not taken very seriously by the villagers.

"I'm surprised that old roof has stayed up so long," said Sammy.

"Have you done them bearers yet?" Albert Groom asked him, "I never knowed anyone take as long as you to make a few bearers. You be 'oldin' up the job, lad."

"What's the great 'urry then, Albert?" Sammy replied, looking for the gauge he had covered up with shavings a few minutes before.

"'Tain't so much of 'urry, Sammy, but a matter of gettin' on," persisted Albert, in the slow deliberate way he had of talking.

"'Urrying ain't the halternative to wasting time. I be doin' it as quick as I know 'ow," said Sammy finding the gauge and beginning to use it. Albert went back to his own bench where he began another task not connected with the work Sammy was doing.

When Mr Hardwick returned it appeared that the situation was a serious one. Jes, Sammy and I accompanied him back to where Fitsy lived. The little house had a small extension to the main square part in which the kitchen and pantry were situated. The roof on this extension was slated, whereas the main roof was thatched. The snow was lying about four inches thick and the timbers under the slates, obviously rotten, had given way. Fitsy had tried to remove what she could, but in fact the powdery, splintered timber, together with snow and slates, had indeed covered the remains of the poor woman's Christmas fare, as well as her immediate food requirements. As we surveyed the scene poor Fitsy wailed of spoiled icing and lost mincemeat.

"Come now, Betsy," said Mr Hardwick, taking her aside, "we'll soon sort it out. No amount of crying will put it right. You make us a nice drink of hot cider on your fire in there and we'll get on better."

We sorted out, as best we could, the pies and jam from the fallen timber and slates, the Christmas pudding and cake from the dust and snow. We carried what we thought might be salvaged into the kitchen end and the rest out to the garden where the hungry birds eagerly picked out anything edible from the heap. We fetched a tarpaulin from the workshop, stretched it across the damaged part of the roof, and tied it securely.

"Timber be full of maggot," said Jes to Mr Hardwick; "reckon it were bad from the time it were put up."

"Needs a new roof right across," he answered, "but we shall have to wait for better weather." Fitsy was buzzing like a real bluebottle, I thought, as she fussed round the larder remains, trying to spoon the pieces of roof out of her preserves.

"Keep the pantry door closed, Betsy, and hope the rest of it stays up," said Jes, as we wedged in two timbers as piers to hold up the kitchen part of the roof.

We sipped the hot cider in Fitsy's parlour where it was warm and cosy. While the men stood drinking and talking, I noticed two pencil and wash portraits, hanging by the fireplace. I recognised one immediately. It was Jenny Hawtin from Lonestock. The other, I thought, must be her sister Maisie, although the likeness was not so good. But of course, my memory of her was based on a single glimpse across a yard and that had been more than a year ago. I would have liked to get a closer look but the cider was finished, so we thanked Fitsy and prepared to leave. Mr Hardwick assured her that we would deal with the roof just as soon as the weather made it possible. After we left Sammy observed to me how thin the cider had been and how he reckoned most of it had come straight from the well behind her house.

"Some folks are never satisfied," said Jes, overhearing what he had said; "better'n cold tea on such a mornin' I'd say."

"Ah Jes, some folks can't tell the difference between hot cider and hot water. No discretion - that's your trouble!" retorted Sammy.

"I'd like you to call in on Betsy tomorrow, Jes, and measure up for new timbers in that roof," said Mr Hardwick; "then you can prepare them for when the weather's better."

As the winter deepened further, work in the shop grew more difficult. Daylight was short and oil lamps were alight most of the time, hanging close to where work was being attempted. Such jobs as planing and adzing were done to keep warm and the everlasting job of pit-sawing was carried on in the bitter conditions of the saw-pit. This was a rectangular hole dug in the ground outside, under a crude roof which kept off only the worst of the falling snow and rain. Each morning it had to be cleared of any snow that had blown in, before a start could be made. Most of the big log sawing was done by a pair of visiting sawyers who were hired for that purpose. Nevertheless, some pit sawing was done by Jes and Sammy and sometimes I had to take the horrible bottom position where a continuous stream of sawdust descended into one's ears, eyes, nose, throat, and mouth, and whence you never dared look up.

The snow continued and I was sent along to Fitsy Bluebottle's house to clear the heavy snow from the tarpaulin, in the hope that the kitchen would not suffer the same fate as the pantry. When I had done I was given a good tankard of hot cider while Fitsy questioned me about my home and anything else she could think of. I asked her if she had done the portraits near the fireplace.

"Bless you no! My sister did them. She's Mrs Hawtin up at Lonestock. Her two girls they be, Maisie and Jenny. Proper young madam that one is too," she added, pointing to the picture of Jenny. I remembered Jenny well enough from when she had helped me with loading the wheelstocks soon after I came to Nether Oldston.

"I went up there to collect some stuff for Mr Hardwick some time ago," I said. "I met Jenny then."

"Oh well, you know how she is then; very much of a handful. My sister wishes she lived nearer to me here so I could have the child sometimes, but I'm thankful I'm not for the same reason! I must say, though, that Maisie, that's the older girl, the one in the other picture, does a lot for her mother. I don't know how she would manage with Jenny if Maisie wasn't there to help."

"I must get back to the shop, Miss Harbottle, or Mr Hardwick will be wondering where I am," I said, draining the last drop of cider and moving towards the door.

"That's right, lad; thank Albert for me and tell him I'll be down to see Gwen later this week." I thanked her for the cider and then trudged back to the shop, carrying my shovel through the still gently falling snow.

The village was silent and the snow had begun to drift, giving it a strange unfamiliar look. My thoughts centred again on Lonestock. I wondered if the Hawtin family might be cut off by the snow. Crash! A snowball smacked hard and painful on my ear, then a barrage of them rained round me. I ran as best I could in the deepening snow. I made out the two figures behind the churchyard wall as Perce Chennel and Jake Pooley, with whom I had brushed before since coming to Nether Oldston. They were a pair of oafs who took great delight in the discomfiture of another being, especially if they were the cause of it. I scooped up snow to retaliate but they already had a store of snowballs behind the wall so I had no choice but to flee, as they laughed and shouted after me. My ear was still stinging when I reached the workshop.

For the next few days I found myself digging snow from the doors of the workshop and yard, from round Mrs Pickvance's house and from Fitsy Bluebottle's roof. The village became cut off from the rest of the world for nearly three weeks and rude sledges were hammered together at Hardwick's shop. Magnolia was used to pull one of these and Jes managed to get through to Remsditch and bring back some provisions just before the snow drifted and became too deep.

One Saturday afternoon Roderick Walker and I had been up on the hill behind the allotments with a sledge and when we arrived back at the stores for tea, Sally was relating how the nurse was at the bakery. Joseph Watts, the baker, was ill with appendicitis.

"There's no way through for the doctor, nor can they get him to hospital," she was saying, smiling and adjusting her hair when she saw Roderick and me. While we warmed ourselves by the kitchen range with its hot coals and dull red iron top glowing in the dark recess where it stood, we ate thickly buttered toast and sipped scalding hot tea.

Sally continued to relate the plight of the Watts family. "The nurse says he's got to be kept warm and still but his lower part," here she indicated her own lower abdomen, "must be kept as cold as possible!"

"Wonder what they'll do?" said Mrs Walker. "Perhaps they'll dig the road through."

"No chance of that. They'd never do it," said her husband. "There's the bakery to see to as well. We'll go round and see what's happening after tea, Roderick." Sally said she would see us there and departed.

We went to the bakery with Mr Walker where things were much as Sally had described them. To add to the difficulties, a day or two later Mrs Watts, while struggling to keep the bakery going, fell, twisting her ankle and breaking her arm. Roderick was sent round to help with the baking and I accompanied him during the evenings when, under the instruction of Mrs Watts, we kneaded the dough, cleaned and fuelled the bread oven, sawed firewood and generally exhausted ourselves.

Sally was there most evenings and when she had finished helping in the house she would come to sit in the bakery with us and relate all the nurse had said about poor old Joseph Watts. After a day or two we got the hang of the bread oven and we managed to produce tolerable bread for the village. However, a certain Mr Grinstead referred to by the Watts as 'Soldier Grinstead' presented himself at the Watts house at about this time. A year or so before he had taken up residence in one of the small cottages near the bakery and, according to reliable sources, was a retired army gentleman living alone on his pension and supplementing it by giving riding instruction at Oldston House. Apart from his ability on a horse and his occasional trips up to London, little was known about him. He kept his triangular garden well and was best known for the loud-checked trousers that he usually wore. Sally reported that he had offered his services and assistance with things. Within a very short time he had taken control, insisted that Mrs Watts rested as much as possible, and was striding around giving orders to Roderick and me.

"Be a little more careful measuring for the dough, you boys; the loaves are not even enough in size," he called out one evening as we arrived. He was sitting in the kitchen by the fire with Mrs Watts. He had already pointed out, on a previous evening, how much he would like to help with the heavier work but due to an old war wound he was unable to do so. His displeasure at our presence was obvious but he had to keep this under control, because we were really needed and also because he wished to appear reasonable, to Mrs Watts. Meanwhile as the days of winter isolation continued, Mr Watts' condition remained serious, even slightly worse. Roderick confided in me that the loud-check trousered Mr Grinstead was after the bakery business and was clearly reckoning on Joseph Watts not pulling through.

"Why don't we point it out to Mrs Watts?" I said, as we walked towards Roderick's home later.

"She wouldn't listen. She reckons as he's a helping her. She can't see as how he's a helpin' his self a sight more!"

The time that Mr Grinstead spent at the Watts' house was noticed by all the village and in the Barley Mow it was said openly "He be waitin' to carry poor old Joseph up the churchyard."

"They tells me as how you've got a new friend," said Jes to me, one midday when we and the other men in the workshop were trying to get nearer the old tortoise stove while we ate our sandwiches.

"Oh, who's that then?" I asked, innocently, wondering why he winked at Albert Groom.

"Why, Mr Soldier Grinstead," he replied in mock surprise. "I hears you spend many an evening in his company."

I scowled. "You know the truth of the situation, Jes Beales, and I'm not being baited by you," I said.

Mr Hardwick came in then with a can of hot cider to warm us all up. It was shared out eagerly, for the biting cold made working very hard to endure through the long hours of the day Catching the name Grinstead, Mr Hardwick said "I hear he's round there most of the day. Is that right Jes?" The conversation then became one of speculation as to what might develop at the bakery.

A certain amount of work was carried on in the workshop during this bitter weather but it was mostly limited to heavy sawing, planing and the trimming of timber with the adze. These processes kept warm the part above the belt but allowed everything else to become stiff and numb with cold. Being young, I was able to move about more quickly than the older men. Horace and George Groom, in particular, suffered even the danger of frostbite as their movements became slower while the temperature dropped lower and lower. Water became scarce as it froze quickly after being drawn from the well. Pumps everywhere had frozen solid with ice. With the workshop doors closed against the weather and snow clinging to the windows it was almost impossible to see to work. Getting to Fitsy Bluebottle's home became more difficult in itself without the added task of keeping the snow from the remaining part of her kitchen roof. However, with the help of Sammy sometimes, I managed to do it.

One afternoon we were up on the roof when a shower of snowballs assailed us. The fluctuating aggression which had developed between me and the two youths, Perce Chennel and Jake Pooley, was responsible for this, for during the snow shovelling period they had managed occasionally to be nearby when I was on Fitsy's roof, offering an easy target for their hard-pressed, forcefully thrown snowballs. Red-faced and shaking with laughter, they would run off, leaving me bruised and sore from their onslaught. Whether they had not seen

Sammy with me this time I did not know, for never before had they attacked unless I was alone.

"Come on, Abey!" shouted Sammy, throwing down his shovel and jumping down from the roof. I followed him and we gave chase, but before we even reached the ground they had gone. "All right!" panted Sammy, "We'll get the sods!" He stood gasping for a moment or two and then after finishing the shovelling we laid our plans for retaliation.

I knew where Perce and Jake usually waited with their snowballs and we made a careful examination of the place. It was on old stone hovel with a poor roof upon it. Sammy and I managed to fix a big old door, which was lying where it had fallen off its hinges, across the roof in such a way that by pulling a rope from outside, we could make the door drop at one side like a trap door. This was all arranged above the place where the two ruffians needed to stand to take aim through an opening in the wall. We then piled snow on the fixed-up door. Preparing these arrangements was a very cold job and we were both almost frozen by the time we returned to the workshop. However, we were lucky, for another fall of snow came that night concealing our work and piling yet more snow on the hanging door.

Jake Pooley worked with the thatcher, Arthur Bourton, and Perce Chennel was employed at Trow's Farm, but somehow they always contrived to get together if one of them saw me making my way to Fitsy's house. I arranged with Sammy to show myself walking towards the house carrying my shovel, that next morning. Whistling loudly, I climbed up and onto the roof. I began shovelling. Perce and Jake crept into the hovel, quickly made a few hard snowballs, then stood ready to take aim directly beneath the spot where we had fixed the door in the roof. Meanwhile, Sammy had positioned himself at the back where he could watch them through a small gap in the stonework. He grasped the rope. Then, just as they were about to let fly, he pulled hard. The weight of the new snow on the door was almost as much as it could bear and it made the catch very hard to move. Sammy pulled again more forcefully. He thought it was not going to work, but then it moved just enough to release the weight above it, and the snow burst through. Snow from a sloping roof behind the hovel followed it and within seconds the two youths and their prepared piles of snowballs were completely covered. They gave a cry of surprise as they disappeared, then all went quiet, until their arms came floundering through and they crawled out spluttering and gasping. I held my sides with laughing as Sammy joined me on the roof, whence we watched them running off, shaking snow from their clothes and looking thoroughly cold and miserable.

CHAPTER NINE

One evening, Roderick and I were sawing up logs for the fire. We were in the Watts' shed working by the light of a lantern. We could hear the wind howling outside even above the noise of the saw. Suddenly the door opened and the figure of Mr Grinstead backed in, clutching his hat in one hand and struggling to pull the door shut with the other. Quite breathless, he asked us, with unusual politeness, if we would help him move some heavy boxes at his house one evening, as they were too heavy for him to manage alone. Not liking to refuse, we agreed to go the next evening.

The following morning I was milking one of the cows when Mr Hardwick came in. "Nip round to Snobbo Pinchin and collect a pair of boots, Abey. He's put some new heels on them. Tell him I'll pay him when I see him. Go when you've finished out here."

Jes was splitting up short ends for the fire when I went through the workshop and Horace was coughing heavily, half lying across his bench and making dreadful wheezing noises. Sammy and Albert Groom were making a coffin for old Seth Mottram, from Trow's Farm.

"Ninety, all but two days," Albert was saying; "'eed a made it but fer this 'ere weather." Sammy was starting to saw the kerfs in the elm boards to allow them to bend to shape for the sides. Hardwick's shop only did undertaking for Nether Oldston, Lonestock and Broughton Dagston. Digging the grave was a problem in such weather. Mr Hardwick was discussing it with Bunker Cobham, the grave-digger, as I put on my coat. There would be at least two feet of snow to clear before he could try to break the frosted ground.

"You wait till the thaw, gaffer," Bunker was saying. "Old Seth won't hurt fer a few days this weather. Put 'im in 'is box and let 'im be till the ground gives a bit."

I collected the boots from the cobbler and on my way back met Sally Pullen going along to help at the Watts'.

"Don't you go up to Grinstead's tonight!" she greeted me. "That man is up to no good, sure as our cat likes gravy."

"It's only to move a few boxes," I protested.

"Maybe, but you keep clear of him, Abey Staughton, or I

won't speak to you again, and that's that!"

"Well wait a minute, Sally -" I began, but she said she must hurry and added as she departed, "But I mean what I say!"

I stood looking after her as she walked carefully on the hard trodden track through the snow. I wondered why she was so definite about it all. She knew that Roderick and I disliked Soldier Grinstead but to move a few boxes for him was hardly likely to lead to trouble.

I went back to the shop where I was given the never-ending task of planing elm boards ready for coffin making. Although it was one way of keeping warm, it was very hard work, the grain being so twisted and awkward. Even with a very small-mouthed plane, little bits of short, opposite grain, would jam up between the cutting-iron and the backiron, which necessitated the removal of both and a re-setting of the heavy beech plane. Our stock of prepared coffin-boards was low and Mr Hardwick felt that with the bad weather we could be in need of some quickly. Later on Bunker Cobham returned red-faced to report his efforts up in the churchyard. Mr Hardwick was underneath the big waggon so Bunker, half bent, with hands on knees and holding onto his cap, called out how he had "even tried a pickaxe!" after he had cleared the snow.

"But it's like trying to dig through a piece of rock," he complained, straightening up to blow his nose. He stood listening for Mr Hardwick's reply but none came, so he bent again. "Did you hear, Albert?" he called.

"Ah, I heard," came the reply from underneath.

Bunker followed it up quickly. "I tell yer old Seth'll keep fer as long as this 'ere weather lasts. Soon as it thaws I'll do it and we'll 'ave 'im in there as quick as ninepence!"

Later on, Sammy and I carried the coffin up to Trow's Farm. It was not very far to the house but we made a forlorn little procession. Mr Hardwick and Jes followed us to do what was necessary when we got there. We walked one behind the other in the narrow track cut out through the snow. We were let in by Seth's widow. The house was as cold inside as the weather outside.

"He's lain in that room fer nigh on ninety years man and boy," she sniffed. "I dare say a night or two extra won't make no odds," and she wiped her eyes with a corner of the big white apron she was wearing.

The men accompanied her to lay the body in the coffin while we lads waited in the hall. We swung our arms about, trying to keep warm, and Sammy caught his fingers on the newel post of the stairs. He cried out at the unexpected pain and jumped around like a madman for a minute while I laughed, adding to his anger.

The others returned and Sammy nursed his fingers silently under his armpit. Mrs Mottram was saying that Greg, her younger grandson, had already said he wouldn't be staying at the farm with his brother now that the old man had gone.

"It's that Betsy Pike from Froglies Green who's put him up to it," she said; "young madam! Our Greg wouldn't have thought of going on his own. But there you are, youngsters today are ready to be up and off without a thought fer anyone else. Look at that poor widow Tasker up the village who's –" But Mr Hardwick interrupted her, apologising for having to hurry away, as work was pressing.

At three o'clock I began the stock feeding. Although I often wished I hadn't the extra winter farm work to do, I must admit I was pleased enough that afternoon to leave the planing of those elm boards until the next day.

In the evening I called for Roderick and as soon as we had done what was necessary at the bakery we went to Grinstead's cottage. In the darkness, as we picked our way through the trodden snow, I pictured Soldier Grinstead waiting for us. Mrs Watts told us that he gone home early to attend to a little business. His slightly bowed legs, hidden by his wider than fashionable checked trousers, would have carried him quickly through the snow. His many years as a soldier culminating as a warrant officer in a cavalry regiment, gave him a bearing quite different from most of the villagers. His straight back and upright stance contrasted with men who had spent as many years guiding a plough or leaning over a bench. We saw the light in his window and walked up the path. Roderick gave a 'crash' on the knocker which made a piece of plaster fall from the top of the small porch where we stood waiting. After a few moments we saw a light coming round the side of the cottage. Grinstead appeared carrying a lantern and bade us follow him. He led us to a shed in his garden and showed us three quite large wooden boxes with nailed-down lids. They had rope handles.

"I want these putting in my kitchen where I can unpack them," he said; "they contain heavy books and such like. I have not had a chance to do anything with them yet but it is time they came indoors." He held the lantern while we took a handle each on the first box.

"Mercy me!" gasped Roderick. "Wait a minute, let me get another grip!" The boxes were very heavy and it was as much as much as we could do to lift one off the ground.

"Careful now!" said Grinstead, as we edged out through the door and put it down for a rest. He fidgeted around us, waving the lantern and making the shadows dance about over the garden path.

"I didn't know books could be so heavy!" I said, during the third rest between the shed and the back door of the cottage.

"Full leather bindings weigh heavy," said Grinstead, smoothing his hair and waving the lantern towards the cottage like a cold country station-master seeing a train off and wanting to get back to the fire in his ticket office.

"Just leave it there," he ordered, when the first box was through the doorway into the kitchen. "Now fetch the next one."

When the third box was at last in with the others, we were quite exhausted. Grinstead thanked us, gave us a few coppers, then wishing us goodnight, firmly showed us out.

"Leather bindings indeed!" muttered Roderick, still breathing heavily from the exertion, as we walked away back to his house. "I've never seen books bound in lead, but I'll wager every one of those was, and probably the pages made of it too!"

"I wonder what they are about," I said.

"What?" asked Roderick.

"Why, those heavy books."

"Army law or something as dry," he answered darkly, still smouldering over the weight of the boxes.

Later that evening when I let myself into Number Three, Mrs Pickvance had gone to bed and Eva had fallen asleep with her head on her paws, waiting for me. She was soon awake and with the usual difficulty I managed to get past her overjoyed tailwagging and into the kitchen, where I spent a few minutes making a fuss of her. She followed me down the garden path to the privy and sat shivering between the shovelled snow on either side of the path until I reappeared. She ate her bowl of food while I had my supper as she seldom touched it before I came home although Mrs Pickvance always fed her earlier. When we were both ready, I carried her up to my room where she wriggled round and round on my bed, blowing down her nose and waving her tail every time I looked at her.

"For goodness sake, Eva, settle down or Mrs Pickvance will hear you!" I whispered loudly in her ear, causing her to lie on her back with all four legs waving ridiculously in the air. She only settled down after I had fallen asleep myself when she was able to creep over the bedclothes to lie with her head on my legs.

That night the thaw came and it came quickly. I was surprised to hear the dripping and gurgling as the melting snow ran from roofs and ricks in the early morning darkness. Instead of the crisp cold air of the last few weeks it now felt very damp and more unpleasantly cold. The workshop field and the grazing pastures along the back of the village were flooded as the stream rose above its banks. Suddenly all the jobs that could not be done before needed attending to at once. There was Fitsy's roof, the stranded waggon along the Lonestock road, old Seth Mottram to be buried, two village pumps needing attention after their icing up, as well as the usual work in the shop to keep going. Mrs Green was at home with 'flu and could not help with the milking and Horace's coughing seemed to take up most of his time.

The truth is, I was quite glad to have the extra milking while the pumps were being repaired, for during cold weather nothing was more unpleasant than helping to do this job which required descending into the well to attend to the 'clacker' valve, when it became stuck after being frozen. Somehow one always got wet and then had to stand about in a cold wind while the work was completed. No doubt I would have had to go had I not been milking when the men left, but Sammy went instead.

A few days later as I was finishing outside, Mr Hardwick

called out, "Take Magnolia round next door, Abey; I forgot to tell you young Peter's a goin' to fix that loose shoe. Bring her back if he can't do it tonight." I frowned to myself, for this meant finishing late and I had arranged to go out with Sally that night, and hoped to get away in good time. Sally was not helping at the bakery that evening as Mrs Watts' mother had come to stay for a few days to help. Mr Watts was now in hospital and at last getting over his appendicitis.

I put the halter on Magnolia and led her round to the blacksmith's shop. "Where yer bin then Abey, lad?" asked Peter Brooks, the blacksmith's assistant.

"He's only just told me," I said, "and I didn't want to be too late tonight."

"Ah well, let's 'ave a look at 'er. Just 'old 'er, Abey, it won't take long." He lifted up the back leg with its loose shoe and drawing his tray of tools nearer with his foot, selected what he needed. Grasping the great hairy hoof between his aproned knees, it was not many minutes before he threw the hammer into the tray again and said, "There you be then, Abey me lad. That won't keep yer long from yer Sally."

"How do you know about that?" I said, surprised and feeling my face flush, as I fumbled with the halter.

"Come on now, never mind that, you get back round there and get finished."

When I had put Magnolia in her stall, all the men had gone home and only Mr Hardwick was in the workshop, as I went through to sweep up and collect my dinner bag.

"You'll have to give a hand as bearer tomorrow, Abey, for old Seth Mottram," he said. "We're burying him at half past two. We shall only need four. There'll be Jes, Sammy and Harry Teemer. You'll have an early dinner-time then we'll go up to the farm at two o'clock."

I nodded and said goodnight, then ran most of the way to Number Three, and after a hasty meal made myself ready to call on Sally Pullen. We were going to a concert in the village hall so I did not want to be late.

It was past seven that evening when I arrived at the door of the cottage where Abe Pullen, the blacksmith, lived with his wife and two daughters. Sally was two years younger than Sarah, but always had enough to say for both of them. She was quick-tempered and quite pretty. Competition was poor in the village when it came to beauty. Ability in the home and on the land was considered most important by a young man seriously considering partnership, but like most of the youths of my age all I wanted was a companion to stroll with who was good for a kiss and cuddle occasionally. Sally was more serious in her approach and I suspect that at that time considered me to be a good bet for the future. Her father was aware of this and although he appeared to have forgotten the time when I had taken Sally home late one morning, after haymaking, he seemed to be afraid of her getting too serious.

"Don't 'ee let 'et get too gone on yer, me lad. 'Er's a good gal but 'er gets too carried away," he said, while Sally went to get her coat.

The big wall clock ticked slowly as I nodded and answered, "Yes, all right, Mr Pullen." Sally appeared wearing the new coat her mother had made. The clock struck a quarter past seven and we set off to the wooden hall where the concert was being held.

The concert was an annual event and usually took place about the end of February, "To help us all through the dreary days," as the producer, Mrs Pinchin, was heard to say almost every day between Christmas and the chosen date. This year it had been postponed for one week as the snow had made it difficult to rehearse. It was the usual pattern, with all the talent coming from the village except for one performer from Remsditch, who played the mouth-organ. There were to be songs, a recitation and a short one-act play, which Mrs Pinchin and Fitsy Bluebottle had written between them and had produced after many weeks of devoted practice.

We managed to get seats quite near the front just behind Mr Grinstead. Sally at once expressed her displeasure at having so tall a creature between herself and the platform, adding in only a slightly lower tone her own derogatory opinion of the former soldier. With the general hubbub of talking and moving of chairs it was unlikely that he heard.

"Shsh, Sally," I said, "change places with me;" but Sally pointed out more loudly that to do so would simply allow her a view of the other end of the stage instead of the one she already had.

The hall was cold in spite of the two big cast-iron stoves noisily stoked by Bunker Cobham. To sit near one of these was to risk getting scorched on one side and being engulfed by a black cloud in the event of a downdraft. The audience came prepared with heavy overcoats, thick scarves and wintergreen sweets. Before long the show started to the accompaniment of fidgeting feet below and a heavy mixture of pipe smoke and stove fumes above.

Herbert Walker appeared first, looking strange without his long, white, fringed grocer's apron. He related his humorous monologues and soon the concert was well under way with vigorous hand clapping and footstamping punctuating each turn to keep the blood circulating in the audience. During the play, which was full of local humour. George Bless, the saddler, laughed so much that he swallowed his wintergreen sweet and had to be helped from the hall, choking loudly and in a somewhat distressed condition. His wife went with him, apologising continuously to those around them, and finally to those on the stage, who had stopped performing and were waiting for them to get out of earshot.

At the end all the entertainers appeared together on stage when the national anthem was sung by everyone, before they departed for home, saying how much they had enjoyed it and what a lot of work everyone concerned had put in. Bunker Cobham, looking important in his white coat with 'Village Hall' embroidered by his wife on the top pocket, started crashing the various dampers on the iron stoves, raking the bottom embers noisily, while new clouds of ash and dust arose.

I managed to say goodnight to Sally outside her front door without making another date for two weeks, then still with the smell of the village hall in my nostrils I returned to Number Three, where, once in bed, I fell asleep to dream of Fitsy Bluebottle shovelling snow down Soldier Grinstead's check trousers and Bunker Cobham squeezing lead-bound books into an enormous cast-iron stove, saying how difficult they were to burn because they kept melting.

CHAPTER TEN

As soon as the snow had departed work began on Fitsy Bluebottle's house, and on the day after the concert old Seth Mottram was to be laid to rest. I disliked the undertaking side of Hardwick's business but sentiment was not allowed to interfere with the course of work and it was naturally considered an important part of apprenticeship to experience all sides of the trade.

Just after two, Jes, Harry, Sammy and I left the workshop to walk up to the farm. Black suits and tall hats were kept for this purpose by Mr Hardwick and each of us wore the size that fitted us best. My braces were pulled up hard so that the roomy trousers came up almost under my armpits and a piece of twine round my waist kept them from billowing out. The long jacket hid most of this and apart from our faces being different, the four of us all looked very much alike.

The track from the farm to the road was very rough so the farm horse which pulled the waggon was led very slowly indeed as it carried the coffin towards the church. We walked two at each side, holding a rope tied to the coffin handles to keep it in the centre of the waggon as it jolted and shook along. The east wind went straight through the thin black cloth of the mourning suits and bit right through to the bone. Harry and I were on the windward side and I can remember wondering if we would get to the road before I became too stiff to walk any further. I could hear Sammy's teeth chattering even above the rattle of the waggon wheels. We tended to jerk our ropes in a paralytic way and more than once I dropped mine altogether when I had quite a job trying to get hold of it again with my stiff hands and limbs.

At last the road was reached and the waggon turned towards the church. The wind now lay behind us and swept along with even more force. Our tall black hats could not be restrained now even by pulling them hard down over our ears and holding them with one hand, so we removed them and put them in the waggon. Harry's frozen fingers let his go and it sped ahead of us to settle in the hedge further up the road. Mr Hardwick who was waiting for us retrieved it and put it in the waggon when we reached him. Just before we got to the church, where the group of mourners waited, we hoisted the coffin onto our shoulders, Harry and Jes in front with Sammy and me behind. A black pall was arranged over the top which covered our heads. Harry and Jes arranged the folds so that they could see enough of Mr Hardwick, who was leading, to be able to follow him. Sammy and I followed by feeling and an occasional glimpse of black boots below. I can remember, even now, the bliss of having that pall protecting my ears from the biting wind. Mr Hardwick clutched his hat with both hands, then at the speed of the slowest mourners, we proceeded towards the church. When we reached the door the pall was removed and I slipped it into a cloth bag before we entered. Bunker Cobham had managed to dig the grave and before long the depressing scene of a burial in a wintry village churchyard, with the wind blowing over the grass mounds, still harbouring traces of snow, and the early darkness already making me think of shutting up the hens, was over.

We returned to the workshop. The pall was hung up over the stove to dry, the black funeral clothes changed and folded away ready for the next time.

I went out to attend to the stock-feeding and found all the hens had already gone to roost. The heavy sky and the little daylight made the length of a hen's day very short, and of course reduced the production of eggs accordingly.

The carpenters finished their work at Fitsy's house and soon afterwards, when she had arranged her kitchen, she stopped talking of her lost Christmas pudding and turned her thoughts to marmalade making; then as spring approached she began her gardening again. Ricks were threshed at the farms in the village and once when labour was short at Crosswood Farm Mr Hardwick sent me up to help for a day. I enjoyed the change although Mrs Pickvance insisted on me getting into the tin bath when I reached home covered in dust from chaff and old straw.

Evenings grew longer and allotments were planted. I noticed their checkered patterns and the increasing number of little wooden and tin huts dotted here and there, and rounded trousered forms bending over to hoe and weed until after dusk when, on fine evenings, the benches outside the Barley Mow were full of animated discussions of the local prospects.

"Haymakin' agen if this 'ere weather 'olds," said Harry Teemer's father to Bunker Cobham, who nodded in agreement. They raised their tankards to a good crop.

One summer evening when I had called at Fitsy Bluebottle's cottage to collect some jam for Mrs Pickvance, I found Maisie Hawtin just leaving. She had been to visit her aunt. Although it must have been all of two years since that day when I had seen her up at Lonestock, and then only for a quick glance when she came out to get Jenny, when I was collecting elmstocks, I recognised her immediately. She smiled as she whisked past me to the road, carrying a basket. I followed her with my eyes, and after she had turned the corner of the house I found myself stopped in my tracks, staring at the spot where she had disappeared from view. I turned again to greet Fitsy who was standing at her door. She told me her neice had just been in to collect jam she had made for her sister.

"She's coming again on Friday for some more," she added and led me into the house to show me where she wanted a shelf fixing in her kitchen. "Now Abey, I need a shelf putting up just here. See if you can find an odd piece of something up at Albert's then come in one evening and fix it for me," she said.

Thinking of Maisie calling on Friday, I quickly agreed to see what I could manage. Fitsy put some jars of jam into a basket for me and after a cup of stewed dark brown tea I left, just in time to see Arthur Bourton driving his sow towards his cottage. He had been to collect her from a visit to the boar at Trow's Farm.

"Third time 'er's bin up there, Abey. Costin' too much 'er is. If 'er don't 'old now, 'er's off to the butcher!"

"Too fat she is, Mr Bourton, that's her trouble," I observed.

"Ah, so old Gill Mottram says, but a pig's got to be fat, I reckon."

We walked behind the grunting mass, as she plodded along with her ears appearing completely to cover her eyes, until we reached the thatcher's cottage gate, where a stick was firmly held in front of her. The sow gave a squeal, dodged past the stick and ran on towards the green. Arthur Bourton swore and tried to head her off, but the fat old waddler had suddenly become transformed into a streak of lightning which, no matter how fast we ran, managed to stay just ahead. Every time we tried to close the gap she broke into a run but if we stopped so did she. On past the green we went. One or two people coming towards us tried to head her off, quite unsuccessfully. Peter Brooks, the blacksmith's assistant, came up from behind on his bicycle and, putting on a sprint, gave her a good run until they reached the pond. Without a moment's hesitation the sow ran in and swam to the middle. There she stayed, floating and grunting with pleasure. Arthur Bourton at first called kindly to her, then threatened her with various kinds of violent death; a long silence followed, during which he fumed and fought to control his anger in the lingering heat, but finally, with the sweat running down into his eyes, he called the blissfully cool, floating sow, every name he could think of.

"Get a long pole, Arthur!" shouted someone. Already quite a number of watchers had gathered. Children were running up the village and old men were hobbling quickly towards the scene, leaning on their sticks.

"Get a rope round her!" came another suggestion. A long pole was found and floated out to try to push the sow to one side. It had to be a very long pole and was difficult to manœuvre, but by standing with trouser legs rolled up and knee-deep in water Arthur and myself, now aided by Peter Brooks, managed to line the pole up and push it hard against the round, nearly submerged, floating sow. Instantly a loud squeal of protest came across the water, but apart from turning round slightly, she remained where she was. After a few more tries during which the sow became more skilled in avoiding the pole, this was abandoned. Two or three people tried to throw a rope over her but the shape of that part of a pig that floats above water is not a good one for attaching a rope to. When a rope did come to rest over her hulk, and very carefully she was being pulled towards the shore, she waited, apparently enjoying the ride, until she was near the side and then simply slipped under the rope and floated back to the middle again, amidst a chorus of dismayed shouts from pursuers and cheers from the crowd. Arthur Bourton seized a stone and hurled it hard at her but missed. He stood shaking his fist, red-faced and swearing.

"She'll come out when she's hungry," said Horace, who

had joined us.

"I'll give 'er 'ungry when she does!" said Arthur, with some feeling.

The Barley Mow, taking advantage of the entertainment, now began to serve drinks outside. The crowd grew. Obviously it was an evening to enjoy. Time went on and still the sow showed no signs of coming ashore. People drifted into the inn. When twilight fell Arthur fetched the sow's feeding bucket and rattled it. Why he did not try this before I do not know, but when he did there was instant interest from the floating hulk. After some movement to shake water out of her ears, she began to glide slowly towards the sound of the rattling bucket. In a few more moments she came out of the water and followed the bucket home.

"You old sod!" said Arthur thickly as he banged the sty door behind her, making sure it caught the fatness of her bottom as it closed. This caused one more squeal as if to say "Leave me alone!" to split the otherwise peaceful, evening air.

CHAPTER ELEVEN

I arranged to fix Fitsy Bluebottle's shelf on Friday evening in the hope that Maisie would not already have called in during the day. As soon as I had swallowed my evening meal I carried a few tools round to the cottage where I had left a suitable piece of softwood on my way home from Hardwick's. I soon gathered that Maisie had not yet come, but her aunt was expecting her at any minute. The fixing of the shelf was not a difficult job and although I took as long as possible without actually stopping I had to finish and clear up without any sign of Maisie. I gladly accepted a glass of home-made wine but even that had been almost drained before the long expected knock came at the door and Maisie looked in. Her big blue eyes opened wide in surprise to find me there.

"Hello!" she said, "I thought Aunt Betsy would be here. I'll just put my bike somewhere." She disappeared again and the door closed. I said "Hello," after she had gone. I felt awkward, standing with my now empty glass. Fitsy heard the door close and came into the kitchen.

"Was that Maisie?" she asked.

"Yes," I said, "she's putting her bike somewhere." I thanked her for the drink and picked up my tools. Maisie came in again as I reached the door.

"Hello, Aunt Betsy. Oh, are you just going?" she said, as I held the door open.

"Yes, I've just finished. Goodbye," I said.

"Oh well, goodbye then," she smiled. As if in a trance I began putting my tools into the basket of her bicycle which she had leant against the wall. Suddenly I realised I had not brought a bicycle and hurriedly removed them, glancing back at the door. Fortunately it was closed. I walked slowly back to Mrs Pickvance's.

Quickly I washed, changed and carefully combed my hair. Calling Eva, I set off with her at my heels along the village street. Maisie's bicycle was still outside Fitsy's door, so I wandered on out of the village along the road towards Lonestock until the sun began to sink. After a long while, and filled with disappointment, I called Eva, who was some yards ahead in the ditch, and as the evening deepened we turned back. In a gateway I stopped and climbed up to sit on the gate. Crickets were everywhere in the warm grass and far across the field behind me I could just make out a herd of silently grazing cattle. A frog croaked not far from me while Eva sat watching a bat swooping near. Suddenly without warning the sound of a bicycle could be heard on the road. I jumped from the gate, Eva stood up expectantly and Maisie Hawtin, with a basket of jam tied to her carrier, pedalled past without seeing us.

It was earlier than usual when I awoke a few mornings later. I lay in bed thinking things over. I had been in Nether Oldston for a long time now and felt I had learned something of the trade for which I was apprenticed, although I did still feel that if more time had been spent with wood and less messing about with livestock, I would have learnt more. Perhaps though, I mused, there was something in what Jes had said about the importance of time being spent in the atmosphere of the work. It was my firm intention to have a shop of my own one day and the experience of living with the people who made up the local trade was obviously important. I lay turning it over in my mind.

The scent of the hay on that midsummer morning, as it floated in on the light breeze through my window and gently moved the curtains, reminded me of immediate tasks. As I turned over to enjoy a last few minutes before rising, I saw Eva's eyes open and close again. I thought of the months ahead. Perhaps this Michaelmas I might go to Remsditch fair. I wondered if Maisie ever went to fairs. A pity I had missed her the other evening. My mind drifted, half dreaming of what I might have said to her if I had met her along the road. If only her bike had had a puncture or perhaps the jam might have come loose on her carrier, or perhaps - oh well - I lay in bed musing for a moment longer. Anyway she was bound to visit her aunt again, so resolving to keep my eyes open for such a happening, I got out of bed. Perhaps a bicycle might be a good investment for me, I thought, as I stood stretching and pushing Eva away with one bare foot as she tried to lick the other one.

The morning was warm and when I had done my stockman's round, which at this time of the year was at its lightest, Mr Hardwick told me to go with Harry Teemer to see a waggon that had broken down during haymaking on the Oldston House Estate, most of the land of which lay up behind and beyond Oldston House and the church. Normally Ben James went with Harry to attend to such tasks but the shop was crowded out with repairs just at that time, and all the farmers wanted their work done immediately, so Ben could not be spared.

"Take Abey, Harry, and get back as soon as you can," said Mr Hardwick. I was pleased, for besides being a good day for outside work, it indicated some confidence in me on the part of my master.

I quickly harnessed Magnolia, then brought the cart round to load up with the tools, wedges and blocks that Harry had made ready. As we swung off the village street and along the drive up to Oldston House, we picked up Billy Bourton, brother of the thatcher. 'Funny in th'ead' was the description most folk gave him. He was dressed, this particular morning, for summer work in the fields, as the estate was glad of extra help during haymaking. The leather braces over his collarless flannel shirt allowed maximum movement for the large grey trousers and held them well up under his armpits. His sleeves were neatly rolled up and his voluminous workingman's cap pulled on firmly and straight.

"Over the back field just by that bit o' plank over again' the ditch," was his description of the whereabouts of the broken waggon. "Full up wi' 'ay 'er was, overloaded I'd say an' all. I said as much afore 'er started off. Won't be told, some folk though." He nodded to himself.

We rumbled on over the hard broken ruts, turning away from the house and towards the fields. Billy got off before we reached the breakdown. We found it with one wheel broken, and, where the felloes had crashed sideways from the iron tyre, two broken spokes, still firmly in the centre stock, were buried deeply in the hard baked earth. Harry stood nodding slowly as he surveyed the damage.

"Usual trouble! Let 'er git too dry!" He stooped lower and examined the damage more closely; "We'll 'ave to git 'er off some'ow."

I crawled underneath to join him, pushing a clump of stinging nettles down with my boot before kneeling to examine the wheel. I could see what Harry meant about dryness. If no grease was put on an axle over a long period, the stock seized up and became dead tight on it. Also, in very warm weather if a waggon stood for long hours in the sun it was necessary to pour water over the wheels and hang wet sacks over them to stop excessive drying out and shrinkage of the wooden parts which would collapse under stress.

While we were both under the waggon we heard a voice calling. In a moment or two the figure of a man, wearing a dressing-gown and boots and carrying a stick, came along where we were working.

"'Tis Mr Purton-Hentis," said Harry, looking out from beneath the waggon.

"Lost my cat!" Purton-Hentis shouted, as he approached. "Come and look for it with me!"

Harry said "'Mornin' sir," and went on peering at the broken wheel. "I've lost my cat," the man repeated; "better find him quickly before the mower has his legs off. I've looked all round the house and sent cook and the others off to search in the village. I think he may have come up here. Help me look around. We'd better go over where they're haymaking." Harry and I crawled out and began peering into the long grass around the waggon.

"He won't be here, where you are working!" said Mr Purton-Hentis. "Let's go towards the fields over there." He pointed to where we had set Billy down earlier.

"I don't rightly know if we should leave this what we be a doin', sir," said Harry awkwardly.

"What? Why not? Good Heavens, man, it won't take you but a few moments. I'll tell Mr Hardwick I instructed you." The breeze stirred the long folds of his dressing gown and he pulled the girdle tighter. "Come now, the cat might be anywhere here." He poked around in the grass with his stick, calling "Porter, Porter, where are you?"

"We're very short of time, sir. Mr Hardwick told us to be quick in returning as the haymaking is held up for want of repairs."

"Yes, of course, just look over the fields where they are working, then. It won't take long," Mr Purton-Hentis persisted and Harry and I followed him, leaving Magnolia beside the broken waggon with its wheel in the ground.

We peered under hedges, calling "Porter!" if Mr Purton-Hentis was near enough to hear us. We separated, then eventually came to the place where the farm men were preparing for the day's haymaking.

"Have you found him?" shouted Mr Purton-Hentis.

"'Fraid not, sir," said Ticker Benson, the estate foreman, pausing for a moment from adjusting the front rave on a waggon. The sun had been up long enough for the hay to be ready any minute now for collecting. The rows stood waiting and men were spitting on their hands and feeling their fork handles.

"Come along, you men, take another quick look round before you get started!" ordered their employer. Benson appeared not to hear and went on with what he was doing. The men drifted about poking the hay with their forks. We went on with Mr Purton-Hentis. I caught part of a disgruntled comment, from Harry Teemer, as he passed one of the other men, including the words, 'time-wasting', 'cat' and an unrepeatable adjective.

Presently he sidled up to me and said in a low voice, "Keep close to me, lad, and tuck your head down when we gets the other side of that hedge." He worked his way towards the side of the field, poking a bit of hay here and there, and making as if to peer into the hedge; then with a furtive look round, he dodged out of sight through the hedge and set off back to our broken waggon. I followed him at what I felt was a discreet distance, but when I emerged on the other side of the hedge I was amazed to find Harry talking to Mr Purton-Hentis, who was searching round there and into whom he must have run in his dash to get away.

"No, he's not through this side as far as I can see," Purton-Hentis was saying. "I wondered, too, if he had dodged us and was round here, but I am sure he would come if he heard me calling him." I tried unsuccessfully to catch Harry's eye, but he nodded at Purton-Hentis and turned back the way we had come. I could almost feel his frustration as he climbed back through the hedge.

"Don't give up, Abey, keep your eye on me," he muttered through clenched teeth, as he passed. He waited until Mr

Purton-Hentis had set off again towards the other men, then grabbed my arm.

"Quick now!" he said and doubled back again through the hedge with me on his heels. Once through, we ran hard along the other side, jumped a fairly wide ditch, slid down a grassy slope, Harry swearing as he passed through some thistles, and on until we reached Magnolia and the waggon.

"Right lad, now let's get that wheel off before he comes back lookin' fer 'is blasted cat!" he panted.

We set to, jacking up the axle and lifting the embedded wheel from the ground. I drove wedges under the sound wheels to prevent any movement and then, after removing the rusty pin from the axle, Harry forced the dry, tight stock reluctantly from its place. We put some big blocks of oak under the axle, removed the jack, and loaded the broken parts and all our kit into the cart.

"Let's be off, young Abey," said Harry, sitting on the tailboard with his legs swinging beneath while I led Magnolia back past Oldston House, and out on the road to the workshop.

Work was under seasonal pressure with two farm men actually waiting while repairs were being made to their waggons. One was a broken rave and the other a longer job where a shaft had snapped and was being replaced. Mr Hardwick had promised it for that morning and we'd had it there for two days. Now George and Ben were fitting what was called the long staple. They had replaced the offside shaft. The long staple on that side had three hooks on it, one for the draught chain which fixed to the horse's collar, one for the breeching chain, and a centre one for the chain which was attached to the other shaft and supported the weight of the shafts over the saddle. The long staple was about eight inches long with its ends driven through the wood and cleated over. It was usual to make a new one for a new shaft, but the old one was not badly worn in this case so, as time was short, the old one had been taken from the broken shaft, its ends straightened, and was now being fitted by driving hard through the two holes previously drilled by George. Then, while he held a 'dolly' (a heavy piece of iron) against it, Ben cleated it over with a heavy hammer.

"There yer be then, lad; take 'er away," said George, from under his moustache; "we ain't a stopped fer tea yet, 'ave us Ben?" Ben shook his head.

"'Ere Abey, move these 'ere trestles and stuff, so as we can get this waggon out." The way was cleared quickly and the waggon rolled outside, where its horse and man were waiting.

"Get the rest of the stuff in from the cart, Abey!" called Harry Teemer, taking a swig from his bottle of cold tea. The wheel was broken beyond repair so Ben and Harry, with a little help from me, set about making a new one.

That evening, walking towards the green with Sammy, I noticed some swallows swooping low over the wall that divided the Oldston Estate from Jethro Pinchin's cottage. We watched them for a few minutes as they continued swooping and squeaking.

"There's something there," I said. Sammy climbed far enough up the wall to peer into a hollow near the top, and sure enough there was Porter, the missing Purton-Hentis cat, curled up and hiding from the swooping swallows. Sammy gathered him up and brought him down. We took him to the house and handed him to a maid.

A few days later when we were in the back yard adjoining the blacksmith's, shoeing the new wheel, Peter Brooks said, "The old man says you can have that bicycle, Abey. Needs a bit of doing up, though."

I was pleased with this news. The old bicycle frame that he referred to was hanging on the wall of the smithy and I had shown some interest in it one day when I was in there. It was in poor shape and would need some time spending on it, as Peter had said.

I left the men tending the circular fire as the iron rim was heated. There was still much to be done in the workshop. "I'll collect the bike after I've finished, then," I called.

As I went along to the workshop Maisie Hawtin passed by on her bicycle. She smiled at me but I was dismayed to see Perce Chennel close behind on another bicycle. He also smiled at me but in quite a different way. In fact 'smirked' is a better description. They were heading out of the village towards Remsditch and Lonestock. I felt my chances of taking Maisie to Remsditch Fair were receding, but I forced myself to turn towards the workshop in what I hoped was an unconcerned manner, shrugging my shoulders.

The men all worked late that night as the weather had turned wet and there was no haymaking to be done. When we did at last finish I collected the old bicycle from the smithy. As I carried it through the doorway Sally Pullen appeared. "Will you be going to Remsditch Fair this year, Abey?" she asked.

"Well I don't know yet," I said hesitatingly, as I did not want to commit myself to going with Sally; "anyway it's not for ages. What do you want to know for, so soon?" Ignoring this, she persisted.

"When will you know then? Sarah says she will be going with her boy. I thought we could arrange to all go together."

"I can't say yet," I said, thinking of Maisie Hawtin with Perce Chennel.

"What are you going to do with that old bike then?" asked Sally, looking disdainfully at the wreck in my arms.

"Mend it," I said.

"What for?"

"I need a bike."

"Where will you go on it?"

"Anywhere, I suppose."

"I shan't come with you."

"So what?"

"What do you mean by that?" Her voice showed that she was put out by my cavalier attitude.

"Well," I replied, "you don't go everywhere with me, so what does it matter if you won't go where I go on this bike?"

"I'll tell you what, Abey Staughton, if that's how you feel, I won't be going anywhere at all with you," she retorted furiously.

"Well I'm off to get my tea," I said, getting a new grip on the bicycle frame.

"What about the fair?" called Sally.

"We'll see nearer the time," I said over my shoulder, and set off for Number Three.

On the green were two waggons of hay with tarpaulin sheets over them. The men who would have been haymaking were in the Barley Mow. A steady drizzle had set in and water was dripping from the thatched roof as I put the bicycle in the shed at the back of Mrs Pickvance's house. After shaking my jacket and hanging it up to dry I went into the kitchen to have my tea.

Later that evening I set about repairing the bicycle, first taking it to pieces and removing the front fork which was twisted. Tomorrow I would take it to Peter Brooks to be straightened.

Towards sundown the weather cleared and a break in the clouds let the sun's orange rays stream over the village roofs. The thatch steamed and puddles everywhere glinted bright colours. Cats ventured out and the front door of the Barley Mow stood open wide again, letting the jumble of voices and chinking of glass spill out over the green. Roderick came round for me and persuaded me to leave the bicycle. Together we set off along Tiptoe Lane, cutting ourselves a stick each from the hedge. We sat on the bridge, watching the fish jump below us until dark. The nocturnal life of the countryside in summer played all around us as we sat staring down into the dark water until the church clock struck half past nine.

CHAPTER TWELVE

Mr Hardwick's wife's brother, Henry, lived with the Hardwicks. He had been a deaf mute from birth and was also confined to a wheelchair. If Gwen Hardwick was away for long she pushed him to the workshop where an eye çould be kept on him. Not that he needed much watching, poor man; he simply sat where he was put and smiled at everyone. His head shook slowly from side to side constantly and if you paid him any attention, he would point at you and wink excitedly.

Towards the end of summer Gwen went away to stay with a sister for a fortnight so Henry was wheeled to the workshop each morning and back again at night. He obviously enjoyed the change and was put in a position where he could watch the proceedings. Mostly no one took any notice of him and he would sit quietly. If Mr Hardwick went past he would point excitedly and wink at everyone who was looking. From my bench I could observe him without his being aware of it. He never appeared unhappy but sat, hour by hour, excited by any little happening, sharing meal-times and nodding and winking with any of the men who spoke to him. When no one was looking his smile, although still there from habit, faded and his eyes looked far away. I could not bear to watch him for long as I felt I was taking advantage of him. His sadness, when he thought he was unobserved, was so pitiful in his gentle old face that I had to turn away from it. Mr Hardwick helped him to the privy when he indicated his need and sometimes one of the men or I would wheel him out to sit in the sunshine. There an old mongrel dog from a cottage nearby would sense his good nature and come and lie down at his feet, slowly wagging its tail and looking up at him every time he pointed at anything.

One morning, after Henry had been wheeled outside, he sat dozing in the sun with the dog lying full length at his feet. There was hardly any breeze, even high up in the tops of the tall elms in the churchyard. The scent of freshly-planed oak floated gently in the air, and the brown leghorns behind the workshop raised their sonorous sounds even higher, in their strutting contentment. Henry was awakened by the crunching of carriage wheels drawing up outside the workshop. A well-dressed young man entered to speak with Mr Hardwick who, after a few moments, accompanied him outside to look at the carriage, which had been slightly damaged at the back. The young man asked anxiously how long it would take to put right. I could hear the conversation quite clearly as the big workshop doors were both wide open.

"Well, it will take a day or so, I suppose, but I couldn't do it before next week," said Mr Hardwick, stroking his chin. Obviously he was wondering who the young man was, for the carriage was no ordinary affair and indeed it was not the sort of vehicle that our shop dealt with.

"Couldn't you possible do it now?" the young man pleaded. "It is terribly urgent!"

"Oh dear, no. I couldn't leave what I'm doing now. Why, what's the hurry then?"

The young man's earnest face was tense and he lowered his voice. The workshop noises had dropped to nothing as every man strained to hear the reply. However, the conversation continued inaudibly, and it was only some time later that we learned that the young man was the Honourable Pearson Grantle, a son of Lord Grantle from Sendersby. At present his father was away and due to return in two days. The young man had taken the carriage without permission the day before, and apparently Lord Grantle allowed no one to use this carriage except himself, and thought highly of it. Mr Hardwick walked round the carriage, looking more closely. The young man followed him.

"Some fool backed into it last night whilst it was stationary. Can you possible do anything? I'll pay cash here and now, whatever you ask!"

Mr Hardwick took out his watch and studied it, then he looked back into the open doors of the workshop. "Wait a moment," he said, and came back inside to fetch Ben James. They looked at the carriage together.

"Well," said Ben slowly, "it's not a job you could do in half a minute. That deep scratch'll want a bit o' fillin', too. Paintwork can't be 'urried neither." He put both hands in the long pocket across the front of his white apron and stood looking at the carriage for a few more minutes before returning to the workshop.

"Call back tomorrow evening and I'll see what we can do," said Mr Hardwick.

"It is most kind of you," the young man said gratefully. "I'll put up for the night in Remsditch."

At that moment a shout was heard along the street and a herd of young cattle came round the bend by the church. They were running quite fast and the man behind them was running too. Mr Hardwick and his customer moved anxiously to head them off from the carriage.

"Hold the horse!" he shouted. "Harry! Abey! Sammy!" he called loudly, but before any of us could get out to help, the cattle were upon them. The leading beasts stopped for a moment as Hardwick and the young man shouted and waved, but the following creatures barged heavily into the leaders from behind, sending some crashing against the side of the carriage. At that point the force of the densely packed herd swept the vehicle forward, just as we ran outside. Sammy went to hold the horse as the carriage turned sideways and crashed over. The dog at Henry's feet sprang up, barking loudly, and fortunately kept the cattle from him until Harry Teemer reached the chair and wheeled him inside, still pointing and winking excitedly at the scene outside.

In a few moments the cattle had gone. The shouting, swearing and barking died down, the dust settled and the flies followed the sweating beasts. Sammy and I helped Lord Grantle's son to free the wide-eyed horse from the twisted and broken shafts of the carriage. We led the nervous creature acrossd the yard and tied it to a ring in the wall.

"Get that carriage off the road and clear up. I'll look at it in a minute," ordered Mr Hardwick. Then he took the arm of the dazed young gentleman and led him inside to sit down in his office. "Make us some tea, Abey," he called, as he closed his office door.

When I took the tea in, all his papers, or so it seemed, had slid off the desk and were strewn everywhere. Mr Hardwick and Mr Grantle were crawling about picking them up and piling them back on the desk.

"Gather up those papers, Abey," said Mr Hardwick, and he took the tea from me. As I started to pick up the papers another shower slid down, and the iron bar laid across them fell noisily to the ground. Mr Hardwick glanced irritably at me as though I had done it.

"I fear I'll be in big trouble over this," Pearson Grantle was saying. "My father and I have not seen eye to eye over anything for a long time now. It's a great pity this had to happen, but what's done is done and can't be undone. I've no doubt he will want his own carriage-makers to attend to this now, so I'll contact you again shortly, when I have discussed it with him. I do apologise for the inconvenience I have caused you, Mr Hardwick. May I ask you to keep the carriage until we send for it?"

"Of course, and one of my men can take you home when you are ready. Abey, slip round and get the pony and cart from next door, and be ready to take Mr Grantle back to Sendersby."

I quickly placed the last of the papers in a pile on the desk and left them, to get the pony and cart ready. The young man stood up, and not being able to find a ledge or place to put his empty cup, handed it to Mr Hardwick.

"Thank you again. I'll send for the horse and call in to settle with you for any costs I have incurred." He shook hands with Albert Hardwick, and went towards the workshop door.

When I brought the little dogcart round to where the badly damaged carriage stood, Mr Hardwick told the young man he should take his horse, which seemed to be all right.

We removed the animal's head harness and replaced it with a rope halter.

"Bring this back with you, Abey," the boss said, as he tied the carriage horse to the back of the dogcart. Pearson Grantle collected a case and coat from the carriage, thanked Mr Hardwick again and climbed into the dogcart beside me. I jerked the reins and we set off.

Sendersby was about six miles the other side of Remsditch. The afternoon was warm and the movement of air as we trotted on was pleasant indeed. Mr Grantle was deep in his own thoughts until we reached Remsditch and neither of us spoke. As we wound our way through the little market town he leaned over the back to hold the halter of his horse. He made clicking noises with his tongue, then when we stopped for a herd of sheep in the main street for a few minutes he pulled the

horse closer and rubbed its nose.
"A nice creature, sir," I said.
"Yes, he's won a few rosettes with his looks in the last year or so. I'm thankful he came to no harm this afternoon. At least the carriage can be put right or even replaced."
We continued on through the town and out again along the winding quiet road to Sendersby. "So your work is connected with coach-building?" my companion suddenly asked.
"Well, yes, I suppose it is, although I'm only in my third year of apprenticeship yet. Also the work is really more waggon and wheelwright's than coachwork," I explained.
"Interesting, though. We have a coachman on the estate who does small work on the carriages and looks after them. It was he who suggested I bring the carriage to Mr Hardwick. He told me he would make an excellent job of it and would do it quickly if I explained the circumstances."
"Oh yes, well we have got one or two good men," I replied. "I sometimes wonder why we don't specialize more and give up the smallholding and general carpentry, but I expect the boss enjoys the variation as well as the local contact."
As we neared Sendersby Pearson Grantle became quiet again. He pointed out the way to Sendersby Hall and I drove the cart through the big wrought iron gates up to the main doors. A man in livery came out to take the coat and case.
"If you drive round to the stable-yard we can leave the horse there," said Mr Grantle. As we drew up a groom took charge and led him away to a stable. The old coachman whom Mr Grantle had mentioned to me looked enquiringly at him.
"I'm afraid there's been an accident, Jim. The carriage is smashed up."
"I am sorry to here that, sir!" said the old man sadly. "I'm glad you are all right, sir."
"Thank you, Jim. I was not in it at the time. I'll tell you about it later. Can we give our friend here some refreshment? I must go and have a word with my mother." He looked at me adding, "Many thanks, Abraham. Go with Jim and have some tea before you return." He disappeared into the house through a side door.
The old coachman stood watching him go and shook his head. His face was grave as he turned to me. "Come along

then, young fellow, we'll see that Cook can find. Just tie your pony to that post. I'll get someone to give him some water."

I was soon sitting at a long scrubbed table in the kitchen, enjoying some large slices of cake and cups of cider. The plump cook who placed it before me said there was plenty more if I wanted it. She told me to leave the plate on the table when I had finished, then she left me alone.

I looked round the big kitchen with its two tables and huge black-leaded, iron oven over which great kettles with trembling lids were gently boiling and sending up faint wisps of steam. Tea-towels were drying on a clothes-horse before a red coal fire, making the whole kitchen extra warm on such a sunny afternoon. A clean, faint smell of boiled linen lingered on the quiet air and I noticed the great salted hams wrapped in white muslin hanging on the walls at the far end, towards what must have been the pantry. All the windows were open and a large black cat dozed on one of the ledges. Everywhere was clean and ready, no doubt, for the kitchen staff who would return later to prepare dinner. I went out, thanked the coachman and set off again with the dogcart.

When I reached the workshop the broken carriage had been moved into the side barn.

"Get on with those coffin boards, Abey. You should finish them today, then you best get back to the waggon end tomorrow. We're getting behind," Mr Hardwick told me, as he met me in the doorway. "They've started cutting that last field of wheat up at Crosswood, so Albert Lane will be wanting some help come the end of the week."

It was too warm for planing coffin boards. I stripped to the waist and set about the wretched job. The sweat ran down my back as I struggled to remove the shavings from the heavy elm boards with their difficult twisted grain. I could see no beauty in the pattern of their formation as my big wooden jack-plane, even with the back iron set very close to the cutting-iron, still jammed awkwardly against the ever-changing grain direction and knot formation. I cursed beneath my breath and wished that I had taken longer getting back with the dogcart. Time and again I stopped to sharpen and reset the plane. Eventually I did finish, then I put on my shirt and went outside to call the cattle for milking.

CHAPTER THIRTEEN

The four bells in Nether Oldston's twelfth-century church were rung every Sunday before morning and evening service. The tenor bell only was tolled before Holy Communion. One Sunday in early September I arrived to ring the early morning bell at about ten minutes before the service began. I usually walked to church to perform this duty on the second Sunday in each month but this particular time I arrived on the bicycle that I had been repairing for so long and had at last finished. Usually a relief-milker or Mr Hardwick himself did the milking on the second Sunday, when I was bell-ringing, but the vicar never really knew if I was milking or not and sometimes, if I did not see him before the service, I would slip out quickly as it started. On this particular Sunday I was planning to try out the newly-finished bicycle as soon as I had rung the bell. However, just before eight o'clock, who should come in but Maisie Hawtin accompanied by her aunt, Fitsy Bluebottle.

From the gallery above where the ringers stood, I watched over the panelling with interest. I immediately postponed the bicycle test and went down the ladder to sit in a pew a little way behind them. Although Maisie never once turned round, by the end of that half hour service I had become convinced that a prettier girl did not exist. Once when Mrs Pinchin dropped her handbag and a coin fell out to roll slowly past Fitsy and into the aisle I caught a flash of her eyelashes from the side where I sat.

I planned to reach the church door at the end of the service at the same time as Maisie and her aunt. I could easily do this by keeping an eye on their progress and by pretending to arrange hymn-books in the pews until the right moment arrived. In the event, Maisie reached the door before her aunt who was having a word with Mrs Mottram. I saw a great opportunity as I left the hymn-books quickly, intending to meet her in the porch.

"Ah, Abraham, I wanted to have a word with you about the bell for next Sunday," said the vicar who had appeared next to me so unexpectedly that I dropped my own hymn-book over the back of the pew and had to go round to get it.

"Oh, er, yes, er, well all right, sir. I think I could manage that," I stammered, edging away.

"Poor John, who usually does it on the third Sunday, has mumps and it would help enormously if you could come. Will you mention it to Mr Hardwick and arrange about the milking?"

"Right, sir. I'll be here then," I said, looking anxiously towards the door. Maisie would be waiting there now for her aunt, who was slowly moving in that direction with Mrs Mottram. 'There is still time!' I thought.

"Oh yes, Abraham, there is one other thing. I promised to send a curtain from the vestry for Mrs Pickvance to repair," went on the vicar. "Perhaps you could help me get it off the rail. It will not take a minute."

"I'll just move my bicycle, sir; it might be in the way of people going out!" I said, in desperation, and taking a step away from the persistent man.

"Nonsense, my dear boy! Nearly everyone has gone. Come, it won't take long if you stand on a chair for me and unhook it."

"But sir, I er, oh well, I . . ." I glanced again towards the door. Fitsy had almost reached it.

"Thank you so much, dear boy," the vicar was saying; "I nearly forgot it again and Mrs Pickvance always asks me when I am going to send it to her." He beamed, seeming totally unaware of any reluctance on my part. "Bring that chair from under the Oldston Memorial."

I saw Fitsy and Mrs Mottram disappear through the church door as I followed the vicar into the vestry.

"Thank you again, dear boy, it's so good of you. Do tell Mrs Pickvance that there is absolutely no hurry for it," he added after I had removed the wretched curtain and folded it ready to take away. "I'll expect you next Sunday then, at seven twenty."

I hurried from the vestry through the church as the early morning sun was just breaking through the mist outside, sending long rays in through the small panes of leaded windows, making the dust sparkle and lighting up the pews where it fell with a deep rich mediæval gold. I reached the door. The porch was empty except for Bunker Cobham, who was waiting to see the vicar when he came out.

"Mornin', Abey," he said.

"Morning, Mr Cobham." I was much inclined to ask him which way Fitsy and Maisie had gone but I knew the grave-digger would put two and two together with the usual speed that the inhabitants of Nether Oldston displayed when two and two were handed to them. I grabbed my bicycle from against the wall outside and pedalled off along the village, past the cottage where Fitsy lived just across the road. There was no sign of them. I rode on slowly towards the green. The heavy mist of the early morning was lifting and the sun was filtering through as I passed Number Three. I could just make out Mrs Pickvance shaking her doormat and there was Eva tied to the fence. She barked once in protest as I passed and Mrs Pickvance told her to stop it. I remembered the church curtain and realised that I had left it in the porch. Oh well, I would go back and get it in a little while.

There was routine activity at the farm where waggons of sheafed corn stood sheeted over in the rickyard, waiting to be built into ricks on Monday morning. In the strengthening sun the wet mist on the waggon sheets steamed gently. Milch cows, having wandered out from the cowsheds after being milked, stood unconcernedly on the green and across the roadway, almost blocking the way.

I pedalled on. A rut in the road set my mudguard rattling. The road rose gently ahead and after a little while I stopped. The mist continued to rise as the sun grew stronger. I could see over the hedges to where the corn stood stooked. The church bells were traditionally supposed to ring three times between stooking and stacking. Now, the corn was wet beneath the unveiling mist, and the familiar scent of fresh cut, damp straw reached my nostrils. Away behind me, I could still faintly hear Will Auger calling to his cows, whilst the road to Froglies Green lay silent except for the dripping of the mist-moistured trees in the hedgerow.

A sadness came upon me as I rested there above the village. I was conscious of time passing. Up here I felt apart from everything. The usual timelessness of life in the village now seemed somehow to be ticking away as I watched. It was as though I had stepped off a roundabout and was watching it go on round without me. More than two sets of seasons had passed since I had come to Nether Oldston. I mused, and I thought of the different folk I knew down there, living out their simple spans. Each one of them toiling and striving as day followed day until they were packed away into the past where other days were already bundled into history. A cockerel crowed down in the farmyard. Now the sun began streaming through upon the hill where I sat on my bicycle, with one foot in the grass. A rabbit darted across the road in front of my wheel. I balanced the machine, put my feet on the pedals, released the brakes and slowly free-wheeled back to join the imperceptible turning of Nether Oldston roundabout.

I remembered the church curtain and pedalled back past Fitsy's cottage to fetch it. The village street was deserted as I cast a casual glance towards her windows. There was no sign of anyone. The curtain was no longer in the porch so I pedalled back again. After about half an hour I decided to try once more and rode both ways again past the cottage. Nothing. Then just ahead of me, I saw Jonah Gathercole leading a horse. He had recently come to live in the village to be with his old father who lived along the Broughton Dagston road. He was going to work for Mr Hardwick, having completed his apprenticeship as a carpenter a year or so before. He walked with a slight limp as one of his legs was in an iron. Some sort of deficiency, as a child, had been the cause. His father kept a few chickens and pigs and made sheep hurdles. I greeted him and rode slowly alongside as he walked.

"I'm starting tomorrow," he said.

"Pity you didn't come last week," I said; "you might have saved me from planing some coffin boards, although there's always a few more waiting to be done."

"I'm coming to do the skilled work!" said Jonah.

"Yes, and I'm going to learn to become a wheelwright!" I answered with a little bitterness. "You can milk and tend livestock I know, so watch out. There's sure to be pressure on you to leave your honourable profession to pursue the husbandry of Old England!"

"Ah, you won't catch me at that lark," he laughed. "I see enough of that at home these days." He looked at me, and hesitating a little, asked "Would you give me a hand moving some hens, Abey?"

"When do you want to do it?" I asked.

"Well, now," he said.

"Yes, all right then. I'll go and change out of my Sunday clothes and catch you up again." I rode back to Number Three. Mrs Pickvance met me at the door. "What happened to the church curtain then?" she asked.

"Oh, I'm afraid I left it in the church porch," I said.

"H'm . . . Fine thing to do when the vicar had asked you to being it to me!"

"Well, I did go back for it and it had gone."

"Don't know what you were thinking about. I expect it's having that bike. You were better without it, dashing about everywhere and leaving things when you've been specially asked to take them. Good thing somebody saw it and brought it to me!"

"Have you got it then?" I asked.

"Oh yes. Mr Cobham saw it in there and so did the vicar. Mr Cobham walked up here with it specially."

"I'm sorry," I said, as she turned to let Eva out of the kitchen to welcome me.

When I had changed, I caught Jonah up just before he reached home.

"Good of you to do it, Abey. Father has been poorly again and things are a bit behind. Old Simon Langton has got a new son-in-law moved in with him and he is proving a bit difficult. He's told us to move the donkey out and he doesn't want our hens wandering into his field. I'm going to move them across to the other side of the house and hope they will stay over there."

Simon Langford's daughter had married a man from Remsditch only a few months before and brought him to live on the farm next to Jonah's father. He had owned a small market garden before but now was beginning to re-organise the farm in a rather ruthless way.

The hen-house was not very big, housing about fifty birds. They were still shut inside, for only by carrying them in their house could we be sure they'd accept the new site to which we were to take them. If we moved it when they were outside, they would all roost on the ground where the house had stood before, and be in danger from the fox.

The wooden structure was built upon skids so that it could be pulled along over the grass. Jonah had borrowed a horse to do the pulling, so we fixed ropes from its collar to the bottom frame of the house and slowly started drawing it along. It needed care, especially when we reached the gateway where we guided it out and along the grass roadside towards the Gathercoles' cottage. Every time the house lurched or jolted, the low, slightly protesting murmur of the hens could be heard. Occasionally, a louder squawk would register a protest at this outrageous treatment.

"Whoa!" I called to Jonah, who was leading the horse. The front of one of the runners had struck a tree root and caused the hen house to turn slightly sideways. We tried pushing with our shoulders to move it but it was too heavy. We could not pull over that way with the horse because we were too close to the hedge, so we decided to try using a piece of timber as a lever. Jonah fetched something suitable and we set about easing it over.

Mrs Pinchin, dressed for chapel at Broughton Dagston, came along the road. She stopped and frowned at us.

"What's this then? Moving a hen house on Sunday? What's your father say?" She added, looking at Jonah.

"It's a matter of no choice. There's no other time I could do it," he said.

"Oh, and what's wrong with tomorrow evening? Or yesterday evening for that matter?" Ignoring this, we continued to push hard at the wooden lever, producing some impressive grunts and straining noises.

"Does your father know what you are at?" she persisted.

"Mrs Pinchin" - Jonah straightened up with a look of resignation - "he knows it has got to be moved and he's left me to see to it, all right?" He tried to lead the horse on a little, but the root still stopped the runner. Mrs Pinchin watched and continued frowning. In a few more minutes Mary Sanders from the Barley Mow joined her.

"Are they moving a hen house?"

"Yes," said Mrs Pinchin, "on a Sunday too. Those hens won't do no good, you'll see!"

"What will Wilbur say? Does he know?" Wilbur was

Jonah's father.

"'Course he doesn't. That's why he isn't out here!" said Mrs Pinchin.

Jonah said loudly to me. "Must be nearly eleven, Abey."

I took out my watch. "Quarter to," I said. Mrs Pinchin and Mary Sanders looked at each other.

"I don't hear no bell yet," said Mary and they went on watching us. Suddenly out came Wilbur Gathercole waving his stick.

"What's all this then?" he shouted. "Are those hens still inside?"

"Well, they must stay in 'till we get the house round to the new place," said Jonah.

"You'll put 'em off layin'. They won't get no food nor nothin'! You let em out!"

"Don't be ridiculous, Father. We can't let them out here!" argued Jonah.

"You let them out when I say!" shouted his father.

"I'll let them out in a minute," Jonah said and tried the horse again. This time the hen house lurched on for about three yards before it stuck again. The confined birds squawked and chattered and Wilbur Gathercole waved his stick, while the two ladies said the whole business was disgraceful.

"Those hens won't no good after you moving them on a Sunday!" shouted Mrs Pinchin.

"No they won't, if they don't come out and get some food!" he called back.

"I'm surprised at you allowing it, Wilbur!" said Mary Sanders.

"Go on," he said, "you'll be late for chapel! You get along with you before I get nasty!"

"We'd a needed to have gone back a few years to avoid you being that!" said Mrs Pinchin sharply, as she took Mary's arm and led her off.

We strained again at the lever but made little difference to the runner's position.

"You should've put the wheels on it!" said Mr Gathercole.

"I didn't know you had any wheels for it," Jonah retorted.

"' Course I have, but you never told me you were goin' to move it now."

"I'll go and find them if you say where they are."

"They be over in the barn on the wall by the donkey harness." Jonah went off, and I tried the horse again, but nothing moved.

"You go and tell 'im one of the wheels is under those sacks under the bench," said his father, after Jonah had disappeared, so I ran after him.

We found all the wheels and, taking a big spanner, carried them back to where the house was stuck. As soon as we approached we realised that the hens were out. Wilbur Gathercole had opened the door and they were trooping out down the little sloping board by the doorway.

"You're mad, Father!" shouted Jonah. "You'll never get them back in again."

"They'll be all right. They needs a bit o' grub and a bit o' daylight. Put those wheels on and leave it until this evening. They'll go back in there come dusk and then we can move them."

"I've got to take the horse back," said Jonah.

"Take it back. When we've got the wheels on, the donkey can pull it the rest of the way if we push from behind." It took some time to fix the wheels on and we had just finished arguing about it when Mrs Pinchin and Mary passed on their way back from chapel.

"Still there then!"

"We've been waiting for you to come back and give us a push, now we've got the wheels on," said Wilbur. "Come on, Mary, come on Polly, you'll give us a push, won't you?" He walked out into the road to meet them as they drew level. The two women quickened their pace and pretended not to hear, then looking slightly alarmed they hurried past and out of sight, with all speed.

Wilbur grinned at us. "Old busybodies!" he mumbled, and said we had better come in and have a drop of cider before taking the horse back.

We sat outside drinking the cider and I asked Jonah if he was going to the fair, which was now only a couple of weeks away.

"Yes, I expect I shall go," he answered; "who are you going with?"

"I'm not sure yet," I said, still hoping that I might ask Maisie

to go with me.
"I thought you'd be going with Sally Pullen."
"Yes; well, I haven't arranged anything yet."
I returned to Mrs Pickvance for Sunday dinner and afterwards took my fishing-line down by the stream where I sat quietly waiting for the afternoon to pass and the evening church service to begin, when I hoped Maisie would again attend. I guessed she was probably staying for the whole day with her aunt, having cycled from Lonestock early enough to go to church with her that morning. As I half-dozed by the stream with my fishing-rod propped over the water on a large stone, I pictured the scene at Fitsy's cottage.

When the English weather at its best combines with a Sunday afternoon in late autumn and one is able to spend it sitting in the shade of a big apple-tree in a country garden, one can feel nearer to perfection and the reconcilation of all things than during most of one's experiences in life. So I imagined it would be with Maisie Hawtin, and I pictured her sitting in a deckchair in her aunt Betsy's garden, with her, who had removed her wire-framed spectacles and nodded off to sleep, letting her book drop silently onto the grass. Bees were busy in the asters and wasps gorging clumsily in the apples. The ice-plant near the wall was covered with feeding red-admirals and there was an abundance of colour everywhere. Above them, as above me, dreaming beside the stream, arched the broad blue ethereal sky, high above the thatched roofs, and the warm steady fullness of the sun poured with a sense of timelessness over the scented, contented scene. At five o'clock they would take a little tea outside, and then sit on until the church bells began to ring at six. I imagined them leaving the garden and Fitsy's big gold and white cat walking slowly across the grass from under the stone wall, to curl up on the warm canvas of Maisie's deckchair.

When in fact I entered the church Maisie was already there with her aunt, sitting in the same pew they had occupied for the early morning service. I sat two rows behind, admiring Maisie's small yellow straw hat, its two blue ribbons hanging down where her dark, short hair curled up under the brim. Long before the sermon had ended I had firmly resolved that I would cycle home with her that evening.

After the service, without appearing too hasty, I made sure that I reached the church door in good time. The congregation slowly shuffled out of their seats and with varying pieces of conversation, nods and smiles, made their way out into the warm churchyard. The orange sun was filtering through the leafiness of the deciduous trees and making the evergreen into black silhouettes against it. Moss on the tombstones seemed gentle, and the centuries of church stonework stood warm and comely as the deepening evening made changing colours in the small leaded window-panes.

I fiddled with my bicycle chain. Three times I made it come off and put it on again before Maisie and her aunt came out.

"Trouble with your bicycle chain then, Abey?" asked Fitsy.

"Just the chain come off, Miss Harbottle," I replied. Maisie smiled at me and I wiped my oily hands on my clean white handkerchief.

"Maisie will be riding home soon to Lonestock. Perhaps you would like to see she's all right as far as the turn," said Fitsy. Maisie looked surprised and embarrassed.

"Oh no, Aunt! I'm quite all right on my bicycle."

Unable to believe my ears, I seized this chance eagerly. "Of course, I'll be delighted to. What time will you be leaving, Miss Hawtin?" I spluttered, and wiped my nose on the oily handkerchief, leaving it very black.

"Oh really, it is most kind of you, er, Abraham, but I do not wish to trouble you. You will have your evening planned already, I am sure."

I did not intend to give up now. Fitsy had suddenly become very interested in reading the inscription on a nearby tombstone. "I would very much like to accompany you, Miss Hawtin, if you will let me," I said earnestly.

Maisie flushed and lowered her eyes. "In that case, thank you, I will be leaving at half past eight."

Fitsy joined us again and we walked to her gate where I bade them good evening and promised to return in half an hour.

When I arrived back at Number Three, I found Mrs Pickvance chasing a strange cat out of her door with a broom. "Out! Out! Out!" she was shouting. The cat, which was as black as boot polish, shot out before her like an arrow. Straight up the walnut tree it went, to crouch on a branch just out of reach of the broom.

"Caught the beggar in my kitchen when I got home from church! Large as life sitting on the table!" she said fiercely, shaking the broom at the equally cross cat who stared from between the leaves above her. "Must have sneaked in the window! Just let me catch you in there again, my lad. I'll give you gyp with this broom like you've never had before!"

I followed her inside. Eva had been shut in the parlour while Mrs Pickvance was at church and came out, wagging her tail and looking as if she suspected that she had missed something. She sniffed unbelievingly round the kitchen, out through the door and round the tree. The cat watched from above. As Eva never looked up she did not see it sitting on the branch.

"Come back in here!" called Mrs Pickvance, just as Eva was losing interest in the cat's scent, and was looking with anticipation to the smells and other delights of the great world beyond the front gate, which had been left slightly open. Ignoring the call, she moved whence her nose could twitch in the opening between the gate and the post. There she waited hopefully, but as the voice of her mistress insisted "Come back here, Eva!" her head drooped a little, and regretfully she turned away from temptation with resignation and slow steps. Mrs Pickvance however, visualising Eva away down the village, ran out, still clutching her broom, just as Eva reached the doorway. She fell straight over the poor creature, who darted away with fright.

"Get inside, you wicked dog!" shouted Mrs Pickvance, sitting on the ground and rubbing her knee.

Eva shot into her basket and Mrs Pickvance returned the broom to where it normally stood, just inside the front door. This weapon, of such great adaptability, was kept handy for the numerous occasions that occurred in village everyday life, such as chasing cows or pigs from the garden, dogs from her door when Eva was in season, knocking apples off the tops of trees, tapping the upstairs window of the nurse next door if she thought she had over-slept, and as a ready defence against whatever might turn up without warning at her front door. A separate broom entirely was kept for the purpose of actually sweeping.

I combed my hair, straightened my tie and presented myself

at Fitsy Bluebottle's cottage at exactly half past eight. Maisie was ready with a basket tied to her carrier and the basket on her handlebars full of books and gloves. She wheeled the high-framed bicycle out through the gate and smiled. We exchanged formal hellos and set off slowly along the road out of the village. The road was rough and dusty. There were ruts made by waggons and carts to be avoided, as well as quite big holes. More than once we nearly collided as we both swerved to avoid a large pothole, each of us turning towards the other. We both said "Sorry" each time, then continued in silence. Eventually we turned up the Lonestock road and I began to despair of saying anything.

'We must be half way there,' I thought; 'I'll ask her about Remsditch Fair soon, but I ought to say something else first.'

We pedalled on up Lonestock Hill. 'What on earth do people talk about?' I asked myself desperately, 'I can't say anything about the weather, it would be too obvious. My work would probably bore her but at least it would stop her wondering if I could speak. If only something would pass us on the road I could say something about it.' But the road ahead lay empty and save for the occasional click from our pedals and the rattle of one of my mudguards all was silent. 'I could tell her about Mrs Pickvance chasing the cat!' I thought, 'But perhaps not to start with.'

Suddenly Maisie spoke. "Are you wondering what to say?" she asked, with just the trace of a smile as she glanced at me.

I tried to smile as I admitted, "I can't think of anything worth saying to you."

"That doesn't sound very complimentary," she smiled again.

"Oh er, I don't mean it like that!" I protested in confusion. "I mean, ordinary things don't seem worth – oh dear, I mean I was trying to think of something which you might be interested in."

"You don't really know anything about me so how can you know what I might be interested in?"

"I know something."

"What, for example?"

"Well, I know where you live and I know your sister, Jenny."

"That's not much," said Maisie.

"It's a start."

"I'll add one more thing to your list," she said.

"What's that?"

"I'm starting teaching at Remsditch Church School next Monday."

"Are you? That means you'll be riding there each morning then!" I exclaimed.

"Yes, I'm looking forward to it."

We cycled into the village of Lonestock and I determined to ask about Remsditch Fair as soon as we had finished talking about Maisie's new school work, which we continued with until we reached her gate.

"Thank you for coming with me, Abraham," said Maisie, as she wheeled her bicycle in through the gate of her home. She smiled at me. Desperation descended upon me once again. In a moment she would be gone. There would be no further opportunity probably for weeks, even months, for saying anything and the fair would be over and forgotten.

"Miss Hawtin!" I blurted out, not knowing what I was going to say next. Maisie still smiled but with her head now slightly tipped to one side enquiringly at my sudden cry.

"Please do call me Maisie," she said.

"Oh well, yes, thank you! Er, will you be going to church at Nether Oldston again soon?" I heard myself asking.

"Well, not for a little while. I usually attend here in Lonestock, with my parents. I expect I will when I come over to see Aunt Betsy again one Sunday," Maisie said.

I was lost in her smile. The autumn evening and the delicate scent of roses round the cottage gateway, as sunset streaked behind roofs and over the little valley between Lonestock and the hill beyond Nether Oldston, was too much for me. The bell on my bicycle rang once as my hand fumbled but neither of us seemed to notice it.

"I hope your new job at the school goes well," I said.

"Oh yes, thank you."

"Goodnight, Maisie."

"Goodnight, Abraham." We parted and I rode away slowly into the warm late evening. A mist was just beginning to appear over the pastures, the late poppies had closed and if I had been listening I would have heard the whirrings and tickings of the night season insects, on either side of the road, as they ignored the sound of my tyres upon the rough road. The elation I had felt in the presence of Maisie turned now to disappointment with myself. Why on earth had I not asked to see her again? Just because she was not coming to Nether Oldston did not mean she was not coming out of the house again! What had been the matter with me? What about Remsditch Fair?

She must have thought me strange. And with every reason, I told myself. 'Who but an idiot would enquire if a girl was going to church again in the next village and on receiving her answer, would then wish her well with her new job the following Monday, and at the same time ring his bicycle bell?!' I shrugged my shoulders as I passed an owl sitting staring at me from a gatepost. I'd had my chance. There was no one to blame but myself for throwing it away. I pedalled on round the corner and back towards the village.

CHAPTER FOURTEEN

Towards the end of the week Lord Grantle's son rode up to the workshop doors where, in the warmth of that particular afternoon, much sweat was being poured into the fashioning of rural products. His fine black horse stood glistening outside as its rider slid from the supple brown saddle.

"Go and see to his horse, Abey," said Mr Hardwick. I went outside and took the horse's reins.

"Good morning sir," I said, "Mr Hardwick is inside."

"Good morning, Abraham. Thank you. I'll go and find him," Holding his riding crop and gloves, he walked into the shadow of the workshop. As I led the horse to tie to the wall I could see Mr Hardwick coming forward from his bench, where he had been working, and touch his dust-filled, shapeless hat. I followed Pearson Grantle into the shop.

"My father will send for the carriage in a day or so," he was saying. "I trust it is not inconveniencing you, and I do apologise again for the upheaval my last visit caused."

"Not at all, sir, it is all part of my day's work," answered Mr Hardwick. He removed a bottle of patent cattle drench from his pocket which was bulging uncomfortably and stood it on my bench. "I hope his lordship was not too distressed by the incident?"

"I fear he was, Mr Hardwick. The result of what happened to the carriage is likely to be far reaching in its effects; I cannot say more now. It is all very regrettable but we cannot reverse the happenings of yesterday." I could see his face was grave and there was a touch of weariness in his eyes as he said, "I wonder if you have my bill ready?"

The wheelwright looked a little startled. "Er, no, I'm afraid I haven't made it out yet, sir. Will you leave it and let me send it to you?"

"I'd rather settle it now," persisted Mr Grantle.

"Well, if you will give me a few moment then, sir, I will do it straight away."

"Of course; I'll look round the workshop."

"Yes, all right, sir." Mr Hardwick went into his office to move enough stuff from his desk to be able to make out the bill.

The workshop was warm and the scent of newly-planed elm hung heavily, intermingled with sweat, as Pearson Grantle stood watching the manipulation of a heavy turning axle beneath a nearly completed waggon. George Groom and Ben Steel were underneath and Harry Teemer was helping position it from one side. After a while, he moved to watch me helping Ben James. We were making a set of new raves required urgently to replace a broken pair in a harvest field at Broughton Dagston.

"All ready, sir!" called Mr Hardwick from the office door.

"Ah, thank you, Hardwick." Cash was paid and the bill receipted. The young gentleman thanked the wheelwright again for his help and went to collect his horse from outside. He bade good day to Henry, who was sitting nearby and who stared and pointed excitedly at him, until he climbed into the saddle and rode away.

Towards evening, when I had tended the stock, Mr Hardwick came to the back field where I was closing the gate behind the two cows I had just milked.

"Abey," he called, as he approached, "I have just had a message from Mrs Purton-Hentis. She wants me to call and look at the dumb-waiter. Will you come up there with me?"

"Yes all right, Mr Hardwick," I said, and added something I'd been meaning to mention. "You haven't forgotten that both the cows will be dry in a week or two, have you? Teasel is still giving quite a drop but she ought to be dried off very soon."

"No, I haven't forgotten. I have spoken to Albert Lane about getting a replacement and he showed me a cow I can have. I wonder if I should get something a bit younger, but I don't know. The one he's offering will give a lot of milk; she's just had her fourth calf."

Just then Jes came out to say that two field gates that they had been working on were ready. After Jes had gone, Mr Hardwick locked up and we walked along to Oldston House. In the driveway Bunker Cobham was clipping the high box hedge.

"Beautiful evening, Albert," Bunker called from the top of his swaying steps.

"Good evening, Bunker. Yes, it certainly is. So much so

that Abey and I thought we would take a stroll before supper!"

"Oh ah! Not up this way you wouldn't unless you was up to summat!" Smiling to himself, he went on clipping.

When we reached the house, a maid opened the door and showed us into the kitchen.

"How kind of you to come so quickly, Mr Hardwick," said Mrs Purton-Hentis in the loud voice that contributed to her reputation for being somewhat formidable. She led us to the broken dumb-waiter. The lift, which was operated by pulling ropes in the wall between the kitchen and dining room, had jammed. We went upstairs to a boxroom where a trap-door opened to reveal the pulleys at the top of the system. The pulley wheels were wooden and lack of grease had caused uneven wear, on one wheel bearing in particular. It appeared to have been running tipped to one side for some time and now the rim, which kept the rope in position, had worn and allowed the rope to come off.

"Come up tomorrow, Abey. Take the wheel out and bring it back. It looks as though you will need to make a new one. You can turn one on the lathe. There's a piece of dry beech under my bench that you can use. We'll put a bit of rosewood in for a bearing. Take the measurement of this axle, when you come up tomorrow, and make sure you put plenty of graphite in the bearing."

We mentioned to the maid that we would be attending to the work next day and left the house just as the vicar was approaching.

"Ah, Mr Hardwick," he said, "you're just the man I wanted to see. Can you send a man up to attend to my barn doors? One seems to have dropped off its hinges, and while he's there he could see to the front gate which will not close properly. Perhaps tomorrow? I'll send your seed fiddle back with him. Thank you so much for lending it to me. Good evening, Abraham. Don't forget the early bell this coming Sunday."

"Good evening, Vicar," we both tried to answer and Mr Hardwick began something about, ". . . as soon as harvest was finished," but the vicar had passed on, and was already smiling and waving his hand to Mrs Purton-Hentis, who had seen him coming and had opened the front door to greet him.

Next morning after I had completed my stock rounds I

muttered darkly to Jonah Gathercole as I put a few tools into a bag to carry over to Oldston House.

"Odd jobs and stockman! That's all I'm here for! No wonder apprenticeship takes so long if you never start!"

Jonah smiled and nodded.

The maid at Oldston House, who was a girl from Broughton Dagston and a friend of Sally Pullen, let me in. "I'll make you some tea in a little while," she said.

The nuts holding the axle ends had rusted so the removing of the pulley wheel was a slow business. I put a touch of paraffin and linseed oil on them. While I was waiting a few minutes for that to penetrate, Charlotte Purton-Hentis, the eldest daughter of the family, came upstairs and appeared to be interested in what I was doing. I explained how the mechanism worked and what I was going to do to repair it. After some other attempts at conversation she suddenly said, "I believe there was an accident outside the wheelwright's last week?"

For a moment I could not think what she was referring to. "Oh yes, you mean the Grantle carriage?"

"Yes. Was it badly damaged?"

"It was. Unfortunately a lot of cattle came round when the carriage was there, and frightened the horse." I went on to explain what had happened and Miss Charlotte listened with interest.

"We are not going to do anything to it," I added, "as Lord Grantle is sending to collect it sometime."

"Is Lord Grantle's son coming to collect it?"

"I think not, Miss, although I did not hear the detailed arrangements."

"If he does, will you tell him that I was enquiring and convey my concern over the matter?"

"Yes Miss, I'll do that if he returns."

Sally Pullen's friend, Biddy, brought me some tea at that moment and Miss Charlotte departed. After I had removed the rusty nuts and slid the pulley off the axle, I measured its diameter and carried everything down to the kitchen. Biddy gave me a large slice of blackberry and apple pie which I enjoyed before departing for the workshop.

The big lathe that stood under the front window at the

waggon end of the building was used almost exclusively for turning the elm stocks for wheels. It was a heavy machine with a long wooden bed that had been built by Mr Hardwick's father. There was no power at all in the workshop so the lathe was driven by man-power. For turning the wheelstocks two men were required to turn the wheel which was mounted up above the lathe in the roof. The belt connecting it to the lathe came down through a hole in the ceiling. This hole was big enough for those involved to call up and down to one another. For smaller items, and ones requiring less power than the tough, rough elm stocks, one good man could manage.

I found the piece of beech Mr Hardwick had mentioned, and marked out the circle on it. Taking my bow saw which, under the guidance of Jes, I had made myself a year ago, I tightened the tensioning string along the back and began cutting out the circle. My bow saw was also made of beech, which had been cut some five or six years earlier from the hedgerow not a mile from where I was working. I fixed the beech disc which I had sawn out onto the face plate of the lathe and asked Sammy if he would turn the wheel upstairs.

"Not likely! I'm too busy with this 'ere 'en-coop!" he said loudly, indignant that an apprentice should suggest a skilled journeyman might turn the wheel while the same apprentice carried out the lathe work below.

For a moment Sammy hammered hard and loudly to cleat over the nails holding the front bats of the hen-coop, until he realised that Mr Hardwick was watching him. "You'll have to wait half a minute," he mumbled, frowning.

I kept myself from smiling, to spare Sammy's dignity as he retied his apron and blew his nose before walking over to climb the ladder, muttering about the place of the apprentice these days. In the semi-darkness of the roof space, lit only by chinks of sunlight through the roof tiles and the air holes at the ends, Sammy began to turn the wheel in a disgruntled fashion.

When I had done, I called up through the hole in the ceiling to tell Sammy I had finished. The lathe stopped, he came down the ladder and went back to his bench, sulking and speaking to no one. I had turned a rosewood centre for the wheel and before I finished that day I glued it in position. Next day I planed and levelled it and then drilled out the hole for the axle shaft, using an auger as the lathe had no facility for drilling.

CHAPTER FIFTEEN

Jonah Gathercole had settled in happily at the workshop. Very quiet and unassuming, he worked steadily at his bench in a competent way. He told me he had managed eventually to move the hen-house with his father and the hens had accepted the new position. Simon Langford's son-in-law was keeping up the pressure on his father and they had taken their donkey out of the Langford's field.

"I wonder if Mr Hardwick would let me put him in with his mare until we find somewhere else. We haven't really got enough room for him on our holding."

"I doubt it," I said; "he's getting another cow from Lane's and will need all his grass. But you could ask him. He might know of someone else who could help."

Later that day Mr Hardwick sent Jes and Sammy to fetch the new cow from Crosswood Farm. I met them bringing her home just as I was leaving the workshop to go up to Oldston House with the new pulley wheel. She was quite a respectable looking animal apart from a tendency, as Horace said to me later, to be "a bit cow 'ocked". I helped turn the new creature, whose name was Beatrice, into the workshop field to join Teasel and Thistle and stood watching them for a few minutes.

There was the usual scene of indignant 'just who is this?' looks from the resident milkers and the startled 'don't you dare come near me!' look from the newcomer. Wide circles were paced slowly. Low-strangled noises were emitted with heads held strangely and eyes always fixed on each other. A little pawing up of the grass and then a trial of strength with heads pushing together, then suddenly up went the heels of all three and just as suddenly they stopped and began grazing not far from one another, and that was that. Through all this Magnolia had stood gazing at the stream, completely ignoring them. No doubt she felt that since she had to share her field with cattle, whether it was two or three of them, or whether one of them was a different one or not, made not the slightest difference.

"Bit more milking tonight, Abey!" Sammy said with a grin when we parted.

"If I'm not back in time, you'll have to do it then, Sammy!" I retorted.

It was quite a difficult job to fit the pulley and ropes back into the lift mechanism single-handed. However, the new wheel fitted well and I had started fixing the ropes when Charlotte Purton-Hentis suddenly appeared with a tray of refreshment.

"The maid was bringing this so as I was coming up I said I would bring it," she said.

"Very kind of you, Miss," I said. She looked out of the window across the estate.

"It looks as though the weather is going to hold for Remsditch Fair," she remarked without turning round. I agreed, and after finishing the piece of cake from the plate, I attended to the ropes and pulleys again. Charlotte turned and watched what I was doing. Suddenly from the stairs came the voice of Mrs Purton-Hentis.

"Are you up there, Charlotte dear?"

"Yes Mother, I am just coming down."

"What on earth are you doing up there?"

"I'm just waiting to bring the teacup down from Mr Hardwick's man."

"Really Charlotte! Biddy will see to that. Do come down now!" Charlotte glanced at me.

"I can bring the tray down when I've finished, Miss," I said.

"Oh, all right then." She turned towards the stairs.

"There's no further news about the carriage, nor has Lord Grantle's son been over again, Miss," I said, feeling that her interest in what I was doing was a cover to gain further news of that episode.

"Oh, thank you. How kind of you to remember that I was interested." She smiled at me and went down to where her mother was waiting.

While I drank the tea I looked out of the window. I could see below where Soldier Grinstead sat astride a piebald mare. Charlotte's two younger sisters were also waiting on ponies. A fourth horse was evidently waiting for Charlotte who, after another few minutes, having hurriedly changed, went out to join them. A groom held the horse while she mounted from the stone steps. Sitting sidesaddle, she gathered the reins and the four riders set off.

I finished my work and cleared up, returning my tray to the kitchen.

"Miss Charlotte brought it up to you then!" said Biddy, the maid, pointedly. "Honoured you are I'm sure!"

"Thank you for sending it up," I answered, ignoring her insinuation.

"She's a strange one, that young madam," persisted Biddy, wiping her hands on her apron and whisking away the returned tray to empty its contents into a bowl of hot water. She beat a soap whisk in the water for a few minutes to get a lather. "Last week her mother found her cleaning the sparking plugs from one of the cars. She had oil all over her hands. She came in here to scrub it off. Just after I had cleaned the sink and all, and cook likely to appear at any moment!" Then after a slight pause she said, "I suppose I shall see you at the fair with Sally?" This last half-question came as I opened the door to leave.

"It's possible," I said, trying to convey nothing in my expression.

"Oh, like that is it?" she was saying, as I closed the door behind me so I wouldn't have to see her wide, round inquisitive eyes turning into a knowing look.

As I walked out into the village street I heard a familiar voice calling me.

"Abey! Abey! Catch her!" It was Mrs Pickvance running towards me and chasing Eva, who was very closely accompanied by Miss Betts' terrier. Eva was in season and great precautions were in force at Number Three, The Green, to ensure no contact with the outside dog world.

Joy and excitement were obvious in the eyes of the two tongue-hanging dogs as they approached. They had the whole width of the road to dodge past me.

"Eva, come here!" I ordered. Eva stopped and looked at me. The white terrier jumped on her but poor Eva was uneasy with me so close. "Eva, come here. Come on!" I said. Eva's head hung lower and her eyes changed from abandoned care to guilt. I felt mean and rotten. "Eva!" I persisted. "Eva," I said more softly and Eva lay down in the middle of the road and let me pick her up.

"Good dog!" I said and made a fuss of her. She made an effort to wag her tail slightly although it was down between her legs. She looked so sad as Miss Betts' terrier ran off.

"Take her back home, the wicked dog!" gasped Mrs Pickvance crossly as she reached us. "Go on Abey, never you mind about work! Take her back and shut her in the front room. I'll tell Albert where you are. If only I'd got my broom I'd have given that dog of Miss Betts' a good hiding, that I would!"

Two days later a firm of coachmakers collected the broken Grantle carriage from Hardwick's. Sally Pullen was waiting by the workshop field gate as I went home the same evening to ask me if I was going to Remsditch Fair or not. I had done nothing about asking Maisie and knew that unless something very unlikely was to bring her across my path in the next day or so I would not be asking her. I still pig-headedly refused to close the door of possibility.

"Well, yes, I am going but I am not sure yet who I am going with," I said awkwardly.

"Just what does that mean?" asked Sally coldly.

"It doesn't mean anything other than what I have said."

"Who might you be going with then?" Sally persisted.

"I don't know."

"I hear you cycled to Lonestock the other evening with a certain person," she glared at me crossly.

I met her eyes steadily and asked, "Should I have sought anyone's permission first?" Sally's mouth tightened and she did not answer. "I expect I shall be going to the fair," I continued, "but I don't want to make any definite arrangements about it now. Perhaps I shall see you there."

Sally tossed her head. "Don't bother yourself!" she said and turned on her heel, leaving me feeling mean and awkward yet relieved that the inevitable moment had passed. I thrust my hands into my pockets and walked home to have my supper.

Remsditch Fair lasted for two days. It was usual for local traders in the neighbourhood to close for business earlier than usual on one of these days to allow their employees to visit the fair. Hardwick's closed at four o'clock on the second afternoon, which was a Wednesday. On that Wednesday morning, which dawned misty and silent over Nether

Oldston, Horace Timberlake walked steadily through the nearly invisible village by the path that he had trodden six days of most weeks for just about fifty years. Upon no occasion had he met with anything really unusual between leaving home and reaching Hardwick's workshop which might have fixed it in his memory. For the last few years those living along the way he trod could follow his progress from his racking cough which was always at its worst in the early morning. In the heavy mist it was like a foghorn on a sea vessel sounding its whereabouts constantly to avoid collision. As I heard afterwards Ben had caught up with Horace and they had progressed together through the mist until Ben stopped suddenly.

"'Ark 'Orace!" he said.

"Do what?" wheezed Horace, walking on.

"'Ark!" said Ben more loudly and hurried to catch Horace again. Horace stopped to listen but his noisy breathing prevented him or Ben from hearing anything at all.

"'Old on there, 'Orace." Ben walked on a few steps to listen again. He could hear something in the hedge of the workshop field to which they were now close.

"'Tis a pig in 'ere!" he called back to Horace. Horace joined him and peered hard into the mist where Ben stood.

"There's more than one," he said; "they be down in the ditch, there, but I can't see 'em."

"Nor can't I!" The two men peered down into the ditch, overgrown with summer grass.

"Wonder whose they be?" said Ben.

"No tellin'" rumbled Horace, coughing again and making the hidden pigs go silent as they listened to the noise above. At that moment Jes joined them on his way to the shop.

"Pigs?" he said, "Penny to a shillin' they'll be the vicar's. They're always out lately. I'll go and see." He went over to the vicarage where the vicar kept his pigs in a building at the back. He knew the vicar would still be in bed so went straight to look for himself. Sure enough, the sty was open and empty.

"It's them all right," he called to Ben and Horace when he returned. "I'll tell Albert and get a stick."

I had not started the milking when Mr Hardwick called me. We went out, carrying wide elm boards, and assembled in the wet heavy mist on the side of the ditch where pig-grunting and rummaging could be heard. The ditch was dry so I went down into it at one end, which made the pigs scramble along to the other. My trousers soon became soaked from the wet misted grass as the pigs tumbled over one another and splashed into a drop of water lying at the other end of the ditch. Four of them there were. Young porkers of about seven weeks. One of them, facing the opposite direction to which they were now moving, ran backwards trying all the while to turn round yet unable to do so, for the sides of the ditch were too steep. He kept up a fine noise, too, as I moved towards them. At last he managed to scramble round, plastered with mud, and ran after the others.

"Can you see 'em?" I heard Horace ask Ben as they peered down from above.

"I caught a glimpse of them but that's all," said Ben, wiping the dripping mist from his moustache. "We shall have a job getting them up to the vicarage field."

Horace started coughing again and Mr Hardwick advised him to go inside. "We'll manage all right," he said.

At the end of the ditch, where the water ran under a culvert, the pigs shot up the bank, where it was less steep, and I drove them out. Ben James and Harry Teemer joined the others, then with some difficulty the excited pigs were guided with the elm boards in front and encouraged with sticks from behind, back to where they belonged.

Mr Hardwick helped me with the milking when we returned to the shop but I had to take my trousers off to dry as they were so wet and muddy from the ditch. Fortunately it was not cold in the cowshed as I sat milking in my underpants.

When the milking was finished and we went into the workshop, a farmer from Broughton Dagston was waiting to see Mr Hardwick.

"In trouble I am," he began.

"Nothing desperate, I hope," answered Mr Hardwick.

"Wheel seized up," said the farmer.

"We'll try to get up there tomorrow, then. Don't know which way to turn today."

"But I've got a load on it and I need the waggon for carting corn. I shall have to get someone else if you can't come now!"

"Now?" Mr Hardwick looked horrified. "Where is it?"

"On the road. Almost home but it's blocking the road a bit. I've only got the one waggon. I've told the men to unload it with the carts. It can't stay there long." Mr Hardwick looked round the shop. Every man was working on urgently needed repairs.

"Go and finish unloading it, and I'll come up myself in a minute." The farmer departed. Mr Hardwick turned to me.

"Get the cart round, Abey. Put some ropes in. We'll need levers, wedges, blocks, a sledge and that box of mine under the bench."

Half an hour later we set off. Before we reached the broken-down waggon we passed a farm that was having its driveway repaired.

"I've heard that Lord Grantle's son is coming to live there," said the boss."

I nodded. "Yes, it looks as though he's making a start already."

"Doesn't waste much time. He wants us to start on repairs up there next week. I've known old Jim Henry's been going for some time. Needs some work doing to it."

The waggon came into view round the next bend. There was no one with it. It had been unloaded and was standing well out in the roadway, making it difficult for anything to pass. The wheel needing attention was on the back nearside.

"Chock the wheels and get the jack underneath," Mr Hardwick told me.

A heavily loaded straw waggon approached and stopped. The driver came up to us. "'Ow long yer be?" he asked.

"We've only just arrived. Can't you pass by on the verge?"

"Well, I dunno as I can. Load's a bit wide an' I don't want to get stuck." He removed his cap, scratched behind his ear and replaced it.

"Get the levers and bars out, Abey. We'll see if we can shift her over."

The driver of the other waggon took one of the bars, then the three of us dug the end in under the offside wheels and gradually levered the heavy waggon over, inch by inch.

"You'll get by there now," said Mr Hardwick.

The driver led his horses slowly past and went on. I chocked up the wheels so the waggon could not roll and we soon had the seized wheel jacked up. A little later a cart drew up alongside and the waggon's owner appeared.

"Ah, well done Albert; what's the matter with her?"

"I don't know yet but I expect it's lack of grease," said Mr Hardwick, in reply to the farmer. "See that, Abey?" he pointed to a hardened ridge of grease on the axle. "It's overheated. Get that off with a cold chisel first."

I spread a sack on the road, then sitting on it underneath the waggon I began removing the rock-like grease. Mr Hardwick climbed out to where the farmer stood.

"I hear Jim Henry's place is changing hands," he said.

"Ah, so it is. Young Grantle's coming there. Fact is, I believe he's there a-ready."

"On his own then, is he?"

"Waal, I don't rightly know. They say he and his father have fallen out. He's taken on Jim's two men and all his stock."

"He'll be your neighbour then, won't he?" asked Mr Hardwick.

"Ah, so he will, but only along the lower end. I hope he's going to put that fence right before he does much else."

I stopped hammering after the last piece of grease had dropped away.

"Have you done that, Abey?" Mr Hardwick crawled back under the waggon, grunting with the exertion and holding his dusty hat on his head. "See if we can move it, then." He set to with the sledge hammer, striking gently on the stock from both sides. The wheel remained firm. We put tallow on the axle and then both of us endeavoured to turn the wheel backwards and forwards. It was indeed dead tight.

"Let the jack down and take away the chocks," said Mr Hardwick. I did as he said and then with a little rocking of the whole waggon the wheel showed signs of movement. I put the blocks back and jacked it up again. This time when we put pressure on the wheel we managed to turn it a little. Backwards and forwards we worked it, increasing the movement slightly all the time, then using the sledge again we persuaded the hub to inch along the axle. As it moved across the part where we had applied the tallow it became easier, until at last it was off.

We greased the parts of the wheel well, replaced it and the lynchpin, and then put our equipment back in our cart.

"There you are then. You can get on now, and we must get back," said Mr Hardwick to the farmer. I clicked my tongue to Magnolia and we clattered away in a cloud of dust back to the workshop. The early morning mist had cleared away to leave the day cloudless and warm.

"Mrs Green is coming in to do the milking tonight, Abey, and I'll do the hens so you can get off to the fair," said Mr Hardwick, as he climbed down from the cart and went into his office.

CHAPTER SIXTEEN

The night sky above Remsditch was aglow from the bright and glittering lights of the fair. The warm day had slowly faded into the cooler evening but there were ox-roasting and tests of physical strength which seemed more of an attraction in the cooler air.

"Roll up! Roll up! Roll up!" was shouted continuously from all directions. A pig stood penned between four hurdles, blinking its little black eyes at the hubbub around it, while it waited as one person after another bowled for it. Shooting galleries cracked corks at bottles and darts thudded into dartboards, whilst ball after ball crashed into ever resurrecting skittles. Shrieks of laughter, shouting, and blowing of whistles and stage novelties were mostly drowned by the deafening roar of the great steam organ. This stood brightly painted and proudly attended by two young men in waistcoats and shirt-sleeves, who took it in turns to change the music rolls and check the moving parts, of which there were very many, of the mechanical masterpieces in their charge. Young farmers and labourers from miles around were lining up to pit strength and skill, one against the other. An occasional cheer went up from bystanders as someone topped the record, rang the bell or won a prize. Various tents contained the usual flea circus, the bearded lady, the largest ox and the smallest cow in the world, and, as far from the noisy steam organ as possible, sat Madam Scraviolatti gazing into a crystal ball to tell fortunes.

Perce Chennel and Jake Pooley would no doubt be frightening the life out of some small boy who would whimper that he had only got a shilling. "I'll tell my Dad!" he would cry, unavailingly.

"Give it me! If you tell 'im we'll get yer for it!" the two bullies would threaten, while not far away Sammy Blowfield climbed into the boxing ring to challenge the 'champ'.

"Good old Sammy!" shouted a supporter, then, as Sammy looked round to grin, "Wham!" the champ felled him with one blow to the side of his head. Outside the tent, a cold sponge from a bucket brought him round, spluttering and indignant.

Roderick and I wandered from one stall to another. He carried a grotesque china ornament which he had won at a shooting gallery. We stopped to buy some roasted chestnuts from a barrow and enjoyed the warmth from the glowing coals as the man shovelled each portion into a little conical white paper bag.

As we wandered past the whirling roundabout, with its brightly painted and gilded horses and barleysugar poles going up and down, we turned to watch the swingboats. The light was poor up in the actual boats but after a minute or two I recognised Maisie Hawtin sitting at one end of one of the high swinging ones, being pulled even higher by a smartly dressed young man who was up there with her. They were laughing and talking as the swingboat dipped and rose to hang momentarily almost vertical, before dropping back to rise yet again. In the glowing lamplight I felt my face fall as my heart sank even faster than the dropping swingboat. I must have stood as if in a trance for Roderick, even in the poor light and jostling crowd, was aware of my change of mood.

"What's the matter, Abey?" I heard him say.

"Nothing, nothing at all," I answered as we turned away.

"During the day many young men and girls had sought and found employment, for farmers and their wives attended the fair in the morning if they required a new hand, a shepherd or a servant girl. Usually the engagement was completed with a handshake and a shilling paid to the hired person. Many of these shillings found their way into the pockets of the fairmen before the night was done. Cider and beer was plentiful and as the night wore on, so the merry-making increased. Singing and laughter echoed into the night air and the steam organ music could be heard miles away in the dark fields, where beasts stood under hedges and birds perched silent and still as autumn drifted towards winter once again.

I followed Roderick through the crowds and found we were close to Sally Pullen and her group of friends as they waited to ride on the roundabout. Roderick wanted to go on it, so we joined them and climbed aboard as it slowed down. At first Sally ignored me but as the roundabout went faster and the man in the middle played a concertina faster and faster, above the noise of everything, even the steam organ, Sally moved over to the horse on which I was sitting. She had had quite a lot of cider and laughed as she slipped slightly and I caught her. She climbed onto my horse and put her arm round me. Round and round we went. Everything was a blur. Then, as we slowed down, I saw Maisie and the young man she was with, standing and watching from the side.

Later, when people were beginning to leave for home, I found myself with Sally walking back to Nether Oldston by the light of the moon. It was cold and Sally slipped her arm through mine. She felt warm and I was aware of her generous unsophisication. We climbed over a gate to follow the footpath through the dark-shadowed fields, while the moonlight distorted the shapes of cattle standing quietly in groups. We passed under the black depths of towering new hayricks which still faintly scented the air when a light breeze played round them. We crossed a stile and Sally pulled me close as I helped her over. Her hair fell across her face. Her eyes were soft in the light of the moon. I kissed her and we stood by the stile for a moment. The breeze moved the leaves of the hedgerow near the footpath. We walked on, hand in hand. A rabbit darted out from a clump of grass; an owl swooped low past us. The path wound down past a tin-roofed hovel, silent and full of new smelling clover hay, still warm from the afternoon sun on the tin roof. We left the footpath and disappeared into the shadows and hollows of the warm hay. A pheasant squawked near the road, the roof of the hovel creaked occasionally and the breeze played gently round the wisps of hay sticking out from under the eaves. The yellow moon stared silently, making long, uneven black shadows across the footworn path.

The following Monday morning Magnolia stood at the front of Hardwick's workshop, harnessed between the shafts of the cart. She snorted and tossed her head around, then, after another half hour of waiting, stamped hard with her back foot, making a thud which could be felt right through to the office, where Mr Hardwick was trying to find the list of work to be done at Halfroot Farm, where Mr Pearson Grantle had taken up residence. Jes, Sammy and Albert Groom were going there to work and I was taking the cart with tools and timber.

"Ah, here it is!" the boss exclaimed, pulling out a piece of paper from the assortment on his desk. He went through each item with Jes and said he would give him a copy when he had made one out. Sammy and Albert Groom had walked on ahead. Jes and I climbed onto the cart. Magnolia, glad to be off at last, snorted, and trotted slowly through the village and out along the Broughton Dagston road.

Not far from the village we met a riding party from Oldston House with Soldier Grinstead in charge. Charlotte recognised me and smiled and nodded as we passed. Jes was quick to notice this.

"Hullo! You be gettin' quite well known around here, young Abey, blessed if you 'ain't! That smile from Miss Charlotte in this direction was all for you!"

I felt myself colour slightly. "I said I'd deliver a message for her when I was up at the house," I explained.

"Ah, maybe," nodded Jes, as we swayed gently in the cart. "I be gettin' on fer sixty and I seen smiles of different kinds through most of that time, on and off, like. Handsome young wench she be. A smile like that from a beautiful young woman be a treasure in this 'ere world. At your age you can treat 'em lightly. At my age 'tis different. When you be sixty you'll know what I be meanin'."

We turned up towards the farm. Sammy and Albert were just arriving. A new farm manager directed us to where the first work was to be done. We unloaded the cart and I set off back to the workshop. Urgent repairs created by the harvest had eased off now and the main work in hand at the shop was the starting of a new waggon for a farmer near Remsditch. Orders for a waggon and a dung-cart had been received from Mr Grantle, which meant plenty of work for the coming months.

One morning in October I was riding my bicycle carefully from the workshop, holding in one hand two heavy ploughshares held together by a piece of wire threaded through their peg holes. I had been sent up to the six-acre field that lay along the road to Froglies Bridge, just past Mr Hardwick's garden. Gill Mottram was renting him a little grazing on the other side of the road from the workshop so it had been arranged for Albert Lane to send Billy Shipton to plough up the old grass. The boss had decided to have it ploughed, ready to sow a few oats next spring.

Peter Brooks had brought the shares in that morning, dumping them on the stone threshhold with a clang. "Tell Bill Shipton we'll have some more for him at the farm next week and we'll send them straight there," he called to Jes, who happened to be near the door at that moment.

When I reached the field Bill Shipton was well under way. He was Harry Teemer's father-in-law and had ploughed for Albert Lane for over fifty years. He was at the other end of the field turning his team in the far 'headland', so I waited at the end of his previous furrow for him to come back. I put the weighty shares down on the wet grass. It was a grey heavy morning and the tang of the freshly turned earth brought memories of ploughing at home when as a child, with my brothers, we had shared sandwiches with the men and tried to eat the impossible crab apples from the hedges.

Perhaps because I was born on a farm I had always been fascinated by ploughing. Now, with harvest done, the fields lay quiet and sombre under grey skies. The old leaves of the hedgerow, the rose hips and dark red haws, hanging silent and still, were waiting for the frosts and birds to help the wind to disperse them. I stood in the quiet solitude watching the slow-moving horse team on the far side of the field. With winter ploughing, although the aim was to get on with it as soon as possible, the sense of urgency, so recently a part of getting the harvest home, had diminished and one could stand and stare with some humility. The freshly-turned furrows contrasting with the yet unploughed lands lay before me while the old plough, basically the same tool as it had been for hundreds of seasons, moved quietly along, preparing yet another round of increase and toil.

I watched the multitude of birds settle behind the plough as it set off down the furrow towards me. The field had been set out earlier and a shallow furrow taken out all round it to mark the headlands at each end, which were about four yards wide, enough for the horses to turn on. The rest had been divided into 'lands' and each one had had a ridge opened, ready for the main ploughing to follow on each side until all the land had been turned. The headland would be ploughed last of all.

As they neared I began to hear the clank of chain and the

creaking of harness of the two big Shires stepping powerfully towards me. I could hear their breathing and even the swish of the plough itself as the lively creatures came up onto the headland. With a word from the ploughman they turned the whole contraption in perfect harmony as it tilted in a close arc, skidded round to enter the furrow on the other side of the ridge and was off again, leaving only the smell of horse sweat mingled with that of the earth and the birds crying and swirling just over my head as they again made ready to drop onto the new furrow.

I followed behind the heavy tread of Bill's boots and while I walked along in the straight furrow I could hear the powerful cleaving sound as the coulter and ploughshare thrust cleanly and continuously through the ground, to cut the square-edged ribbon of earth which flowed over the mouldboard, crinkling and settling with a few white stones while pink wriggling worms tried desperately to disappear among the grass roots before the following birds found them. Sometimes the ploughman rested his hands lightly on the handles then at others he gripped them tightly to lean heavily to one side or the other, putting his weight here or there. The sound of the plough changed if it came to a wetter spot or a stony one and there was a subtle difference to the look of the turned furrows in those areas.

Bill stopped to adjust one of the draught chains and I was able to tell him I had brought the shares. He nodded and set off again. I continued behind, collecting mud on my boots until I could scarcely walk. We reached the headland and I scraped my boots. Bill said he would change the share when we got back to the other end. He called to the horses and we continued. I smelt mayweed where the land dipped slightly and was poorly drained. We stopped to cut some of it away where it had tangled round the plough body just above the mouldboard. Bill muttered about it, and we went on to the headland where he stopped and looked at the shares I had brought.

"They'll do. I can't think why Abe Pullen doesn't have more in stock this time o' year. But then you'd think Albert would get on to him earlier."

I gave him Peter Brooks' message and helped him tip the

plough on to its side. He wriggled the old share and tapped the wooden peg out, throwing it onto the grass. After scraping round with a little bit of metal which he carried specially in his pocket he fitted the new share, which looked odd with its red, rusty, rough surface against the shining mouldboard. He took a green oak peg from his pocket and tapped it into the hole through the share and the lug on the end of the mouldboard with his spanner.

After uprighting the plough he scraped some earth off the back of the mouldboard, then using the big spanner he set the coulter right for the share, tightened the nut on the beam and was ready to start. He checked the lines through the rings from the horses and spoke to them quietly. Their eyes were intelligent and alert as their ears pricked, while they put their heads up and down. Bill spoke one word intelligible only to them and they were off. Stepping sideways and slightly forwards they pulled round together perfectly, the newly-fitted share sliding into the earth as it crossed the brown headland mark. The birds which had settled over the ploughing rose together and came down again behind the team as the horses thrust into their collars and the earth twisted over the mouldboards, coming to rest rich and dark against the previous furrow.

I watched for a few moments more as they pulled away. Soon they were out of earshot and while I was left in the quiet of that October morning, I wondered how many miles Bill Shipton had followed behind the plough. He had seen the factory-produced steel plough take over from the individually made, local wooden product and as he would tell you, he had been impressed when the new 'self sharpening' shares had become available. Previous shares had been blacksmith-made from wrought iron which could be sharpened by heating and hammering, then cast iron was used which had to be sharpened on a grindstone but the new idea was to cast them in steel with a process that gave a hardened surface on the bottom. When they were in use the softer upper metal wore away more quickly, leaving the harder part protruding, to maintain a good sharp front edge.

I picked up the two shares from the grass, one rough and new, the other shining, smooth and worn out. I put them near the hedge by Bill's dinner bag.

As I neared the bakery I smelled the day's newly baked bread and realized I had missed breakfast time at the workshop.

CHAPTER SEVENTEEN

Towards the end of October, one morning after the milking had been finished and the stock attended to, Mr Hardwick said, "Abey, I'm going to look at some timber I've bought about four miles away. I want you to come with me."

Most of the leaves had fallen and lay thickly on the road in places. It was cold with an east wind, causing the trees to sway and shed their few remaining leaves. A roadman took a wheelbarrow load of them towards a huge smouldering bonfire, which glowed red under one side where the wind whisked round it and sent the smoke swirling first one way and then the other.

"I'm meeting the men who are going to do the felling," Mr Hardwick told me, as we rode together in the cart. "It's nearly all ash. Four ash, in fact, and one oak. I'd like to get it home before Christmas."

We drove off the road along a winding lane, then away from the lane through a field gate, up a small humped hill to where a spinney stood. A man was waiting for us. The five trees stood amongst some other oaks and one large elm. The bark had been cut round near the bottom of the doomed trees so that the sap would start drying out. In those days timber was only felled in winter, when the sap was down. This made drying easier and was said to yield more durable timber. Mr Hardwick discussed the trimming to be carried out on the tops of the trees and pointed out any big branches he wanted to keep. The oak and one ash were larger in girth than the other three but the fellers would remove all the bark from the oak as soon as it came down, as oak bark fetched a good price at a tannery where it was a principal constituent in leather processing.

The man agreed to fell the trees in the next month or so and to notify us as soon as it had been done. After he had gone Mr Hardwick and I went round the spinney looking at various other trees.

"I might get the chance of some more of these oaks later," he said. "Look at that ash there, Abey; see how it bends slightly in the trunk? That's just right for waggon shafts if it's clean when it's cut. That one over there by the elm is a bit twisted but I think it might provide good fellie stuff. You can never be certain until you see it cut, but you can have a good idea.

"Seems a shame to bring them down," I said. Mr Hardwick stopped for a moment. He looked at me and he looked again at the trees.

"You're right, lad. I wouldn't go with my father to see trees before they were felled when I was a young boy. I've got used to it now. What I say is they're just as beautiful in a well-made article as they are standing, and what's more, they couldn't last a lot longer. So all is well as long as there are more of them growing all the while, to replace the ones we are taking. It's a fine thing to use well what the Lord has provided. 'One of God's greatest gifts to man'; that used to be written up in the workshop in my father's day, under the word 'Timber'."

We stood for a moment looking up into the bare branches overhead as the wind whistled through them. Grey clouds moved quickly across the sky and winter again felt near. The last crop of leaves that these purchased trees would ever produce had fallen over the mould where they stood. After a few more moments in silence, Mr Hardwick turned and walked back to where we had left the cart. Magnolia tossed her head and whinnied. With his hands deep in the pockets of his overcoat and his head well down, the guv'nor looked slightly dejected. I followed him.

With three men working away at Halfroot for most of the month the workshop was quiet at the wood end. Only Horace worked there, for I was occupied with the wheelwrights on the waggon work.

One day was spent outside, sorting timber with Mr Hardwick. The sawyers were expected any time in the next fortnight, so stuff that had been cut some years before was taken out of 'stick' and marked ready. This was timber that had been converted by the sawyers some years ago from the log and had been seasoned by stacking carefully on stickers (strips of wood about an inch square) to allow the air to circulate between the boards and dry them. There was no hurrying this process of seasoning. The ends of the boards were painted with thick heavy oil paint to stop them drying out too quickly at the ends, for that would cause splitting and wastage. The slower the wood dried, the better its quality when at last it was ready for use. The quality of the timber was critical for the wheelwright for the strength and durability of the finished product would eventually be tested to the full. Special boards suitable for curved and shaped work were put aside and marked. These would be sawn out by our men later when the weather would be too cold for less vigorous work in the shop.

Room was made for the new logs coming in soon. Sawdust and chippings were shovelled into sacks. It was a job to be done steadily for the boards were often big and heavy. Big spiders unused to the sudden daylight would scurry away as stacks from long ago were dismantled. Toads liked to sit under the stacks where it was damp and dark; when the last board was lifted it was no unusual thing to find one sitting there. Mr Hardwick never harmed a creature if he could avoid it and would lift the helpless toad in his hand, telling it that everything was quite all right, as he popped it under another stack unlikely to be moved for another year or two.

"There's some work to be done in the church, Abey," Mr Hardwick said, as we lifted a long oak board about two inches thick. I nodded to indicate that I had heard. "Round the front of the organ loft there are some alterations to make where the panelling comes up behind the organ, and where the rails have come apart there's some making good to be done. I'm sending Horace up there tomorrow and I want you to go with him." I had visions of how cold it would be. Nether Oldston church was damp and cold and was never heated. The middle of October could be like the middle of winter in there. "I've told Horace you're going with him. He will finish those two sheep troughs by tonight."

"Did anyone ever do that work for the vicar?" I asked.

"No. Well, there's not been time really, and truth to tell I forgot about it. Perhaps you could slip across and see to it while you are over there. What was it again? A barn door or something?"

"What about the waggon work? Harry wanted me there on that cart this morning," I said.

"Well, yes, I know. But there it is. Can't do everything at once. You won't be up at the church long. We must get that done first. Someone could fall through from the organ loft and

I did say I'd do it soon, some weeks ago."

George Bless, the saddler, came into the yard. He looked round and seeing us over by the timber, came across. He spoke quietly to Mr Hardwick, who looked serious. They walked towards the shop. At length the saddler left and Mr Hardwick came back to me.

"Will Auger's boy's dead. They found him over in the back field down beside that old stone barn. Broke his neck. They reckon he was trying to climb up to an old nest in the roof. I said we'll go up. Get your coat, Abey, and we'll go straight away." We both brushed the dust from our clothes and went into the workshop.

"Which one of his boys is it?" asked Harry Teemer.

"George didn't say." Albert Hardwick took his rule from the pocket of the apron hanging in his office, checked that his notebook and pencil were in his jacket, then nodding to me, we set off along the village.

The cowman's house stood solitarily along Tiptoe Lane. The sky was overcast and the trees, now bare and lonely-looking, stood as if heralding tragedy. The back door was open and Will Auger's two other sons sat at a scrubbed table. They were silent and stared ahead. One looked round as we entered, then looked away again. There was a saucepan of peeled potatoes on the side of the sink and a bowl of water stood with the peelings in it. A churn of water was in the doorway.

Albert Hardwick tapped on the side of the bare wooden staircase. He led the way up and into an open room where Will Auger stood by the window looking out across the fields. His wife, weeping softly, sat on the bed. The young lad lay where they had carried him. His boots, muddy and worn low at the heels, had stained the cheap bed cover. His laces were knotted in many places where they had broken and strands of fresh grass were caught by one partly loose sole from his playing such a short time before, when a stickleback under a stone in the cattle drinking pool had provided his delight and joy. Scratches on his bare legs from briars and trees, and mud on his hands and face told of his young life spent in the fields, when not confined to the schoolroom. His hair, kept cropped short by his mother, was unkempt over the simple, slightly pained face of one of the countryside's sons who had entered this life expecting nothing.

"Bad business, Will. I'm sorry. We won't be many minutes. Sorry to intrude, ma'am," said Albert Hardwick. She did not look up while we ran the rule over the young lad. "Thank-you, ma'am. Thank you, Will." Nobody looked at us as we left the house.

"Go round to Mrs Waddup and say I said for her to go up. I'll get the elm out while you've gone and we'll start right away on the coffin. Jes will help you finish it when he gets back this evening, so you'll be able to go with Horace tomorrow up to the church," said Mr Hardwick.

Mrs Waddup lived alone in a converted disused stable on the Oldston House Estate. One single stone room, cosy and well kept, housed all her needs. She had a wooden box with two iron handles containing her requirements for 'laying-out'. She operated in Nether Oldston, Broughton Dagston and the farms and small hamlets nearby. A heavy, large, iron, sit-up-and-beg bicycle conveyed her and her box, and she was not infrequently seen pedalling steadily as her well-oiled chain passed silently beneath the pleated cover guarding her voluminous dark skirts from getting entangled in the wheel.

Births and deaths in rural communities were proportionately far more numerous then than later. Larger families and greater losses were accepted with resignation. I informed Mrs Waddup of the next summons and as I stood at her door I saw her reach for the huge crinkled bonnet that she always wore, and begin to install it upon her head.

CHAPTER EIGHTEEN

The old stone walls of Nether Oldston church stood cold and sombre as yet another winter approached. A low mist hung over the tombstones and the grass between them looked a greyish green. The vicar's hens clucked over the nearby wall while a red squirrel darted through the damp stillness. Each time it stopped to listen it was as if it were waiting for autumn's dragging minutes to catch up with it. The main door of the church stood open and a smell of old hassocks and beeswax drifted around it. At intervals the racking cough of Horace Timberlake shook and vibrated the wooden, age-loosened tracery of the choir stalls.

Between the coughing, the noise of sawing and hammering echoed round the Early English pillars and arches before sounding out through the open doorway. The solid oak pews, their panels already expanded fully in their grooves, due to the moist air, were silent. Their long wait for next summer had begun. Not until then would they slowly contract again to fill the church with their joyous creaks.

I carried my toolbag across the road from the workshop where I had remained to help Jes finish the small coffin. By mid morning Jes had left for Halfroot Farm and I set off to join Horace in the church.

The organ loft was poorly lit as it had no windows, but after a while our eyes became accustomed to the gloom. Together Horace and I removed all the faulty panelling until we could see what needed doing to restore it. Albert Hardwick joined us to discuss the job. One end of the main top frame had rotted and broken, leaving no good fixing for the whole section of panelling which ran across the front of the loft.

"Shall we scarf a piece in here then, Albert?" asked Horace, wheezing, and beginning another long coughing session.

"Take the whole length out right across, Abey," said Mr Hardwick, turning to me while Horace clutched the side of the organ as the coughing racked his bent frame. "Take it out and put a new piece through. You can prepare it over at the shop and in fact, if you bring the complete section of panelling over, you can make it all up there and bring it back here to fit it, after it's finished." Horace, standing breathing heavily, nodded.

We took various measurements and set about carrying the pieces back to the shop.

"Abey, take the waggon to Remsditch and fetch some timber from the station," said Mr Hardwick the following morning. The waggon was an old affair kept mainly for such purposes as collecting timber from the railway station. Magnolia always seemed to like the waggon better than the cart for some reason known only to herself. It was what was known as a Midlands Trolley and had no sides. Ropes and a tarpaulin sheet would be required and when these were found in the barn and put aboard I climbed up behind the mare and set off for Remsditch. If I had been a little later I might have overtaken Maisie Hawtin on her bicycle, but in fact I saw no one at all. The morning was damp and grey with a cold westerly breeze blowing all the way.

At the station a man showed me a goods van in the siding containing a large quantity of softwood boards. It would take about three loads to get them back to Nether Oldston. The man helped me make up the first load. It was important not to make them too heavy for Magnolia. If the mare became too tired before the last load it would be difficult to get the job finished in one day. The station man was all for loading until no more could be stacked on the waggon, but I knew that such a thing would be foolish.

"That's enough," I said, when about a third of the total timber was on the waggon.

"Put a bit more on. You'll get it all on in two loads!" said the man.

"It will be too heavy."

"Go on! Put a few more on. That won't hurt. Put a good load on while I'm here to help you." But I was firm. I shook my head and began to unfold the tarpaulin. The man swore and accused me of being too clever. "One of those know-alls," he muttered and for this small disagreement he left, telling me to get on with it by myself.

The first two journeys back were slow for, even without the extra timber that the railway man wanted to put on, the loads were still heavy and Magnolia had to thrust hard into her collar, to keep the waggon moving all the way.

So that the last load might be got home before dark, Mr

Hardwick sent Sammy with me, for the station man had not been seen since our difference of opinion that morning.

It was market day in Remsditch and that afternoon as we passed along the main street towards the station, although the greater part of business transactions had been completed, the whole street was still thick with farmers and tradesmen. There were still some horses tied to a chain which ran between iron posts set in the pavement for this purpose. A little further along cattle were penned. The horses' tails and manes were tied with coloured ribbons and every so often someone would run up and down along the street leading a horse, to show it off to a potential buyer.

I led Magnolia through the crowds and as we neared the other end of the street a voice called out to Sammy.

"Hold on a minute, Abey!" Sammy said. I brought the mare to a halt and she champed her bit hard and shook her head up and down, jingling the harness, anxious to be moving in the crowded street, and aware of the nearby presence of many other horses.

A young man, wearing a waistcoat over a thick flannel shirt and kerchief round his neck, was talking to Sammy, who had climbed down from the waggon. I could not hear what was being said but the two young men seemed pleased to see one another. They slapped each other on the arm occasionally and laughed. The waggon was tending to block the street and other carts were crowding past. There were shouts of "Move on!" and "Get over!"

I tried to catch Sammy's eye to get him to come on, but he would not look, so I edged the waggon forward a little. Sammy waved, as if to say he was just coming, but he still went on talking. I moved the waggon again and Magnolia snorted and stamped at the short, frustrating movement.

"Whoa!" I said to her. "Whoa there now!" and she lifted and shook her great head, making the harness rattle amongst the market clatter.

At last Sammy looked towards me. "You go on Abey," he said. "I'll catch you up at the station. I'll only be a minute or two. I haven't seen old Jos for a long time."

I did not like the idea. "You better be quick then, if we're to be back by dark," I told him.

"I'll catch you up, don't worry. You go on and get the waggon backed up to the train." I shrugged my shoulders and led Magnolia on. Round the corner the road was clearer and before many minutes had passed I was again in the station yard with the waggon ready for loading. I set about the job myself and was in the process of extracting a small splinter from my hand when the station man with whom I had had the disagreement came over and stood watching me. I continued loading the lengths of timber. The man leaned against the side of the goods carriage and rolled a cigarette. He lit it, inhaled deeply and slowly blew the smoke out as he pocketed the 'makings'. At that moment Sammy appeared.

He had been to the Six Bells in the town with his friend and conscious of the shortage of time, had quickly taken more than was good for him, while drinking his friend's health. Now he came up to the half-loaded waggon and made as if to climb up.

"Come on, Sammy. Time's getting on," I said.

"Leave him be," said the station man to Sammy. "Let him load himself. I tried to help him but he don't want no help. You let him get on with it!"

"What's it got to do with you?" asked Sammy.

"I told you. I tried to help him before," said the man.

"I'm here to load it with him," Sammy told him in a slightly slurred voice.

"Well, why aren't you doing it then?"

"That's my business!" said Sammy.

"I'd say it looks more like some landlord's business if you ask me!" retorted the man, recognising Sammy's condition.

"Nobody's asking you!" Sammy roared, rounding on the railwayman, "and what's more we'd get on better without your observations." At that, as he made to climb on the waggon he missed his footing slightly, causing the station man to guffaw. Sammy took a step towards him. The man did not move but took another pull on his cigarette, removed it from his mouth and flicked the ash from it.

"Are you asking for trouble?" Sammy said, adding when the man remained silent, "Another clever comment from you and I'll clout yer ear!" The man stared insolently at Sammy, then took another long inhalation while they glowered at each other.

"Come on, Sammy!" I shouted, seeing the danger of the developing situation, "Come and help with this load or we'll not get back by dark!"

The two men on the ground glared at each other for another half minute, then, as I leaned over the top of the load and shouted again, Sammy reluctantly climbed up on the timber and left the sneering man leaning against the railway carriage.

Sammy's condition improved as the timber was loaded and by the time the tarpaulin was spread across the load and the ropes were pulled tightly over it, his head was much clearer. We did not speak as we worked to finish the job and when we were ready to leave there was no sign of the station man.

"What was the matter with that miserable sod?" asked Sammy, as I adjusted the reins and hooked them over the front board ready for driving.

"He wanted me to overload this morning. He said I should make it in two loads instead of three. I don't know why, but he was quite insistent. So much so that when I said I was not doing it he turned nasty and refused to help any more, although no one had asked him to anyway."

"Huh!" said Sammy, "Another word out of him and I'd have flattened his ear!"

"You'd have done better to have ignored him. He's the sort who could make trouble," I said, as Sammy climbed up on the front of the waggon and I led Magnolia out of the station yard. The heavy wheels clattered over the cobbled entrance and the last load of timber creaked and swayed as the strong wooden frame beneath braced against each new stress, as the turning circle was pulled round to face the market street again.

It was much clearer now along the main street, as the market business had finished. The usual clearing up was going on and groups of farmers and tradesmen were standing about. Boys were shovelling up the horse droppings and the occasional honk of a horn from one of the rare motor vans could be heard amongst the goings on.

I led Magnolia right through the town and then sat aboard the offside shaft and let her have her head. Although she was tired any horseman along the road could have told from the look of her head and shoulders that she was heading for home.

Two days later, on a Friday, Mr Hardwick went up to

Halfroot Farm to inspect the alterations and to pay the men. I was told later what happened there. The work was going well and it looked as if another week or two would complete the job. Sammy was nailing some elm boards to the side of a shed. When Mr Hardwick stopped to watch him for a moment he looked round and nodded.

"There's your money, Sammy. When I send you to do a job I don't expect you to spend the time drinking in the tavern, and being objectionable and rowdy afterwards. Things like that bring the firm a bad name and I won't employ a man who uses his boss's time like that. You'll finish with us tomorrow, Sammy."

Sammy took the money in silence, put it in his pocket, and went on with his hammering.

When Mr Hardwick had gone, he went over to Jes and said, "I'm sacked."

"What?" said Jes turning round in surprise.

"Sacked for having a drink when I went to Remsditch station to fetch timber with Abey. Must have been that sod from the station who told him. I'll go and see him!" he added darkly.

"Don't you do any such thing, young Sammy," said Jes; "you'll only make more trouble. You've made enough for yourself as it is. But I'm sorry you're a goin'." Sammy put a few more nails in the elm boards but did very little else all day or the next morning.

When I heard about the dismissal I went to Mr Hardwick and pointed out the provocation that Sammy had received from the station man and that no time, or very little indeed, had been lost in the episode.

"The fact that he was drinking when he should have been working is enough!" said Mr Hardwick. "I'm not having that sort of going-on by any man here, and what's more Abraham, I hear you were none too polite to the staff at the railway station yourself!"

"The only trouble that occurred was caused by the man there," I said. "If I had listened to him we would never have got that timber back here without a lot of trouble and possibly harm to Magnolia!" I could tell Mr Hardwick knew I was right about this, but his anger was roused if any disrepute was brought to his business by the action of his men. He was determined not to continue the employment of a man who went in to a tavern during working hours and that was that. The next day Sammy left the shop and work continued without him.

CHAPTER NINETEEN

Towards the end of the following May when I was preparing to start the morning milking, I noticed that Thistle was standing on three legs only. Her back right foot was swollen and she held it just off the ground. When I turned her out after evening milking the night before, there had been no sign of anything wrong with it. Spring had come late and until only a fortnight earlier the cattle had been kept in at night. The foot looked painful. I milked her before calling Mr Hardwick, who examined it while I went on with the other milking. He spoke quietly to her while he slowly slid his hand down the affected leg to the inflamed foot. Immediately the cow lashed out viciously and then stood with the sore foot quivering in the air.

"Now then, Thistle, come on!" he coaxed, but in no way would she allow him near enough to examine it. "You'll have to give me a hand, Abey; I'll wait till you've finished. How much milk did you get from her?"

"Very little. She's right down from her usual," I replied, from where I sat milking one of the other cows.

When the milking was completed, I went to help. I twisted Thistle's tail, pushing it hard upright, which caused it to pull if she tried to kick. While I held her like this Mr Hardwick lifted the still quivering foot and firmly held on for a moment before she gave a great heave and threw him off.

"There's something in it," he said, rather out of breath. "Make a bran poultice, and we'll put it on."

A bran poultice was made by putting bran into a small sack and pouring boiling water over it. This was applied to the affected foot by making the creature put its foot in it, then quickly tying the top round its leg with a piece of twine. The idea was that the hot bran which retained its heat for a considerable time would draw any poison out of the wound, and indeed whatever else was causing the trouble. The essential part of the whole operation was to get the foot in quickly and the sack tied round even more quickly, before the considerable heat of the poultice was felt by the already suspicious creature. With a little perseverence and loss of breath, we managed to get it applied without mortal damage, but before the twine was tied, WHAM! - the bag of bran smacked against the back cowshed wall. Mr Hardwick flew past me like a thunderbolt and we both landed in the dung channel. I was unhurt and helped Mr Hardwick to his feet. He breathed heavily and leaned against the wall.

"She caught us that time!" he gasped. The bran was splattered over the floor and still steaming. Thistle stood staring and holding up the painful foot.

"Make another, Abey. This time we'll pull her leg up with a rope over that beam in the roof."

While I made the next poultice Mr Hardwick recovered. He found a long rope which we put over the beam and, in spite of Thistle's lack of cooperation, one end of which we attached firmly round her lower leg. By hauling on the rope and tying it to a ring in the wall, we were able to lift and hold the leg up. Although she danced around on the one back leg, we got the poultice on and tied. Quickly we released the rope and poked the bran about with a stick. Thistle jumped about for a minute or so while the hot bran covered her foot. She tried hard to be rid of it but at last accepted it, and we left her tied up for the bran to do its work.

During that same month of May, Maisie Hawtin was pedalling towards Nether Oldston one Saturday morning when she noticed a sheep down in a ditch. The ditch was deep enough to prevent it from getting out. The ewe's lamb of about six weeks was standing close by and was in danger of following its mother into the ditch. If the ewe had walked back along the ditch to the gateway into the field, where the culvert had become rather sunken and trodden, she would have been able to walk out without trouble. But sheep being what they are, she remained facing the high banks where she could not get out. There was a small amount of running water flowing along at the bottom.

I heard the rest of Maisie's misadventure sometime later from Fitsy. She laid her bicycle down and went to see what might be done. At her approach the lamb retreated several yards to bleat to its mother from behind the hedge, whilst the ewe herself scrambled fearfully at the steep sides of the confining banks and got nowhere. The now muddy water splashed over her. Maisie hesitated. She knew that she would not be able to lift or pull the ewe out as it would be too heavy. Perhaps it would be wiser to go to get help from the village, she thought, but then the lamb might get in the ditch while she was gone, and if the mother got exhausted, it would get down into the water. Being a country girl she decided to act herself. Off came her shoes and stockings, then glancing round to make certain that no one was coming along the road, she wound her long skirts and petticoat up and held them under the arm. Down into the ditch she went. The water felt icy on her feet and the stones at the bottom were rough. She splashed towards the sheep which made a frantic effort to escape. As she reached towards it, one arm still holding her skirts, meaning to push it up the slope from behind, the ewe slithered and turned round. Knocking Maisie sideways and bleating it ran towards the shallow end of the ditch where it scrambled out and was reunited with its lamb.

Maisie put out both her hands to save herself from falling; her skirts fell into the muddy water and she sat back against the side of the ditch. Cold and wet, she climbed back onto the roadway. One small handkerchief was useless to dry herself with, so wiping her feet on the grass as best she could, she put her shoes on, stuffed her stockings into her basket and set off for her aunt's house as fast as she could with her wet and muddy clothes clinging uncomfortably to her legs.

On that same Saturday morning, after the poulticing of Thistle's swollen foot, Mr Hardwick had instructed me to go along to Fitsy Bluebottle's house to collect her wheelbarrow which she had asked him many times to repair. Apparently Fitsy had been visiting Gwen Hardwick the night before and told Albert that if he didn't mend it before the end of the following week she would send it somewhere else.

"If I don't need a wheelbarrow in May, I don't need one at all!" she'd said, wagging her finger at Mr Hardwick as she left his house.

The wheelbarrow was in her garden shed, full of flower pots. Seed trays were piled in front and some empty sacks hung over the handles. After extracting it I pushed it up the garden path, making the axle grind roughly in its dust-filled bearings.

"Drink this glass of hot cider, Abey," said Fitsy as I reached her back door. The sun was well up now and although there was every promise of a beautiful May morning, it was still cold and I welcomed the idea of hot cider.

"I mustn't be long, Miss Harbottle," I said. "We've got a cow lame this morning and we're a bit late." Removing my cap, I stepped into the kitchen.

"Sit down and drink it, lad," said Fitsy, closing the door. She was getting out the brushes and blacklead for cleaning the grate when we heard the gate latch click and a bicycle being hurriedly placed against the wall.

The back door opened and Maisie Hawtin burst in, almost in tears and looking very bedraggled and wet with mud plastered over her. "Auntie, I'm wet through and frozen!" she gasped. "I've been into a ditch to get a sheep out and I'm soaked!"

"My poor dear!" cried Fitsy, putting an arm round her and leading her over to the fire where I sat finishing the cider.

"Oh Abraham!" said Maisie in surprise, clearly taken aback at finding me there and probably self-conscious about her bedraggled appearance.

"Hello, Maisie. I'm just leaving," I said, gulping down the remains of my drink. I was embarrassed myself at catching her unawares.

"Take that water-butt with you, from the garden shed, Abey. Albert's going to put a new bottom in it," said Fitsy, as I said goodbye and thanked her for the cider.

I took the wheelbarrow back along the garden path to pick up the water-butt, then, when I had loaded it and pushed it as far as the back door, Fitsy came out to say Maisie had lost one of a pair of shoes she was bringing to the cobblers. It must have fallen from her basket when she put the bicycle down to rescue the sheep.

"Take her bicycle and see if you can find it while the poor girl is getting dry and having a hot drink."

"Mr Hardwick will think I've been a long time fetching your wheelbarrow," I said, slightly worried about how long I had already been.

"Tell him I sent you and that it was an emergency!" said Fitsy. She explained where Maisie had had her adventure down by the ditch. I took her bicycle and set off. I knew Mr

Hardwick was going out somewhere that morning, and hoping he might have left, I pedalled hard past the workshop and quickly out along the road.

It was not very difficult to find the place described by Maisie. I stopped twice at possible places but the third place was obviously the one. I could see where the sheep had tried to scramble up the ditch and where the mud was disturbed. By looking around I easily spotted the missing shoe lying close to the roadside, and picking it up, I rode back as fast as possible towards the village. Unfortunately, as I approached the workshop, the door opened and Albert Hardwick came out. At first he did not seem to notice who was on the bicycle but then looking hard to say, 'Good morning' to whoever it was, he was amazed to see me.

"What's this then, young Abey?" he called, putting his hands on his hips and looking questioningly at my approaching figure.

"I've just been to get something for Miss Harbottle!" I shouted as I passed. "I'll take the bike back and won't be more than a minute!" He watched me pass and shook his head. No doubt he wondered what the world was coming to, and what his father would have made of it.

As I handed the missing shoe in at the door of Fitsy's house, Maisie pulled the big towel round herself by the fire.

"Thank you very much, Abey," Fitsy said and closed the door quickly. I set off with the wheelbarrow and water-butt.

Along the village street I met Mr Hardwick and began to apologise but he held up his hand. "I can't have my men running errands for the village in working time," he said. "Since when have you been apprenticed to Miss Harbottle?" When I tried to say that she had sent me and that it was a sort of emergency, he interrupted. "I'm surprised at you, Abey, and I feel I should write to your father about it! Take the barrow on then and get back to work. There's a sideboard to attend to on the carrier's cart, that's got to be done today. Harry could do with a hand and don't forget to go up to Lanes' for some more bran for Thistle's poultice." He nodded as if to indicate that there was no more to be said and we parted. Pushing the rumbling wheelbarrow towards the workshop I left Mr Hardwick walking towards the green.

The next evening a note arrived for me through the letterbox at Number Three. It was from Maisie Hawtin, thanking me for retrieving the shoe and asking me to tea the following Sunday at four o'clock.

A week of perfect May weather followed and gardeners and farmers were busy with their different shapes of land. With the arrival of spring Horace's cough improved slightly, although he was still racked with it from time to time, especially in the early mornings. Halfway between his cottage and the workshop was a low stretch of stone wall where the branch of an apple tree had grown and pushed the stone out years before. Here every morning now Horace would stop and hold on to the apple branch while he coughed harshly and stood fighting and gasping for breath. When he had composed himself he made the rest of the way to the shop, where he would have a similar bout over his bench.

Since I had carried his pieces of walnut up to the workshop Horace had from time to time done a little work on it in the evenings of the previous summer. Now that it was lighter again, after work, he began to do a little more. Two chairs he had decided should be made from it. He had selected two fine pieces of elm for the seats, cutting out their shape with the big wooden bow saw from his tool kit, which he had made many years before when an apprentice himself. He had hollowed both seats with the curved bottoming adze which hung on the dusty wall over near the window. This was done with a slow rhythmic swing as he stood astride the piece of elm, one foot on each side holding it still while each swing of the adze removed a long curved chip. Working all round, the hollow of the seat slowly appeared. Occasionally he would stop to touch up the edge of the adze with a fine piece of oilstone, feeling the edge with his thumb until he was satisfied with its sharpness.

I was late milking one evening and stopped to watch Horace as I went through the workshop to get my dinner bag. After a period of watching in silence, I said, "They're coming well, Horace."

He went on steadily and carefully swinging the adze until some time later, when he stopped and examined his work closely. "Ah, they'll do," he said. Then after turning each seat over on the bench and running his hand all over them as if appreciating the gentle unevenness of the adze marks and the hollow curve of the worked elm, he added, "I'd better be off for tea then." He put the seats away, to continue on another day when he would finish off their surfaces with with a big scribing gouge on the bench.

As we walked slowly along the village we stopped to look over the gate into the workshop field. Only Magnolia was in there now as the cows were grazing out beyond the blacksmith's cottage. She was just standing down by the stream looking at nothing in particular. She hardly moved at all. There were no worrying flies yet and she was full enough with grass. Apart from keeping her eye on two horses a field away up on the other side of the stream she had no pressing business at all. No doubt after dark she would eat a little more, but much of the night would be spent rubbing her great rear end against the corner of the barn. Just a gentle rubbing but even so the size and weight of what was rubbing was more than considerable if looked at it from the barn's point of view. The ends of the boards had gone completely and the corner post had worn smooth and polished where the mare's rounded rear had passed backwards and forwards continuously. On a dark night when all was quiet, the faint creak that the old barn now began to make in protest, might make a person stop to listen with wide eyes.

"The guvnor will have to see to that corner afore the 'orse brings down the barn," said Horace, nodding towards the damage.

"You mean I'll have to!" I said.

"Ah!" said Horace, straightening up from leaning on the gate. "I shall need a hand on the lathe one evening, Abey. Will you give me a turn?"

"Let me know when, Horace. We're supposed to be fetching that timber in tomorrow: that from up on the top, which was cut after Christmas."

"'Bout time," he coughed; "ought to have been in before Christmas. Probably have a job now." Coughing again, he turned into his cottage, holding up one hand to me.

That evening Mrs Pickvance went out after supper and I took Eva for a walk round the green. I met Sarah Pullen, Sally's sister. She stopped to tell me that Sally was not well, that she had been in bed for the last two days and that her mother was worried about her. I asked if I should visit her but Sarah said she would let me know in a day or so if there was no improvement. I sent my good wishes for her recovery.

The moon was low, and cloud had formed to pass across its face. As it increased so the village became darker. Returning past the Barley Mow, where the rising and falling of general conversation became loud as I passed under the oil lamp, I noticed the light fall across Will Auger as he pushed a wooden wheelbarrow towards his cottage. It was piled high with steaming cow manure pulled from the big ripe manure stack in the dairy yard. Its wholesome warm aroma floated on the night air as I remarked, "That smells good, Will".

"Ah, no trouble with its quality. It's gettin' it where it will do most good that worries me!" We went along together to the top of Tiptoe Lane, Eva mostly running up and down all along the ditch, snuffling with excitement but never finding anything. Once, a rabbit jumped out just ahead of her, hid behind a clump of grass on the top of the ditch while she danced past below, then returned to where it had been previously. Eva's nose led her on from one scent to another. I wished Will goodnight and heard him trundling away into the darkness with his load. I called Eva who came reluctantly, one ear bleeding from a low bramble in the hedge. We turned into Number Three. Mrs Pickvance was not back yet, so after feeding Eva I went to bed.

CHAPTER TWENTY

The huge timber-bob that Albert Hardwick was hiring from another wheelwright had almost reached the spinney above Nether Oldston. It consisted of not much more than an enormous pair of wheels, six foot six in diameter with a strong construction between them carrying the axle and pole and roller for lifting the weight of a fair-sized tree. The wheels were specially made and extra wide for use on soft surfaces, and the shafts with which the horses drew it forward were extra long to allow the log to hang well forward between the wheels. A second pair of wheels was attached to a short beam and pulled along behind. The big wheels turned slowly, pressing and grinding over the poor country road surface, but Israel Parker could not have heard the birdsong which accompanied him all the way, even if the wheels had been silent, for he was stone deaf. He sat half sideways on the nearside shaft just behind the horse, with his feet swinging clear above the road surface. The four fine draught horses and Israel had been borrowed from a farmer for the day.

I met him along the road to guide him to the spinney where Albert Hardwick, Jes, Harry and Albert Groom were already gathered with Magnolia. Nearby stood our own pole-waggon which was kept for the purpose of transporting logs of not too big a girth and which could be loaded with levers, chains, ropes and ring-dogs.

Israel Parker nodded to Mr Hardwick as he pulled the big, wide-nostrilled horses in a half circle and reined them to a stop. The dry earth crinkled and dropped back into the ruts behind the heavy wheels. Magnolia whinnied to the strange horses and as the reins dropped and the light breeze of the fine May morning stirred their flowing manes they turned their heads to look at her with their blinkered eyes.

The five trees had eventually been felled in February and now lay silent and heavy on the remains of old black and brown leaves. The one oak lay stripped of its bark and had turned almost black. The early sun climbed higher. From the spinney the fields and hedgerows lying below could be seen to be streaked with clear shadows and strong colour. A thrush sang from high in the branches of a tall larch while a watchful blackbird emitted his warning short note continuously as his young brood hopped about under the brushwood.

"Mornin', Israel!" shouted Mr Hardwick. Seeing his lips move, the old man nodded again.

Three of the ash logs were of middling girth and with some manœuvring could be carried home by the pole-waggon one at a time once loaded. However, the remaining oak and ash were of a greater size and would need to be moved singly by the timber-bob, which carried its load slung beneath its wheels. Albert Groom and Harry Teemer were already moving the first of the smaller logs. Levers were used to position it at the bottom of two strong timbers placed sloping against one side of the pole-waggon. Jes and Mr Hardwick attached guy ropes from the front and back of the waggon to pegs driven hard into the earth. Now Magnolia was led out of the shafts and round to the other side of the waggon. A rope was tied to the top of the waggon, threaded under and over the log to be lifted, back over the waggon and across to Magnolia's collar. A man stood at each end of the log. I led the mare forward inch by inch. She strained at her collar. The waggon looked as if it was going to pull over. Mr Hardwick pushed a prop against it and Jes drove a peg in to hold the prop. The log creaked on the sloping timbers. Albert Groom and Harry eased it with their levers and pushed, always ready to spring sideways if the rope broke, for such an accident could cost a man his life. Slowly the log was raised until it reached the top of the slope and was lowered slowly with the help of levers into position on the waggon. Magnolia was put back in the shafts and the waggon was taken down to the road to wait while we loaded the timber-bob. With their levers and a ring-dog, an ingeniously simple device consisting of a metal ring and hook which gripped and levered against the curved bole of the tree, and with the help of the horses and chains, the men turned the first of the larger trees on the ground before loading it.

The men had brought their breakfasts and now they leant against the great butts while they ate and drank, passing judgement on the quality of the timber. I went down to give Magnolia her nosebag while Israel Parker attended to his Shires. The work was heavy and the moment of rest short. As the men drank their cold tea, the trodden earth where they had hauled the logs with horses and chains lay rich brown and scented the breeze. A trampled twig slowly rose again and blackbird, robin and thrush were busy in the newly-exposed soil. Broken and crushed bluebells still peeped brightly here and there. The horses shook their nosebags and pressed them to the ground, acutely aware of each other although hidden by blinkers. Albert Groom walked round the big ash log.

"Best get on. There's rain a comin'," Israel Parker said; "we won't get out of here if that comes wet."

"There won't be no rain this side of midnight!" said Albert Groom, finishing his drink. Israel nodded but he had heard nothing. As the horses' nosebags were taken off the men assembled round the timber-bob and handled the big wheels and shafts slowly into position over the ash. One of the horses was backed into the shafts and a stout chain was rattled down, threaded under the log, then attached to the roller. Ropes were now arranged from the pole which operated the roller by levering it round, to the place where the men positioned themselves on either side of the shafts. When they pulled, it would lift the log.

"Right, when I say, then!" called Harry. The men stood ready. "Now!" We all pulled and strained. The log lifted a little, a little more. It hung about two inches from the ground.

"Pull!" shouted Albert Hardwick, "Pull!" We strained harder. The trunk lifted another inch then slowly the pole came down and the great weight of the tree hung under the strong timber-bob frame. The wide wheels sank well into the earth. The pole was secured and the log chained in position.

The other horses were brought round and harnessed one in front of the other. The second pair of wheels was fixed to the back in a similar way by levering the log up with the beam attached over the wheels, although being right at the end of the log the weight was not quite so great. Everything was fixed securely by chains before the hauling to the road began. Israel Parker led his front horse.

"Come on now! Giddup! Giddup!" he encouraged them. The horses snorted, leaning into their collars, their wide feathered feet pressing their iron wrought shoes deep into the soil. The cumbersome timber-bob lurched forwards, cutting two great grooves into the ground. Chains creaked, and earth flew and flurried round the straining horses' legs.

"Giddup! Giddup!" shouted Israel Parker. The hindquarters of the horses sank lower; they grunted and heaved. The slow bulk inched forward, and then the ground began to slope gently down towards the road. Still the weight sank into the field track so even though it was downhill it still needed hard pulling to keep it moving. A wide swing was necessary to get onto the road and here the horses had to be kept moving as fast as possible as the earth was softer where they left the track to make their slow curve round to the road. "Come on! Come on! Git on! Git up!" Israel Parker continued to urge them.

Once on the road, they stopped. The horses steamed and nodded, champed at their bits and shook their heads. They were excited and trembled slightly. The men praised them and rubbed their noses. They enjoyed it all, rattled their harness and blew down their noses. Israel now led them slowly along the road whilst Harry and Jes walked alongside, carrying skid-pans ready to put under the wheels if the horses could not hold the load back on the downhill slope. Magnolia followed with the pole waggon and smaller log. Mr Hardwick and I accompanied her in the same way. Albert Groom went ahead on his bicycle to warn anyone of the heavy load approaching, for if stray cattle or a flock of sheep met the descending loads there could be trouble. Dogs barked as the timber-bob entered the village and old men came out with their sticks. Boys followed, shouting at the dogs. The clatter of hooves and chains, the creaking of straining timber and the dreadful pressure of the iron-straked wheels on the road surface, filled the air with excitement.

Just past the bakery, opposite the churchyard, there was an entrance to a short but wide lane which led round to the workshop field, across which the timber could be hauled straight into the yard near the sawpit. Here they pulled across the road in a wide sweep into the lane. The horses could not easily turn to get back with the timber-bob but there were gates on the far side of the yard which allowed them through the blacksmith's yard and out again through Cut Lane. The horses stood steaming, while the log was lowered. The back wheels were attached to the front bob and the horses then set off back with it to the spinney to collect the oak log. Magnolia's load was rolled off and she followed the bigger team back through the village.

Mr Hardwick told me not to return with them or I would be late for milking, so I went into the workshop to give Horace a hand with some timber preparation until it was time to help him put another poultice on Thistle's foot and then prepare for milking. The foot was very tender now and when approached, the cow lifted it tremblingly. We cleaned it with hot water and examined it. I pushed her tail up high while Horace held firmly onto the foot as she tried to kick.

"'Ere, 'ere now! Come on girl! There now!" wheezed Horace, stifling a cough. He pressed the inflamed area which was swollen and drawn to a head by the poulticing. It burst and the thick white pus shot out like paste from a squeezed tube. "There, there now! Ah, that's more like it!" coughed Horace.

He washed the foot again and put another hot poultice on it.

Mrs Green had helped Horace do the milking that morning so that I could go straight up to the spinney and while we were attending to Thistle she called back to collect her gloves which she had left in the cowshed.

"They say young Sally Pullen's having a baby," she said.

"What?" I looked up. "Where did you hear that?"

"'Tis all round the village," she said; "some lad from Remsdich I was told."

"Are you sure?"

"Well, that's what they're a sayin'." She went out.

Horace said nothing and I wondered if it was true. We gave the cow some hay and I started to clear up. The rest of the men in the workshop were getting ready to leave so I started sweeping round the benches. I thought of the time when I was summoned by Abe Pullen after I had taken Sally home in the small hours of the morning after haymaking. I felt sorry for the boy responsible for Sally's condition, if what Mrs Green had reported was true, for the blacksmith was a formidable man when angry. Pondering my thoughts deeply as the last of the men left, I was surprised to see Pearson Grantle enter the shop.

"Good evening Abraham, is your master here?" I stopped

tipping the shavings into the sack.

"Good evening, sir" I answered; "he's up in Hawkes Spinney collecting timber. I think he will be back very soon."

"Very good. I'll wait for a few minutes then. I want a word with him." He stood looking out of the doorway and I continued with the broom. After a little while he turned towards me.

"What do you think of the building up at Halfroot?"

"Very good, sir. Have you got much stock up there now?"

"Only what I took over. I'm culling most of that now and will be bringing new stuff in very shortly."

Mr Hardwick arrived, saying that the large oak had presented some problems. It had been just too heavy to lift near the middle so they had to do this nearer one end which meant more weight would now be on the smaller set of wheels. Apparently they had at last loaded it and brought it down as far as the road. They had also loaded one more of the smaller logs onto the pole-waggon and now they were bringing that home with Magnolia. Israel Parker had taken his team away until next day.

Seeing Mr Grantle, he greeted him and apologised in case he had kept him waiting.

"Not at all, Hardwick. I just wanted a word with you about a godson of mine who wants to be apprenticed to a man such as yourself. Would you consider taking him on, Hardwick? I think he might be a good lad."

"Well, I might consider it now that Abey's getting on," said Mr Hardwick; "in fact I might very well. Let me think about it for a day or two." They both went towards the doors and stood talking just outside.

Jes, Harry and Albert Groom came back with Magnolia and I went out to take off her harness and feed her after they had taken her out of the shafts. The log was left for unloading next day. She drank deeply from the water trough while I measured out her food. The men took their dinner bags and called "Goodnight".

"Albert said to tell you he'd lock up," said Jes as he went out through the field gate; "he's still out the front a talkin'. Israel Parker is comin' back to the spinney tomorrow and will bring the oak down. It's all ready. Then we can go back for that last ash with Magnolia. I expect Israel will give us a hand loading it before he goes home with his 'osses."

I went back to put the broom away, having left it behind a big waggon, and to get my bag. I found the front doors had been closed and as I took up the broom from that rather darkened part of the shop I heard the voice of Abe Pullen calling across the yard to Mr Hardwick, who was coming in at the back door.

"You got a minit' Albert?" he was saying.

"Not more than one!" came the reply. I hesitated for a moment, by which time the two men were inside the workshop.

"I needs to talk to you, Albert," the smith was saying. He was breathing heavily. My hesitation at the sound of Abe Pullen's voice had been due to what I had just heard from Mrs Green about Sally and now I stood waiting behind the waggon for them to go round to the office when I would be able to slip out quietly.

"What's up then Abe?" asked Albert.

"You've heard, I expect, about my gal Sally?" breathed the smith, sitting down heavily on a trestle not far from the door.

"What's that then, Abe? I've heard nothing."

"Ah well, you must be the only one then," Abe replied, getting up and pacing towards the door and back. "She's got herself into trouble, that's what!"

"What, you mean . . ." began Albert, sitting down on another trestle.

"What I mean is that some scoundrel from Remsditch has got her into trouble and what I've come round here for is 'cos I don't know what to do about it!"

"Do you know who it is, then?"

"Certainly I know his name and where he lives. That's where I've just been. I went as soon as I could get young Sally to name him, but when I got there he'd gone. Left a note saying he'd gone for a soldier. I saw his mother. She was a cryin' and I could get no sense out of her. If I could get hold of him I'd give him a good hiding. That's what I went to do but I were too late!" He banged one big fist into the other and walked up towards the waggon and back again.

"I'm sorry to hear this, Abe. If you could have found him

you might have persuaded him to marry her."

"That's what I went for. To tell him to do the honourable thing or have me give him a good hiding!"

"Now Abe, sit down a minute. You'll have to think quietly about it."

"It's the disgrace, Albert, as well as the expense. Who's goin' to keep em both? I can't turn 'er out though, can I?"

"Of course you can't. Nor will you, Abe." Albert rose and put his hand on the blacksmith's shoulder. Plunged into despair, his friend sat with his head in his hands. "As for disgrace Abe, put it out of your head. The world is full of disgrace. It's only at times like this that we seem to notice it. No one could stand up and say with sincerity that they knew of no disgrace within themselves. Many hidden acts of disgrace have led to monstrous evil doings. What you are now seeing as disgrace, because it can be seen by all, can end there, and by the grace of God can be turned to a blessing. Let the world see your love for your daughter. Never mind about good hidings and blame. Those things are an indulgence; if you satisfy them now you might very well regret it later. Go and comfort your wife and daughter, Abe. Let them see where you stand. Tell them that if this child is not to have a father, he'll have the best of grandfathers!"

Abe Pullen sat with his head still in his hands. "Come on now Abe, we've known each other for more than a few years. Do you remember when we first went up to Dagston Mill, with your old grandad for the fishing? Remember how you slid into that mudbank and he pulled you out of the river? Who's going to teach this youngster to fish and pull him out of the river, Abe? And who's goin' to show him how to light the forge and hold a horse's hoof between his knees? Won't it be you hammering the red iron and sending the sparks flying in the autumn dusk while he watches, longing to try himself as he waits for you to go in to tea with him?" The smith nodded. He pulled a red spotted handkerchief from his pocket with a scrubbed but iron-grained hand, blew his nose and went on nodding.

After a few minutes of sitting quietly they went out and Mr Hardwick walked across the yard with Abe Pullen to his cottage, enabling me to leave but feeling very guilty indeed and regretting the foolish hesitation that had led to my reluctant listening.

CHAPTER TWENTY ONE

Sunday was wet. At half past three I put on my oilskin and set off from Number Three, on my bicycle. "You hang those waterproofs up in the shed when you gets back!" called Mrs Pickvance, holding tightly to Eva's collar as I left.

The wind was dead against me. The rain drove into my face and I pulled the oilskin hood tightly round my head, although as soon as I returned my hand to the handlebars it blew open again, allowing the rain to drive in. It was not cold and pedalling hard against the wind, tacking backwards and forwards, I became very warm inside the oilskins. As I left the village it blew even harder along the open road. Mottram's cows stood together with their heads down and backs to the driving rain. Halfway to Lonestock came a cloudburst and I was forced to shelter under a chestnut tree for a few minutes. I could not get at my grandfather's watch without removing the oilskins. I wished I had started a little earlier, although I did not want to reach Maisie's house too early. She had said four o'clock and but for the rain I would have reached there in good time. However, I thought it must ease up soon. It did, and although the rain continued to fall and blow against me, I was able to ride on again. When I turned right to Lonestock it was a relief to have the wind against my side for a change, although the road was now uphill. At last I came to Lonestock. The yellows, greens and blues of spring-time, so glorious in the last few days, had completely disappeared and had been replaced by the grey, blowing desolation of this wet Sunday afternoon.

A figure came out from the house as I opened the gate and pushed my bicycle through. It was Maisie, enveloped in a huge mackintosh and hood.

"Put your bike in there," she said, pointing to a shed near the house. We stood inside for a moment and I pulled off my oilskins. I hung them up on a nail to drip on the shed wall. Taking out a handkerchief, I wiped the rain from my face. My hair was very wet. "Come inside and use a towel," said Maisie. "I thought you might not come as it was so wet."

"It wasn't too bad when I left," I answered, following her across to the house. Not come! I thought to myself, if only she knew it I would have come even if there had been snow six foot deep!

Inside it was warm and cosy. I was tingling all over from the exertion of wind and rain. My face felt stiff from where it had dried and my hair, I felt sure, was standing out alarmingly above my red, glowing face. I was introduced to Maisie's mother and father, whom I recognised instantly as the man I had helped with the waggon load of stakes along the Remsditch road, the day I arrived from home. He had supplied the elm stocks that I was collecting when I first met Jenny and caught a glimpse of Maisie. He remembered me too.

"Oh, it's you again, is it?" he remarked from his chair by the fire.

"Do you know Abraham then, dear?" asked Mrs Hawtin.

"We have met," he answered.

"Yes I helped your husband reload a waggon . . ." I was glad of something to talk about, but Mr Hawtin turned away impatiently and poked the fire as if I had said nothing.

"He's a little deaf. Come and let Maisie show you where the washroom is. You can dry your hair there."

"You're still with Albert Hardwick, then?" Mr Hawtin asked as I was leaving the room.

"Yes, that's right," I replied, waiting for him to say more, but he looked away again at the fire so I followed Maisie to the washroom.

"Tell him which towel to use, Maisie," called her mother.

In the privacy of the washroom where there was a small wooden-framed mirror with its silvering coming off, I was able to examine my appearance. The mirror was not large enough to see my whole face at once but by moving my head about I was able to see that it was very red and my hair wet and bedraggled. The mirror was placed on the wall in a very high position for some reason. If I stood on my toes I could only just see the top of my collar. I noticed a nail in the wall lower down and thought that it must be an alternative position for the mirror so removing it, I hung it on the lower nail. Inspecting myself further down, I found that my tie had disappeared round my neck out of sight and my collar was crumpled and creased, with one of its points standing up. I hastily made some adjustments and dried my hair as far as possible on the towel. Fortunately I had brought a small comb with me in my pocket and managed to flatten my hair somewhat. My trousers, crumpled and wet round the turn-ups, would have to do, all signs of their straight, pressed-under-the-mattress smartness having gone completely. The leather of my shoes was soaked too, looking dark and wretched; but there it was, I thought, shrugging my shoulders at the mirror which reflected only the tip of one of them.

I remembered I had moved the mirror and in transferring it back from the lower nail to the higher one I dropped it onto the enamel water jug. It broke cleanly into two triangles and fell out of its wooden unpolished frame. The crash brought Maisie to the door.

"Are you all right, Abraham?"

"Yes, but I'm afraid I have broken the mirror."

"Never mind, it was an old one."

I opened the door and Mrs Hawtin joined us to examine the pieces of mirror. "Oh well, it can't be helped, I suppose. I'll get the dustpan and brush." She tried fitting the two pieces of glass together while I stood with Maisie, watching uncomfortably. "Seven years' bad luck they say," she murmured nervously while Maisie looked at me and managed a weak smile. I felt like saying that mine seemed to have started earlier in the afternoon, but remained silent. I tried to return Maisie's smile but my stiff red face strongly opposed my efforts.

When we returned to Mr Hawtin, now soundly asleep, Maisie brought out a large pair of her father's slippers.

"You must take those wet shoes and socks off, Abraham. You will catch cold if you sit about in them." I took them off and after drying my feet put them into the slippers, which were at least four sizes too big.

"What about your trousers?" asked Maisie, noticing the wet turn-ups.

"Oh they're all right. It's only on the outside," I answered hastily, as I envisaged myself in her father's trousers or perhaps sitting by the fire, clad only in a towel.

"You must sit nearer the fire so they dry out quickly," she said, leading me to a chair next to the hearth.

"Bit wet then," said her father, opening his eyes from the

chair opposite.

"Yes, er, yes, it is," I said, watching the steam already rising from my trousers.

A door banged somewhere upstairs and within seconds Jenny Hawtin appeared. "Hello Abey! I didn't know you had arrived yet! Nobody thought you would come in this rain. Nobody except me, that is. Did you get soaked? Those slippers are much too big for you. You look funny in them with your hair all wet and your face so red!" I felt everyone looking at me and shuffled my feet in the shapeless slippers.

"Don't be rude, Jenny!" said Maisie, "you would look awful if you had got as wet as Abey."

"I wouldn't have come up here in all that rain. Why did you, Abey?" persisted Jenny, looking at me with a wicked smile on her face.

"I came because I was invited to tea and because I wanted to come," I answered boldly, glancing at Maisie who was watching me.

"Now stop it, Jenny," she said; "go and find something to do."

"Run along to the kitchen, dear," Mrs Hawtin suggested, "and see if the clock says twenty past. If it does, you can take the eggs off the boil."

Jenny went to the door. "I saw you last week with that old horse of Hardwick's. She looked overloaded to me!" When she had closed the door behind her Maisie asked me if I was comfortable and I felt like an old man as I nodded and smiled. Her father had closed his eyes again. The newspaper he had been reading slipped to the floor. A struggle for conversation began.

"Are you getting on well with your teaching?" I jerked out, feeling a drowsiness overcoming me from the warmth of the fire and the exertion of the hard pedalling.

"Yes," I heard her say; "the Easter holiday starts in a short while. I am going to stay with an aunt in Oxford."

"Oh are you? How long for?"

"Just a week."

There was another pause. Then, "We have been carrying timber from the spinney over by Broughton Dagston this last week," I said.

"Oh have you?" Maisie tried to sound interested.

Maisie's mother looked up from her sewing. "I hear Sally Pullen's having a baby. Is that right?" she asked.

"Er, I don't know. I have heard she might be," I answered, cross that I felt embarrassed by the question.

"She will be getting married then, I expect," persisted Mrs Hawtin. "I wonder where she will live. She's young to be married." She went on sewing, and apart from the deep breathing of Mr Hawtin and the occasional crack from the fire, silence fell again. I pulled the bottoms of my trouser-legs round so that the wet side faced the fire. The steam continued rising.

"They *are* wet, Abraham," said Maisie.

"They'll soon be dry," I answered, staring into the fire and wishing I had not come. Maisie rose and went out to the kitchen. I could hear her telling Jenny to wash her hands ready for tea. Jenny argued with her and let their big shaggy sheepdog in from outside. He shot into the living-room, dripping wet and wagging his tail over everyone.

Oh Jenny, take him out!" shouted Mrs Hawtin, jumping up. Jenny came in and hauled the dog out by the collar. Mr Hawtin murmured in his sleep, then continued peacefully breathing deeply.

"He's soaking!" shouted Mrs Hawtin.

"Really, Jenny!" Maisie was saying, "Put him out in the shed until he's dry! Hurry up and then wash your hands and help me with the sandwiches."

I wondered if the rain would stop before my return home. I took out my watch when I thought Mrs Hawtin was not looking.

Tea was served and Mr Hawtin was shaken and told to sit at the table. "Still raining then," he murmured.

Jenny passed me the egg sandwiches. "Special these are, because I made them," she said, grinning at me. Maisie said nothing. I asked Jenny if she liked school.

"No. I hate it!" she said fiercely. "I wish I could leave and do something properly."

"Like what?" I asked.

"Anything. Anything, that is, except teaching!" she said loudly, looking across at Maisie who closed her eyes and turned her head away. "Did you know Maisie's teaching? I expect you do. She could have been a nurse or a . . . well a . . . well anything! But she's a teacher! Ugh!"

"That's enough of that, Jenny," said Maisie slightly crossly.

"Why don't you talk to him then?" Jenny rounded on her sister. "You're always getting boys in to tea and then we have to sit here while you say nothing, and I get told off if I say anything!"

"Do stop it, dear," said Mrs Hawtin.

"What do you mean, always get boys in to tea?" demanded Maisie crossly.

"Well, there was that Arthur who came and said nothing and just looked at you all the time."

Maisie turned red. "That was because he was a friend of Mother's friend in Remsditch," she retorted.

"Hmmmm," said Jenny and smiled wickedly across at me again. I was busily eating sandwiches and thinking that somehow Maisie was not really what I had thought, but I did feel a little sorry for her as Jenny was being pretty rotten.

Mr Hawtin passed his cup for a refill and said, "There's water collects in the yard. I'll be going out to clear it when I've had my tea. Perhaps you'll come and look at it with me." Against my will I nodded. What on earth should I want to go and look at water in the yard for? I was barely dry now. To go out into the rain again and stand around in a flooded yard was hardly how I had envisaged spending the afternoon. I felt a depression rising within and wondered how soon I might suggest leaving. If I went outside with Mr Hawtin to the yard, I thought, I would not come back inside. I would make some excuse about shutting up hens or something . . .

Mrs Hawtin said, "Abraham is going into the front room with Maisie now he's dry. Go through there now, you two, and Jenny and I will do the washing-up." Jenny's face dropped and she let out a howl of dismay. While Mr Hawtin put on his boots to go outside alone, Maisie led the way through to the front room, and I followed. The front room smelt damp. Maisie took a box of matches from the shelf above the fireplace, knelt down and lit the prepared paper and sticks. I sat on the sofa and watched the trickle of smoke curl and develop into an orange, blazing, crackling fire. But the yellow flames sent out no heat. Maisie shovelled small coal on from a copper bucket. The fire gasped, flickered low and changed into a black smoking mass while tiny cold flames licked weakly out at the bottom. The damp room was filled with the acrid fumes of the match, and smoke from the spitting pine. I felt pinched and cold. Maisie continued looking into the struggling fire for a while then turned and smiled at me.

"Do you play cards?" she asked.

"A little, not very much." I did not say that I hated card games.

"Shall we play gin rummy?" she asked, going across to the sideboard and taking out a pack of cards.

"Yes, all right. You'll have to show me how to play, though." We sat at a small oval table facing each other. The fire went on struggling beneath the black coal and as we played I shivered from time to time as the cold room remained just as cold and my trouser turn-ups were still damp.

"Are you cold?" asked Maisie as she shuffled the cards for another deal.

"No, I'm all right," I said, smiling at her and thinking how attractive I had always found her when I had met her before. Now, in the over-fussy dress she was wearing, she irritated me.

"You are very quiet," she said, after another hand.

"I'm sorry, I was concentrating on the game." I wondered if it was still raining and glanced at the window. "I must go shortly. There are the hens to shut up."

"Oh it's not late yet. You must have another drink before you go," said Maisie, "I'll go and make one." She left and I went over to stand in front of the fire. My legs were very cold. I looked round the room, which was well furnished but had a never-used look and reminded me of Mrs Pickvance's front room, which was in fact never used. The fire scorched the back of my legs, so I moved away about two feet where I could feel nothing of its heat at all and the draught from the door soon cooled my legs again. When Maisie returned with the drink I sat with her on the sofa.

"Perhaps I'll see you in church next Sunday?" she enquired and I agreed to look out for her there.

When I said good-bye to her parents they both told me that

Jenny had gone for a walk with the dog. I thanked Maisie, out by the front gate, and set off back to Nether Oldston. It had stopped raining and as I free-wheeled down from Lonestock in the gathering dusk, I breathed deeply of the rain-soaked countryside. I felt disappointed. A sense of disillusion came upon me. A low moon was already visible as I pedalled past the shuttered doors of Hardwick's workshop and then got off my bicycle by the field gate. I stood and looked over it down towards the stream. In the half light I could just see Magnolia, already in position by the barn corner, with her great rear-end angled for her ecstatic nightly rub. I rested my bicycle against the gate and went across to the mare who gave a gentle, quiet whinny as I approached. I spoke to her and she blew down her nostrils. I felt alone and the presence of the cart-horse helped my loneliness. I stood rubbing her nose, thinking of Sally Pullen with a child; Maisie Hawtin playing cards in that cold, damp room with its smell of spent matches; Horace coughing over his walnut boards and Henry in his wheelchair pointing and winking. It was dark. I could only make out the shape of Magnolia now if I looked at her against the sky. I pondered on the total humility of this great creature which, if I chose to lead her now onto the road and put her into a cart, would without question haul it as far as I might demand, or just as readily stand tied to a tree all night. But here she would remain, indulging in a gentle rub until she was required next morning. I sighed. What was I doing in Nether Oldston, I wondered. Was I serving any purpose at all here? I walked in the darkness back to the gate and Magnolia followed me. I climbed the gate, rubbed the mare's nose and rode my bicycle on towards the green.

CHAPTER TWENTY TWO

Wheelmaking was the supreme task of the wheelwright and was only achieved by constant practice and at first by watching and helping and handling the successes of the masters. Ben James was considered the number one man at this job, with Harry Teemer a close second. Mr Hardwick himself often worked on the wheels and prided himself on his product with some justification. I was only allowed to help from time to time, but as the days passed, my experience grew and the feeling for the trade developed until, although I had never made a wheel from start to finish, I had contributed for one reason or another to all the various processes and methods for the production of a growing number of different wheels. There had come a point at which, if necessary, I could have made a complete one myself. This is how an apprentice learnt his trade. Over a period of years he would be involved increasingly in the skilled processes: hardly noticeable at first with the feeding of livestock, the sweeping of the workshop, the fetching and carrying of timber and ladders, sawing and stacking and sorting of boards and logs, together with hours of planing, helping with harvest and haymaking all involving him in the complete life cycle of skilled country craftsmen. As Jes had told me many months before, an important part of the useful tradesman's role was understanding what was required of him. The most successful men were those who learnt how to use their skill to the best advantage and how, with experience, to combine purpose, requirement and material to produce useful objects of grace and even beauty.

When a wheelwright stood with his hands on his hips in the doorway of his shop as a new waggon or cart was wheeled outside, he would eye it critically both as a craftsman and also as an expert in its use. The beautiful chamfering applied to edges throughout were not simply to satisfy a delight in its appearance, but to lighten the weight without loss of strength. The run of the grain was all important for the stresses it would have to bear and for use with hand forks and shovels. The paintwork and the position of holes drilled for the ironwork were derived from the experience of generations of skilled workers. As the first horse was backed between the new shafts, the wheelwright and his colleagues would stand watching critically, in the knowledge that the vehicle would spend its working life in the near vicinity and be judged accordingly. Time and use and sometimes abuse would test their product to destruction, before their eyes. When one returned for repair any fault would be discovered and the workman who had been responsible for its origin would have his attention, and everyone else's, drawn to it.

Ben James was working on a pair of heavy wide wheels for the back of a new waggon. When the spokes were ready and the stock turned and drilled and morticed, they were driven dead tight into their positions. A perfect fit for each one was essential for once driven in they could not be removed. When ready, each stock in turn was held steady between two heavy trestles by myself, while Ben drove the spokes in with a sledge hammer. Each one was tapped first into its position, and then Ben would look at it squarely, draw his lips tightly in a line, swing the sledge above his head where it seemed to hang for a second while he snatched a quick breath and then brought it down 'crack' upon the waiting spoke, which would shoot in with a 'never-to-move-again' squawk. Once only he hit every spoke and every time it went home perfectly.

While I stood waiting for the sledge to descend on the fourth spoke, Mr Hardwick came from his office carrying a piece of paper. He waited until the hammer had struck the spoke, then showed the paper to Ben. Ben stared at it for a moment and put the sledge hammer down.

"As soon as you've finished this wheel you can get started on it with Abey. There's not a lot of work in it. The wheels are on the fine side but I don't mind if you make them a bit heavier." I moved closer and caught a glimpse of what was on the paper. It was a drawing of a simple dogcart.

"I'm getting a pony from over near Broughton Dagston. It will be useful for getting about more quickly," Mr Hardwick explained while Ben studied the drawing. "I'll leave it with you, Ben, then you can look at the drawings as long as it suits you. I've ordered the springs and ironwork. They should be here soon enough for when you want them." He went back to his office and Ben carefully folded the paper, went across to his coat hanging on the wall, put it in his pocket and returned to the task in hand. He continued, without a word to me, to drive in the rest of the spokes.

That afternoon the godson of Mr Pearson Grantle arrived with his father at the workshop to arrange with Mr Hardwick the details of an apprenticeship.

"Another one to help do his farming!" said Harry Teemer to George Groom. My hopes rose as I foresaw the tasks of egg collecting, feeding and milking diminishing. I said nothing but Harry came across and said in my ear,

"I've heard he can't tell one end of 'os from t'other nor can't he milk!" I smiled, and moved the set of felloes over to where Ben was working. Later, as the men cleared their benches and I went to get the broom, Mr Hardwick told me that the new apprentice would start in a fortnight.

"I'm going to put him in your charge, Abey, for doing as much with the livestock as possible. Jes will occupy him when you don't need him. Get him to do as much as you can with the aim of leaving him to do it himself as soon as possible. He's done little or no milking so it will take a while, but I want you in here more now. He lives in Remsditch and will bike over each day. Have you seen the drawing of that dogcart I gave Ben?"

"No, not yet," I said.

"Well, he'll be showing you. I want you to pay particular attention to how he sets about it because I might want one or two of them making."

I felt pleased at the prospect as I walked to Number Three, The Green and consequently, after supper, I cut the grass round Mrs Pickvance's house whistling loudly enough to make Eva's eyebrows twitch to give the appearance of some concern, as she lay watching me from under the laburnum.

Ben James finished the wheels he was making and I took them round to Peter Brooks for tyring. When I returned Ben was studying the paper that he had been given previously by Mr Hardwick. I peered over his shoulder and said nothing. After a few minutes he handed the paper to me and walked over to run his rule over some pieces of timber leaning against the wall. The dogcart that we were to produce was the sort of everyday transport used much at that time. It was of simple construction and all over the country variations of it were made locally to satisfy a steady demand. Hardwick's had not produced anything so light before, as farm waggons and carts had been their speciality. Ben returned and looked again at the drawing.

"We'll use that inch elm over there fer the sides and ends," he said; "plane them and saw out the side shapes, Abey. I'll sort out some stuff fer the bottom frame."

We set to, and within a few days the body of the little dogcart stood waiting for the ironwork to arrive. Ben's skill as a wheelwright had been developed on the heavy farm wheels sometimes three or four inches wide. This small cart required a much finer job altogether and so he took his time over making this first pair of dogcart wheels. He tended to leave everything thicker than was suggested in Mr Hardwick's drawing; nevertheless the finished wheels were a credit to him and were much admired by the men in the shop. When completed, we took them round for shoeing and assisted Peter Brooks, who also was more used to heavier work.

The light cart body was carried out to the paint shop and given two coats of goldsize. The ironwork arrived and was duly fitted. Four more coats of goldsize were painted on with a rubbing down of pumice powder between each coat, then it was given three coats of varnish. The ironwork was painted a dark blue and when finally the dogcart stood finished, it was a proud Ben and myself who wheeled it outside ready for harnessing to Jiffy, the new pony Mr Hardwick had bought specially for it.

Mr Hardwick backed the pony between the newly-varnished shafts, passed the saddle chain over to me, coupled the draught reins and made ready for a test drive. He climbed aboard, shook the reins and Jiffy was away like his name, with his feet stepping high. They sped along the village, up the the green, down the lane over Froglies Bridge and up as far as Froglies Green, then all the way back again to the shop where all the men had turned out to watch.

"Well done, Ben. Well done, Abey!" called out Mr Hardwick. "It's a very nice job. A real treat to drive! Light and easy! Take her round the village, Ben." But Ben was already shaking his head. "Well, you take her, Abey. Go on, see for yourself!"

I was eager to try. "Come on Ben, let's give it a test!" I said.

Ben looked doubtful. "Well, I don't know," he murmured half-heartedly.

"Come on Ben," I urged. "Up you get."

Ben climbed up on the step with a hand from Mr Hardwick. "No, you drive, Abey!" he said, as I climbed up and handed him the reins.

As he refused, I took them up and the lively pony needed no encouragement to be off again. Round the village we sped, waving to Mrs Pickvance in her garden and Billy Bourton standing open-mouthed by the churchyard. Ben held on with one hand to the seat that he had fitted only a few days before and to his cap with the other.

"Steady now, young Abey!" he called out, "Slow down now!" as we approached the shop again.

Mr Hardwick was delighted with the dogcart and gave it yet another run, this time along the Remsditch road to Lonestock Turn and back. Later he had George Groom paint the words: A. Hardwick. Wheelwright, Carpenter and Undertaker, Nether Oldston, on both sides, then he set Jes and Albert Groom to build a lean-to shed from elm weather-boarding where the smart little cart was to be kept.

Jiffy, the pony, settled down quickly with Magnolia, after the first couple of days, during which he attempted to nip the big mare on her backside, if he could get close enough to do so. This ceased abruptly when the old mare landed one of her back hooves, like lightning, squarely on one of the pony's shoulders, sending him staggering away with a limp that lasted some time. This episode caused Mr Hardwick some concern and he even threatened Magnolia with extinction, but after this initial sorting-out the two creatures became inseparable. In the field there was seldom more than a yard or so between them, and they both protested loudly when one was taken away to work.

CHAPTER TWENTY THREE

War had been declared on Germany. The perceptive had seen it coming for years. Even the ostriches with heads firmly buried in sand were not really taken by surprise. Campaigns were launched to attract men into the fighting services. The talk was increasingly of beating the Germans. Young men flocked to join, many anxious that it should not be over before they could get there.

I wondered about going myself and mentioned it to Mr Hardwick, who did all he could to dissuade me. I set aside the idea for a while. The new young apprentice, Pip Horner, had arrived and this absorbed much of my attention. He was a shy young lad, fourteen years old, and although he was ignorant of most of the work required of him, he was keen to learn and quick to grasp. Mr Hardwick told him quite firmly that he was to take orders from me and that if he was not showing promise by the end of the month he would not be able to stay. For a while his presence was more of a hindrance to me than a help but as time went by the simple things like collecting eggs, feeding stock and cleaning out could be left to him. The care of the milkers and the milking itself took longer and indeed it would be some time before he would be able to handle the situation entirely by himself. Nevertheless, my time spent with the stock was much reduced and after a month or so when Mr hardwick sought my opinion of the new boy I said, "He's a good lad and works hard. I think he will do well."

"Good!" said Mr Hardwick, "Jes says the same. I'll keep him on, then. Now Abey, I've been telling Ben that I've got two orders for dogcarts. You and he can make them both together. I've ordered enough ironwork for six. My cart has been much admired all round. I think it's going to be popular. Ben is outside looking at the ash. Go and help him. He's going to sort out enough for six pairs of shafts."

After lunch Mr Hardwick told Ben and me to go over to a farm at Broughton Dagston to look at a waggon which had collapsed under a load. We left the work on the dogcarts and set off with Magnolia. At the farm we were shown the damaged vehicle by the farmer who told us that, when we were ready to go, there were some bags of potatoes to be taken to Mr Hardwick. We did not stay long as it was quite apparent that the waggon would need to be taken home for repairs. Part of the chassis had split and had allowed one of the back wheels to move out of alignment, causing difficulties in pulling straight. The farmer agreed to send it down to the shop next day, after being assured no further harm would be done if it was moved steadily.

"My daughter's in the house; she'll show you where the potatoes are," he said. We took Magnolia round to the farmhouse where we were shown a shed whence we collected the potatoes.

"My husband has gone to France," the young woman said; "only married six months and now he's gone fer a soldier. He was home last week fer three days. He says everyone's going – or will be before long. Do you think it will be over soon?" she asked Ben.

Ben was pulling a sack of potatoes onto his back; it was halfway across his shoulders, but he stopped, looking round at the young woman's anxious face. Her eyes were moist and her lip trembled as she waited in the vain hope that Ben might have some unlikely good news of the war coming to a quick end. Ben shook his head slowly and I stopped where I was for a moment to hear his reply. He made as if he were about to say something, then just shook his head again slowly. We went on loading the potatoes and the young woman turned and went into the farmhouse.

On the way back to the workshop Ben called over to me, sitting on the tailboard of the cart, "There's Archie Bowles' new bull!"

Over the hedge we could see a herd of shorthorns grazing. Near an oak tree on one side of the field stood a young bull, probably between two and three years old. Purchased recently by Farmer Bowles from a sale up north, to improve his stock, he already had a reputation for being a 'bit of a sod' with villagers who had to run for the gate when crossing the corner of the field in which he was grazing. The bull was a fine looking animal, deep-chested, with massive front legs and a huge wide head set well onto a massively thick neck. His horns were well balanced in size, although one turned slightly down, giving him something of a Henry the Eighth look. He liked to rub his head on the tree under which he was now standing. He would slowly force first one horn hard under the oak bark, then when he had gored and broken well into its surface he would hook it out sideways making the tough bark fly out and splinter, and then he would repeat the process with the other horn. The muscles rippling in his neck and the powerful thrust of his shoulders would be an awesome sight for anyone unfortunate enough to be near him when he was roused. The red eyes, showing their whites, could look angry as his head went lower and the deep, heavily breathed, low sonorous roar resonated across the fields, in expression of his dreadful exertion.

"Won't do that oak much good," I called and Ben nodded.

When we reached the shop, Ben went back to his work inside while I took the potatoes on to Mr Hardwick's house. Henry saw me coming from his position in the front window and pointed and winked at me. Gwen Hardwick gave me a cup of tea and left me to talk to Henry while she went to the shop. Magnolia waited patiently outside, resting first one leg and then another.

Very few motor-cars were seen at this time in Nether Oldston. Mr Purton-Hentis owned a 'horseless carriage' but seldom used it. When he did, he chose a good fine day and usually went to visit friends in it, avoiding any trip which demanded reliability. Although, for its time, it was a good machine, and the groom who looked after it was devoted to it, the older method of travelling by horse and carriage was, at any rate in his mind, more reliable.

However, on this occasion, as I drank my tea and stood by Henry looking out of the window, the Purton-Hentis motor-car could be seen approaching. Magnolia was not a nervous or highly-strung creature although such a noise as the car made was an unusual one in the world in which she dwelt. Her ears strained at various angles from the moment its first sounds were heard. Her head and neck were held questioningly as if to ask if she had heard correctly. Eventually the machine went slowly past, by which time I had reached her bridle and was explaining that the commotion was purely momentary and that such sights as this were something for today's 'up-to-the-minute' horse to be getting used to.

On the front seat next to the driver sat Charlotte Purton-Hentis, who was trying to discover how one drove the thing. Whether Mrs Purton-Hentis knew that her daughter was out riding in this fashion was doubtful. As they passed, Charlotte smiled at me standing by Magnolia's head, and I admired the smooth running of Nether Oldston's first motor-car with its beautifully polished brass and spotless paintwork. I smiled back at Charlotte, then as the machine disappeared I saw Gwen Hardwick coming back from the shop.

"Thanks for the tea, Mrs Hardwick. I'll get back now," I said, and turned the horse and cart round.

Back in the workshop Pip was waiting to see me. "I need some more hay, but I can't find the hay-knife anywhere," he told me.

"Oh yes. I brought it inside to give it a good sharpen. There was a hollow developing in the blade so I put it on the grindstone. It's all right now. Keep it sharp. The stone's in the side of the rick." Pip took the big knife and carried it up the ladder to where the rick had been previously cut into great square steps. The sharpened knife cut beautifully with each thrust. The compressed, light golden fibres crunched deliciously as the boy drove the steel hard down into them. Fodder for the beasts was carried down the ladder with a pitchfork on his shoulder.

The iron work for the new dogcarts arrived and prompted Mr Hardwick to press Ben to get on with their construction.

"We ain't 'ad no time, Albert," Ben said slowly, without looking up from under the waggon where he was working, "We've been at these repairs ever since you said about them."

"All right, but soon as you've finished that waggon, you can get straight on with them. Abey's going up to Halfroot with young Pip to take those racks and troughs, now that Horace has finished them. Soon as he comes back he's going to be with you until those two carts are finished." I heard what he said from where I was grinding the cutting iron from a spokeshave.

"Go straight away, Abey," he went on, calling across to me; "have a look at the gateway on the left before you turn into the farm. Measure up for a new gate and see what the posts are like. He wants a new one making. If you make a note of what's needed, Jes can get on with it while you help Ben. Let young Pip harness and drive Magnolia. Don't let him go too fast, but I want him to be able to take the horse and cart himself as soon as possible. You must be at the waggon end more now."

At Halfroot Farm much activity was in evidence. As Magnolia turned into the gateway and Pip reined her to a halt, a farm man standing nearby came over to warn that some young cattle were coming out.

"Hold Magnolia, Pip, until they have gone past," I said. "I'll go over and measure that gateway." On my return I met the cattle coming out. Just beyond where Magnolia stood, Pearson Grantle was talking to his foreman.

Pip called to me, "These mangers are to go over in that end barn." While we unloaded, two more lots of cattle were driven past us. The yard was splattered with cow muck as was our cart.

"Lot of moving about!" I called to one of the drovers.

He nodded. "Most of 'em are new stock. We're sortin' 'em out and checking for lice." Men with shovels began clearing up after the last of the cattle had gone, and Mr Grantle came across to where we were unloading.

"Good morning, Abraham. One of the surrounds has been broken off from my dining-room fireplace," he said. "It's been gone so long nobody remembers it. I've mentioned it to Mr Hardwick but he says he's too busy to do anything about it now. He did tell me you were doing some carving these days and that you might like to have a go at it after work sometime."

I banged up the tailboard and dropped the pins in. "Well, I don't know whether I've done enough to take on anything like that," I said. It was true that I'd been trying my hand at some carving, but I was not aware that Mr Hardwick had seen any of my work for it was in the evenings when I had gone in to help Horace that I had begun to use the carving tools that I had bought at the sale all that time ago.

"Come and have a look at it," said Mr Grantle.

I called to Pip, "Roll the ropes up and get the cart over to the gate. I'll be back by the time you get there!"

In the house two huge pointers met us with overwhelming delight, standing on their hind legs and trying to lick my face.

"Get down, Gerald! Get down, Borneo!" was shouted at them at least six times before we could make our way along to the dining-room and shut the dogs out. The fireplace was a big open hearth with a fire-basket. On one side under the oak mantlepiece was a heavy slab of oak fixed flat against the wall and carved with figures in a harvest scene. It had been done by some earlier craftsman in a good bold open way much like the sort of carving that can be found on the ends of early church pews. With the passing of time, regular polishing and dusting had produced a beautiful colour with the high parts of the relief carving reflecting a dull patina. We stood looking at it for a few moments until Pearson Grantle asked me what I thought.

"Well," I answered slowly, "I'd quite like to try something. I'll think about it for a little while, and draw out my ideas. Do you want to depict anything special?"

"Something to do with the farm, perhaps. Whatever you like really," he said.

I quickly ran the rule over the area. "I'll come and show you when I have done some sketches," I said, "but I must go now or young Pip will be waiting."

As we left the room and walked towards the door a young woman came out of another doorway and almost collided with us. I recognised her immediately as she exclaimed "My goodness! It's the white-faced demon from the roadside!" Although over three years had passed since that day when I was walking towards Nether Oldston with my big cases, Mr Purton-Hentis' sister Daphne had evidently not forgotten the incident when her horse had been frightened by a boy resting in the grass. Nor had I forgotten her forthright language. She lived up north somewhere and only visited her brother occasionally.

I had turned bright red at her exclamation and said somewhat faintly, "Oh, er good morning, ma'am," and made my escape as fast as I could.

CHAPTER TWENTY FOUR

The following spring, a poacher was shot dead in the woods near the village. One of the estate's gamekeepers found his body during his early morning rounds, and later a man was charged with the shooting. Apparently both men were army deserters and were living rough in the neighbourhood. In an effort to obtain food there had been an accident and one of them had been shot. Such news caused a great stir in the village. It also forced the reality of what it meant to be a soldier, upon the quiet community. The war was well into its second year now and news had come recently of two local men who had been killed. One of Will Auger's boys was missing and a nephew of Miss Betts' was a prisoner-of-war. I felt more and more that I should join up. Pip could manage the milking and stock now, and workshops all over the country were managing to run short-handed. More and more young men were going. One of my brothers had joined the navy and Perce Chennel had gone into the army last week. But I knew that Mr Hardwick would try to dissuade me if I mentioned it again.

Two more dogcarts had been completed and Ben and I were making two more. After work, with the lighter evenings, I had started carving the oak for the fireplace at Halfroot Farm and was able to give Horace a hand with turning the lathe for his chairs. One fine morning, after an early frost had cleared, leaving a dazzling blue sky and straight columns of wood smoke from the village hearths, Mr Hardwick told me to take one of the dogcarts to a customer at Lonestock.

"Pip will follow you with the cart. There are some fencing posts to collect from Hawtin's and you can come back with him. Go straight after dinner."

While we were pulling up the joints on the next dogcart frame, I mentioned to Ben about going to the war. Ben as usual said nothing for some time after I had told him what was in my mind, then, as he stropped a wide firmer chisel on the palm of his hand, he said slowly, "I know how you feel, lad. 'Tis a big decision fer a responsible young man. 'Tis only you as can decide, but a man 'as to do what 'as ter be done." Then after another long pause, "'Tis a 'ard life in the army and if you goes you'll never be the same man as before. It will do in six months what this 'ere village won't do to yer in sixty years!" He said no more about it and we went on with our careful woodworking, sending the ash chippings and shavings steadily onto the floor, but I felt he was glad I had mentioned it to him.

Later, when the men finished their dinner Pip went out to harness Magnolia and I fetched Jiffy in from the field to put her in the new dogcart. I called to Pip that I would meet him at Hawtin's yard, then after wiping my boots clean, climbed into the little vehicle with its still strong smell of new varnish. Jiffy sped away and as we left the village we passed Sally Pullen with her small son in a perambulator. She waved as I went past. Up the hill went the high-trotting pony, making the new springs bounce joyfully over the rough road while I looked over the budding hedges at the faintly green haze now appearing on the oak trees. There on the road to Lonestock on that beautiful afternoon, war seemed very far away, in fact totally unreal. It was strange that my thoughts still turned towards it and what I should be doing about it.

In Lonestock I drove to the quiet house of the local innkeeper, whose wife would be using the dogcart for going to Remsditch and back. They came out to admire their new acquisition and told me they would give it a good test later, before coming to settle up with Mr Hardwick, probably the next day. I helped put the cart in a building round the back, then bidding them good-day, I set off, leading Jiffy along the road to Hawtin's yard. Magnolia had taken longer than Jiffy to reach Lonestock but Pip had already taken the cart into the yard and was loading the fencing posts, when I joined him.

Tapper Chalk, who was helping to load the posts, called to me as I approached, "Tie that pony over by the barn. Look, there's a ring over by that there water-butt. That's it! He'll be all right there until we've done." Magnolia and Jiffy exchanged noisy greetings as if they had been parted for a number of years and I joined in the loading of the cart. There were only three dozen posts to collect so with the tailboard down on its chains they stacked neatly together, overhanging the back.

"I thought you might be gone fer a soldier when I seed this 'ere lad with the cart," said Tapper; "they be startin' to call up young fellas now, ain't they? Young Sanders along 'ere went last week. 'E volunteered though. Gone in the Gunners, they say." I nodded, and threw the rope across to Pip on the other side of the cart to tie to one side of the tailboard. Pulling it tightly, I wound it round the overhanging posts, then lashed it to the cart. Tapper Chalk pulled out his pipe and tobacco pouch. After slowly filling the pipe he returned the pouch to his pocket, put the pipe in his mouth and felt about in another pocket for the matches.

"I expect Albert will miss you when you goes," he said through clamped teeth; "the paper says the war is likely to go on fer a while yet. I did 'ear that the Germans be movin' forward again and that our generals be all in the wrong places! That's what I 'eard but no one's supposed to know." Pip and I looked across at each other behind the cart as Tapper disappeared in a cloud of blue smoke from which he could be heard coughing.

I fetched Jiffy and tied him with a long rope to the tailboard, then called to Pip to pull out onto the road. Tapper's smoke cloud cleared as we moved towards the gate. We called goodbye to him when we climbed up on the cart after closing the gate, but he was already enveloped in a new cloud of smoke.

"What ever does he smoke in that pipe?" asked Pip.

"Damp sawdust, I should imagine," I answered, looking far away over the fields. "Better walk down when we get to the hill," I said a little later.

When we were approaching Nether Oldston, sitting up on the load of posts, we could see over the hedges. Looking across the field we were passing, I caught sight of Sally Pullen sitting over on a tree stump near a piece of thicket. She had left her perambulator and walked across to sit in the sun while she fed her child. Then to my horror I saw Archie Bowles' bull. It was not a hundred yards away from her on the other side of the thicket. Until that moment both the bull and Sally had been unaware of each other and Sally still showed no concern. However, the bull's head was up and sniffing the air. He had heard the young child's cry and was slowly moving towards the sound.

"Look, Pip!" I shouted, pointing across the field. "Open

that gate while I throw off some of these posts!" I wrenched the rope off one side of the tailboard as Pip jumped off. Quickly I released the rope on Jiffy, who started to graze by the roadside. I hurled the posts off onto the grass, then as Pip opened the gate I drove at some speed through the gateway. Pip jumped on the cart as it passed. We left the gate open and headed towards the spot where Sally still sat unconcernedly feeding the baby. The bull, which had been steadily heading towards her round the clump of trees, now stopped when he heard the rumble of the cart.

I stood up like a chariot driver on the front board, urging Magnolia who was trotting powerfully and heavily, to cut between the bull and the stump where Sally sat. The bull's nostrils dilated and he pawed the ground, sending up pieces of turf, as if to beat out a furious demand to know what was going on in his field. Sally heard the bull bellow and the rumble of the cart. She appeared round the edge of the thicket. Her eyes widened in terror as she saw the bull. He bellowed again, his powerful, huge frame a single throbbing mass of energy, then with a snort, he put his head down and charged. Sally clasped her baby and stood frozen. I urged my steed on. Magnolia never hesitated for a second. She thundered on, cutting across the path of the bull who charged as if he would go right through us. Seconds before he would have hit us he suddenly swerved to the side, his head turning alongside the cart. We heard his enraged breathing as he turned to run parallel with us, his thick, slightly down-turned horn within inches of the cart. Pip's face was white as he hung on tightly. I pulled Magnolia hard round in a circle to cut off the bull from Sally who had now run back to the trees. The frustrated and infuriated bull now circled the other way, trying to get round the cart. Suddenly he stopped, bellowed loudly, then snorting furously he watched from his red-rimmed eyes as the cart swung round to the thicket.

As Sally moved towards the cart the bull began running towards her. "Wait! Sally!" I yelled.

"Take the baby!" she screamed. Pip leant over and grabbed the child from her arms as she held him up. The bull was almost upon us, his head well down and obviously bent on attacking the cart. Sally ran back between the sparsely growing trees and hid behind one of them. I flicked the reins and called to Magnolia who was well aware of the need to move. The cart jerked violently forward, nearly throwing me over backwards while Pip, who now sat on the floorboards with Sally's baby held tightly in his arms, slid from one end of the cart to the other.

This time the bull made contact with us, his great head butting against the turning wheel. He was blind with rage now and ready to charge anything. Hoping his attention had been diverted from Sally, I drove the cart a little further and stopped. The bull, not liking the wrench his head had received on impact with the turning wheel, stood for a moment watching us. He raised and lowered his head a few times then began running towards us again. I waited a few seconds, then urged Magnoloa on until she was galloping hard with the bull chasing behind. Across the field we went until the bull had to stop. His great weight and bad temper began to tire him. He slowed down and stopped behind us, then, as if his slow-thinking brain began to remember something, he turned round and slowly walked back towards where Sally was waiting.

I turned the cart round again. Magnolia was blowing quite hard by now. She was not used to such violent movement especially after going up and down Lonestock Hill, but she seemed to know what was required and thundered past the bull who was steadily walking towards the thicket.

I shouted with all my might to Sally, "Come out now Sally, quickly! We're picking you up!"

She emerged from the trees as the cart neared. The bull also began running again. At the sight of Sally his head went down and his speed increased as he gave a blood-curdling bellow. I pulled hard on the reins to stop Magnolia, as we reached the white-faced girl. Her legs could hardly bear her as she watched, petrified, while the enormous bull bore down upon her. So terrified was she now that I had to let go of the reins as Pip was still clutching the baby. I literally hauled her over the side and she landed hard on the bottom of the cart next to Pip. Magnolia needed no instruction. She started off again just as the bull, angered again by his prey's sudden departure, drove his horns into the side of the cart, splintering it badly and just missing the rear end of the mare, as she pulled forward. The deep-throated roar of the disappointed bull and the dreadful neck and body, only the thickness of the cart-side away from us, was indeed terrifying.

Seizing the reins again I headed Magnolia for the gate. The bull, still not ready to give up, followed slowing slightly, and blowing hard. Pip thrust the baby into Sally's arms and hung out over the tailboard. As we crashed and swayed through the bumpy, rutted gateway he sprang down, grabbed the gate and dragged it shut as the bull lumbered up, snorting and pawing at the ground behind the oak bars.

"Thank God!" Pip said as he sank down on his hands and knees, the relief of being safe again leaving him weak and shivering. Sally was crying and I found my teeth chattering as I jumped down on trembling legs to calm Magnolia, who with wide nostrils quivering, was trembling and champing her bit with excitement.

"Well done, old girl!" I said, patting and stroking her neck. "Come on Pip, get Magnolia out of the cart and walk her up the road and back. She needs calming down and she might get a chill if we let her stand here!" Pip started to unbuckle the harness.

I helped Sally out of the cart and she sat on the grass weeping and hugging her baby. She could hardly speak but managed to say, "You saved us, Abey! Thank God you came!"

I put my arm round her. "Come on now, Sally. Let's get you home where you can get a good strong cup of tea."

Pip walked Magnolia up the road a little way and back again, and we hitched her back in the cart. "We'll take Sally home first, Pip, and then come back for these posts and Jiffy," I said.

We tied Jiffy to a piece of fencing across the road and after putting the push-chair in the cart we all climbed up to ride the short distance to the Pullen's house, where Sally again burst into tears as the fearful episode was related to her mother.

We returned for the load of posts and to collect Jiffy who was still grazing the grass verge, having taken no interest in the dramatic events over the hedge in which his bosom companion had played so heroic a part. Through the gate which had slammed such a short while ago to end that drama, we could see the bull quietly grazing not far away. He did not even look up as we leaned on the gate and relived those heart-stopping moments when his powerful thick neck and heavy horned head, now swaying quite gently over the grazed grass, was so near to tearing little Sally Pullen to pieces.

"We were lucky, Pip!" I said.

"We certainly were," he answered, "and Sally Pullen more so. If we'd taken three or four minutes more to do anything up at Lonestock there wouldn't be much of her or her baby now." We both stood looking at our adversary for another half-minute then quickly reloaded the cart, tied Jiffy behind again and continued our way to the village. "Mr Hardwick won't be pleased with the damage to the cart, that's for sure," I said, as we unloaded the posts and stacked them by the barn.

We rubbed Magnolia down with some old sacking. She was none the worse for her experience but I knew the danger I had subjected her to, for the bull would have driven his horns into her just as readily as into the cart during the attack. Gratefully I led her into the stable and whilst praising and fussing over her, I emptied a very large bowl of rolled oats and maize into her manger. She snuffled her big soft nostrils gently with pleasure, and plunged them into the fodder, blowing away husk and dust as she crunched steadily into the delicious, special treat.

CHAPTER TWENTY FIVE

"I don't expect to have my cart damaged when you are out with it, young Abey," said Mr Hardwick later, when I related briefly what had taken place on the return from Lonestock. As we walked round inspecting the damaged cart, Pip followed us.

"You can get on, Pip," he added impatiently; "see what Jes needs if you've done out here. It doesn't need three of us to be wasting our time looking at what you and Abey have managed to do to the cart I trusted you with!"

The cart was not structurally damaged but where the bull's horn had dug into the side, just behind the place where the shafts entered the body of the cart, it was quite badly splintered. The wheel, too, where his head and one horn had caught it, was marked on two spokes and part of the rim.

"I don't think it's badly damaged," I said, as Mr Hardwick stood looking at it.

"I'm quite able to judge that for myself," he replied testily; then after walking round it again, added, "Do you expect me to send a cart out like that? What sort of advertisement for a wheelwright would that be? Get it out right straight away, and I don't want it just patched up. When I look at it again I don't want to be able to tell where you've repaired it! And what's more, I don't expect you to play the part of a hero when you're out on my work, nor to set a bad example in front of young Pip!"

"But surely you wouldn't have had me leave a person to their death to save a few minutes of your time and protect your cart!" I blurted out angrily. "I did what you yourself would have done, and heaven knows what sort of example it would have been for Pip if I had told him to drive on past!"

Mr Hardwick knew I was right, but of course he did not like being spoken to like that by me.

"I don't expect talk like that from you, Abraham Staughton, but no doubt you're upset over what's happened. We'll say no more about it now." He walked away, leaving me glaring after him and muttering about a few old scratches on a cart not being so important.

One fine evening when I had at last managed to get round to fixing the oak panel I had carved for Halfroot Farm, and was standing back from it to judge the effect of the work now that it was in place, the door opened and Charlotte Purton-Hentis came in.

"Hello, Abraham. I have come up with my aunt to ride the horses but heard that you were here so I came to see what you are doing."

"Oh," I began, rather taken with surprise," I'm just fixing up a piece of carving."

"Did you carve that?" asked Charlotte, going closer to the new oak panel.

"Yes, it's supposed to be showing reapers in the fields."

"How did you learn to carve like that? It's lovely. I wonder if you could teach me to carve? I would so like to try."

"I don't think I've done enough to teach anyone else," I replied; "but really it's mostly a matter of having the right tools and getting on with it."

"What are you going to carve next?" asked Charlotte.

"Why, nothing. There's nothing else to be done."

"You must do something. It's something to develop that sort of skill. I'll see if Daddy would like something carved."

"It's not something I do much of," I said.

"Charlotte!" called a voice outside the door, "Charlotte, where are you?"

Charlotte opened the door, "I'm here, Aunt. I'm coming Goodbye Abraham." She was gone, and a little while after I saw her on horseback, accompanying her aunt Daphne as they went past the house.

The next evening, after the men had all gone except for Jes who was finishing off a coffin and Mr Hardwick who was in his office, I went out to give Pip a hand at finishing the milking.

"You're late tonight," I said.

"Yes, I was late starting and Teasel had caught her udder on some brambles in the field. As she's a bit sore she took longer to milk." We finished off together, then loaded the cow dung in the barrow and got the fodder for next morning.

"Have you got something on your mind, Abey?" Pip asked me.

"How do you mean?"
"Well, you seem sort of far away sometimes. I thought you might be thinking about something else."
I looked across at him. "I'm thinking of joining up," I said.
"I guessed you might be," said Pip, "I shall as soon as I am old enough."
"I feel I should," I said, looking out through the cowshed door; "it's just that," I hesitated then went on, "well, I don't know really, what to do."
"I would quite like to go," said Pip. "Get away from here and see something of life and the world. I expect it will be all finished before I get there!"
"I wonder what life and the world are really like," I said quietly, still looking out through the door.
"More exciting than this, that's for sure!" Pip replied, brushing the cowshed floor, energetically.
"You could be right," I said, putting away my shovel.
Later that night when I lay in bed listening to my window rattling very slightly in the westerly breeze I stared up at the dark ceiling of my room for a long time before turning over and saying again before I went to sleep, "You could be right, Pip . . ."

CHAPTER TWENTY SIX

Roderick Walker shook Chaucer's reins and drove him at a fast trot as we left Remsditch. He had been to collect supplies for the shop and had picked me up in the town.

"I've got to report next Wednesday," he said; "funny to think I won't be doing this any more for a long time. They say they cut all your hair off as soon as you arrive. I'm glad it's not winter!"

"I wonder where they'll send you," I said, then after a little while, "Do you think you will be able to kill people, Roderick?"

"Kill people?" he said, turning round and looking as if such a thought had never entered his head.

The cart wheels rumbled over a bad piece of road surface and drowned our conversation for a few moments. "I thought that's what it's all about," I answered eventually.

"Well, yes, I know, but, well, it's not just that, is it?"

"No, I dare say it isn't," I said.

He looked at me again. "You said you were going soon. You won't be going just to kill people will you?" he asked.

"No, but it's a fact that that is the main outcome. I know the overall cause is liberty and the defence of right. One needs to defend one's country and what one believes in, of course. It's just I don't know what it will be like to send into eternity, other mothers' sons."

We both stared out at the passing hedgerows without seeing them. Chaucer's quick hooves pounded the road and the cartwheels rumbled on, leaving Remsditch quickly behind. On both sides of the road hay was lying cut and awaiting the sun's pleasure. The scent of the drying grass drifted unnoticed to our nostrils as our thoughts dwelt on the far off battlefields which the reports of newspapers and gossip conjured up in our minds.

As we swayed about between the fast-turning, locally-made wooden wheels, the birdsong, Chaucer's rippling black back, grazing cattle and sheep dotted far over the fields, and Nether Oldston church tower ahead with the flag of St George flying above it, made the reality of carnage and terror, of fighting and dying, quite impossible to envisage. But without glory and hope, without visions and dreams, the security and peace of the countryside that we valued would never have been established. It was still these ever-present qualities, strong in the breasts of youth, that steadily called Roderick and me to leave our business and go to defend our country.

A flock of sheep blocked the road as we approached the village. Greg Mottram was driving them; he waved as Chaucer picked his way through the sea of white wool and between the bleating creatures as they darted unpredictably round his legs.

When I jumped down from the cart outside the workshop I called to Roderick that I was going haymaking that evening if the weather kept fine. He nodded and with a flick of the reins, Chaucer was away.

Horace was ill with severe bronchitis and Mr Hardwick was working on his bench. Pip was helping him and I was working beneath a heavy hay waggon with Ben. We jacked it up at the front to take the weight off the worn turning-circle which was binding so badly that it was impossible to turn the waggon. The shop was very full of repairs and carts and waggons were waiting outside for attention. As usual, most of these had stood at their various farms through the winter months, until they were needed again, just when there was so much other work urgently required.

Mrs Green was doing most of the milking and stock work for a few days to release Pip for other jobs. While work continued on the waiting waggons, the sun came out from behind the clouds to stream in through the wide-open doors, giving colour and sparkle to tools, timber and even the dust. The carrier's cart stopped outside with some more metal pieces for the next dogcarts. A few words about the weather and he was away again. Men appeared regularly to take away repaired waggons and carts, as they were finished. Albert Lane came along to request some help with the hay, and Mr Hardwick reluctantly said he would spare two men, both from the wood end of the workshop.

In the evening I met Roderick up at the farm where we finished our day pitching the warm, sweet hay onto one waggon after another. Horses that had been working all day still continued until dark, when rick and waggon-sheets were fixed securely down to wooden pegs; then after some cider-drinking all the men went home.

Quiet was the night sky over Nether Oldston as I lay tired but wide awake in Mrs Pickvance's house; quiet and warm, silent and still. In winter when one came indoors the outside world was shut out but in midsummer the inside and outside were not separated. There was no beginning of one and end of the other. Through the wide-flung window I could see the clear wide sky. I got out of bed and leaned out of the window. There was the view of the village that I had looked at on my first night in that room, not changed at all since that first early-spring when I had arrived and the following summer when I had fallen asleep after haymaking, in the field with Sally Pullen.

How many miles east would one need to travel before hearing the guns in France, I wondered. But what was that? The cows from Crosswood Farm were out on the road. I could see them just emerging round one side of the green from Tiptoe Lane. I put on my trousers and called to Mrs Pickvance as I went. Eva followed me in delight as I ran out. Taking my bicycle I pedalled hard to Will Auger's house and threw a handful of gravel at his bedroom window.

"I'm coming!" I heard him shout as the window opened.

The cows had strayed from their gate and were mostly round the ricks in the farmyard, licking and poking about round the waggons. One young milker seemed to have drunk a bucket of old gear oil but with very little trouble they were turned when Will and I approached, and walked back into their field.

"Thanks Abey," said Will, as he fixed the gate securely; "that would be young Robin's doing. He put them in last night. I've told him he must always check the gate. You might as well talk out of your backside." I whistled for Eva, who came with a noseful of thistles from down by the dark stream. A dog only gets there in the night season when fortune smiles and presents it with such irresistible opportunity.

I was sorting ash out in the timber yard with Ben, for the making of a new turning-frame for the big waggon standing in the shop. It had been worn so badly that a new one was to be made. Some of the finest ash was required for this work. Great boards, four inches thick, were turned over and scrutinised. Templates were laid on the surfaces so that waste was reduced to a minimum while the pieces themselves were adapted to the grain formation for maximum strength. Such boards had spent at least six years standing open to the drying winds and various temperatures. They had been part of the scene at Nether Oldston long before I had left home to come here as an apprentice. I glanced at the ash in another pile that I had looked at with Mr Hardwick last winter. Already covered with dust and neatly stacked with half-inch stickers carefully placed between each board, it waited quietly for the years to pass until it would at last be selected for good waggon work.

"Good bit of stuff, this," said Ben through his moustache. I nodded. "Came from over near Jailer's Barrow. We fetched it one Christmas Eve when the ground was solid with frost. That same Christmas was when Harry Teemer's boy was born." Frank Teemer was now at the village school and I knew he must be all of ten years old.

"Should be dry, then," I said, as we edged one big piece slowly round, to get it onto trestles for sawing.

"Oh ah," breathed Ben, at length, "'tis dry all right."

Mr Hardwick appeared. "You'll have to leave that and go up to Halfroot, both of you. They've a waggon gone in the ditch. They say they've unloaded it. Take Magnolia and get it out and see what's broken. Sounds like one wheel at least has gone. Get back as quickly as you can."

In the shop, when we went to collect our tools and tackle, Mr Hardwick was taking George Groom to task. "There's no call for mending a broken tailboard," he was saying; "leave it and see to one of those hay carts out the front."

"But I told old Joe I'd do it this morning," George began to explain.

"You've no business doing so, George. You know how much there is that's pressing. A tailboard can wait till the hay's finished."

"I've nearly done it," persisted George.

At Hardwick's order to "Leave it!" George threw down with a clatter a big hammer he was using to drive a bolt through the ironwork on the tailboard. He had told Joe Rawlins from Broughton Dagston he would do it straight away and Joe had promised him a bottle of his home made wine. He walked slowly out of the workshop.

Along the village Mrs Broughton was talking to Fitsy Bluebottle. As we passed in the cart, old Ben remarked mostly to himself under his moustache, as he nodded to them, how wonderful it was that certain folk never seemed to run out of things to say. I stopped the cart at the shop to tell Roderick I might not be back at dinner-time to meet him in the Barley Mow.

There was no one about at Halfroot Farm when we reached there except for the housekeeper, a Mrs Jennings. She told us where to find the damaged waggon so we proceeded through the rick-yard to look for it. The waggon had been turned too sharply over an old culvert and the back wheel had cut across the corner, causing the culvert to collapse. The driver had seen what was happening and stopped. The waggon had rolled backwards and tipped sideways into the ditch where the heavy weight of the load had broken the wheel, leaving the waggon pitched half over in the ditch.

"That would be Jim Parsons," said Ben; "he's always in a hurry."

"We won't get that out with Magnolia," I said, looking down to where the wheel had collapsed. "If you get the ropes on, Ben, I'll go and fetch another horse from over there, where they are working."

"Ah, right you are. We'll 'ave t'pull 'er out sideways afore we can get that wheel off."

Three fields away I found the men loading hay. They argued about which horse should go, but in the end a big mare called Delilah was released on the strict understanding that she was to be back within half an hour. I led her round the fields back to where Ben was waiting. With the ropes attached to the waggon, I led the two horses carefully forward as they pulled it sideways up to the firm ground, where we could examine it. The back wheel was badly broken and would need to be replaced, but nothing else seemed to have been affected.

"Better take their horse back, Abey, and I'll be gettin' the wheel off," said Ben, after we had pulled the waggon out of the way and jacked up the axle.

When I returned the horse and they were backing her into the shafts again, one man turned to me and said, "Not in the army yet then?" Another told me that Sammy Blofield had gone to France.

As I went back across the fields to Ben I stopped for a minute to look across the slightly shimmering view of the countryside. There lay a typical piece of England. Two starlings squabbled near me for a moment then all fell silent. I could just hear the faint clack clacking of a distant elevator where a rick must have been being built in a field some way off, down the valley from where I stood.

Cattle stood close together under a hovel, not far from me, their tails and heads ever battling with the flies. The sky was pale blue with cotton-wool specks high up. I was looking towards the east. France lay further over. Perhaps those specks of cloud were what gunshot looked like. I stepped on a twig but did not hear it crack. The scene faded from my eyes altogether, although I continued looking. I saw my mother's kitchen at home. The two dogs, Rip and Curate, were lying by her as she stood mixing at the table. She was wondering what I was doing. Rip stood up and went to lie near the door . . . then I heard Ben hammering by the waggon across the next field, and started walking quickly in that direction.

"Sammy's gone to France," I told him.

"What?" He paused a second in the work of driving off the big wheelstock. "Oh ah," he added, nodding, then continued with his work.

Before we had finished loading the broken wheel two young lads came past, over the culvert. They walked aimlessly and beat at the growing vegetation by the side of the track with sticks cut from the hedge.

"Young varmints," said Ben; "they be playin' truant. Ask 'em why they b'aint at school, Abey." When I questioned them they looked surprised and lied convincingly about being sent out to find some wild flowers for their drawing class. Then they disappeared very quickly behind the hedgerow.

Back at the workshop the broken wheel was handed over to Harry Teemer while Ben and I went back to work on the ash turning frame.

"I expect you be a playin' on Sat'dy, Abey?" said Jes.

"Oh yes, Jes, but they tell me it's starting at three-thirty this time. You'll be opening bat I expect?"

"Yes, I'm opening with Will Auger. If the weather's good fer cricket it will be good fer 'aymakin'! I reckon the 'ay 'll be short-'anded."

When the big boards of ash had been selected and placed on the trestles, the laborious job of cutting out the pieces began. There were very few straight lines and so the sawing was mostly done with the big bow saw known as 'the Betty'. Ben took out his files and selected a triangular one to touch up the teeth on the long thin steel blade. I fetched another Betty from the wall in the shop and gave it to Ben to sharpen while I made a start with the first one. The secret of sawing consists of two things. One is to keep the saw razor-sharp so that all effort is turned into cutting, and not into friction caused through a blunt blade, and the other is thoroughly to accept the job as it is. Never hurry; saw steadily and enjoy feeling the kerf being cut as the teeth crunch deep and forward through the fibrous hardness while the scented sawdust streams out underneath.

When Ben started sawing his rhythm was slightly slower than mine. Gradually the shapes were cut out, true to the line and square to the face. Mr Hardwick wheeled Henry out from the workshop to sit under the shade of the barn to watch us. The dog from across the road followed them and settled down by Henry's feet. The hens squawked indignantly when the dog appeared but forgot him immediately he lay down.

The steady sawing droned on through the warm day, with the murmur of voices drifting from the open doors of the workshop, the quiet crooning of the hens, and an occasional swish of shavings when a piece of scented yellow pine curled long and spiralled to the craftsman's heavy leather boots beneath his bench. Man's spirit seemed for that brief spell no longer to strive with his Creator. The man who is physically fit and well-used to his task finds an exhilaration in his work. Provided that his mental attitude is peaceful, the act of sawing can be therapeutic as the regular movement links effort with result. So it was with me, and in my heart I felt a strange peacefulness for I knew the path I was about to take.

CHAPTER TWENTY SEVEN

The cricket match which took place that summer between Nether Oldston and Remsditch would have been, to a casual observer, more interesting than usual, although no casual observer was ever present at this annual event. The rules of the game had long ago been bent to allow for the peculiar social circumstances of the two teams. Every year it alternated between the two home grounds, and this year it was to be played at Nether Oldston. The vicar captained our team and organised the batting order which, when published, was criticised heavily in the darker corners of the Barley Mow although never openly disputed. An 'over' consisted of twelve balls so that time was not wasted walking about the field. This was so that the match might be played completely on a Saturday afternoon and evening. Nether Oldston were allowed fifteen men although only eleven could be fielded at once and only eleven could bat. This was to allow for the seasonal and stock work which had to be done during the match and also to compensate for the Remsditch team being drawn from a much greater selection of cricketers than the village team. A small marquee was hired for the day, by the committee. This was used to protect the refreshments from bad weather. Early on Saturday morning a large number of village women would arrive to start preparations. Bunker Cobham would have the two big coppers of water boiling when they arrived and would arrange his 'kitchen' and store for the continual supply of hot water and general help for the day. The previous evening, while the marquee was put up, the coppers and trestle tables were collected by cart from Oldston House. Bunker Cobham usually had two boys to help him; this year it was Nathan Brummer from Lonestock and Frank Teemer, who was a little young for the job but reliable.

The day dawned bright and clear, as crusty loaves, home-cured ham, local tomatoes and lettuce were converted into sandwiches. As each dish was filled it was placed with the others on the trestle tables and covered with a damp white cloth. Homemade cakes, buns and trifles were arranged; cups, glasses and tankards set out. The steam rose steadily whence Bunker Cobham bent over his little wood fires, poking the ash and instructing the boys in the art of field brick fires. The gentle scent of close-cut grass mingled with the smoke; the tent canvas warmed as the sun went higher and the butter got softer. The smell of spring onions and radishes tingled the noses of all who came near. Our senses became intoxicated with the delicate promises of the summer's day ahead, when friendships and competition would intertwine with old memories; a chance for the old folk to stand and stare; a chance for the simple pleasures of love-making and courting, and an opportunity for the still younger ones to fall about making eyes at each other.

The weather had never been known to stop the match. Once started, it was played on until finished through rain, wind or anything else. More than once had a thunderstorm descended upon the players, driving everyone else into the marquee or away home but the bowler, batsmen and fielders stood their ground, soaking and slipping in the mud as the heavy rain lashed upon them, completely obliterating one end of the pitch from the other for a few minutes.

This particular year, however, the weather looked very promising as the morning progressed, and a few benches were set out in front of the marquee. Tapper Chalk arrived on his bicycle from Lonestock to help Greg Mottram arrange the toilet facilities. Two canvas enclosures were erected with buckets placed inside. Two notices were hung up, one saying 'Ladies' and the other 'Men'.

At Hardwick's shop that morning the wheelwrights and carpenters were as usual busy at their several tasks, but a slight air of excitement hung over them as all the doors stood open back and front, and a sort of low whistle was gently breathed out of more than one mouth as saws, gauges and chisels and the multitude of various woodworking tools were manipulated deftly in strong capable hands. A fine new waggon stood, almost complete, just inside the front doors and Mr Hardwick nodded, smiled and occasionally banged the dust from his old hat on one of the benches as he walked round the shop checking on the various work being done.

The turning frame for the big waggon was progressing nicely and while Ben and I were working steadily on it Albert Lane came into the workshop to find Mr Hardwick. "Mornin'

Albert," they both said. "I'm desperate for men for the hay, Albert," said the farmer; "it's the last lot of that late second crop, and I don't want to risk losing it. There's talk of rain coming."

"Well," replied Mr Hardwick, "I don't know as I can help much today. We're very busy and there's the cricket match this afternoon."

"Folks pay more attention to that damn cricket than to anything else. I've been told that three-quarters of my hay crop is to go to France. How am I going to manage? Most of my men want to be at the cricket and here it is with the sun streaming down just right for that hay."

"Well, there it is Albert, my men will want to be there this afternoon. You can see if any of 'em will give you a hand if you like."

"Folks need to get their priorities right," went on Farmer Lane; "our men in France fighting for us here need that hay for their horses and we need it as fodder for our own stock too, yet they'll still go on with their important cricket match!" He went round the shop asking for help but no one would say for sure that they would come.

"Ah, maybe I'll get up there fer an hour or two, but there's the cricket, you see," was the reply from nearly every man.

As Albert Lane left the workshop I remembered how Sammy Blofield had surprised everyone a year ago on this same day when he turned up to help with hay making, and never went near the cricket match. Where was he now? I wondered. Somewhere in France. I thought of how he'd laughed on the day when I arrived in the village and Mrs Pickvance had smelt the cow muck on my coat, and again when he and I caught Perce Chennel and Jake Pooley out with our snow trap one winter.

While I was remembering these things, Mrs Hardwick came into the workshop and went across to her husband who was standing near us.

"Sammy Blofield's been killed in France," I heard her say.

CHAPTER TWENTY EIGHT

Crack! Will Auger drove his bat hard at the fast approaching ball and sent it hurtling for the boundary. A burst of clapping sounded round the field.

"Good old Will!" said a voice somewhere. The over ended and Jes faced the bowling again, then after a 'wide' he was clean bowled, having made two runs. He came back to where we waited to bat, mopping his brow and saying how hard the pitch was. When my turn came, Will Auger was still at the other end. I made seven runs and was caught. Mr Hardwick met me as I came off and asked me if I was going up to Lane's to help with the hay. I said I supposed I was, and after a quick half-pint of cider in the big tent, I set off leaving others to do the fielding. Pip, who had come to watch me bat, said he would come and make hay with me.

Farmer Lane was pleased to see us and we straightaway joined the loaders in the field. There was little talking. It was very hot and I had brought no drink with me. I gladly accepted a sip from one of the men's leathern bottles. Deep in thought, I toiled steadily through the hours into the late evening. Mrs Lane and Mrs Pullen brought out cider when we had finished.

That warm evening, after having heard the result of the cricket match and saying goodnight to everyone, I had a feeling of unreality as I washed and lay down uncomfortably upon the hot bed in my room.

Two days later I enlisted for the army, and was told to be ready in a fortnight. When I told Mr Hardwick he said "I knew it wouldn't be long. I don't know how we shall manage but I expect we shall."

None of the men mentioned it, except Ben, and yet I felt that they were all, almost imperceptibly, ready to nod and smile more readily. Ben said, slowly and seriously, as we raised the big new turning circle up into position under the jacked-up waggon, "Things won't be the same when you comes back, Abey."

I was straining hard under the weight of the circle, but after a minute I gasped, "How do you mean, Ben?"

Another minute passed. "Ah, you'll see. When you comes home after this 'ere war things will 'ave changed. T'will be all motors fer one thing."

After a longer spell during which the turning circle was secured and we were able to relax more I said, "When do you think that will be, then?"

Ben looked across at me and took out his snuff box. He tapped the lid and opened it. "When the powers that be, decide. 'Tis all nonsense as far as I can see. Greed and jealousy are the cause of wars just as they were the cause of the devil being thrown out of heaven."

Mr Hardwick came out to where we were working and said, "Hawtin from up at Lonestock and Soldier Grinstead have been arrested!" Ben and I looked at him in amazement. "Caught transporting stolen property," he said.

At first I could not believe it, then I suddenly thought of those great heavy boxes that Roderick and I had helped him move one night. "What sort of stolen stuff?" I asked.

"Mostly silver, I believe. It seems that Grinstead stored it until searching had cooled down, then Hawtin took it to someone who was getting it to Harwich and across the Channel. They caught him with it in his cart."

'That box', I thought, remembering the day I had arrived in Nether Oldston four years ago and had helped Mr Hawtin ro restack his load on top of a big wooden case. No wonder he had not been pleased with my persistent help! He must have been doing it for years.

"They've taken them both into Remsditch," Mr Hardwick told us. I thought of Maisie and Jenny and Mrs Hawtin and I wondered what they would do if he was sent to jail.

"Might 've guessed Soldier Grinstead was up to no good," said Ben.

"Ah maybe, but I'm surprised about Hawtin," answered Mr Hardwick.

Two days later I met Maisie in Daisy's shop. She walked out without a glance in my direction. I thought perhaps that she had been preoccupied and had not seen me but later, when I walked past Fitsy's cottage, I bumped into Jenny.

"Maisie says it was you who gave our Dad away. She says he told her you must have done. I'm glad you're going to the war, and I hope you don't come back!" She turned her back on me and marched away, leaving me open-mouthed, staring after her. I went back to Mrs Pickvance's feeling sick. Surely they could not really think I was responsible for their father's arrest? Not that he was innocent, but all that time ago, and even then, why should they imagine I knew what he was up to? It was shattering to feel so hated by those girls with whom I had been so friendly.

I told Mrs Pickvance what had happened and she said, "Take no notice, Abey. They're fools if they think that, and what's more he was caught doing a criminal act so it serves 'im right. I'd have told on him if I'd known!"

I spent my last day in Nether Oldston saying goodbye round the village. I avoided going up to Lonestock but when I called to see Fitsy she said, "I've told those girls not to be so soft in the head. I'm very cross with them for saying those things about you. I told them if their father was a fool there was no need for them to go soft in the 'ead as well!" I thanked her and she wished me well.

Mrs Pickvance shed a few tears and asked me to send her a letter sometimes. "Eva will miss you so much," she said, and I patted my faithful and devoted little companion who sat tightly against my legs as if she knew I would not be putting her to bed that night.

"I'll be back again soon, I expect," I said; "you tell Eva that every night, when you go to bed."

"I will Abey, and when I say my prayers every night I shall ask the Lord to keep you safe." She wiped her eyes on her apron, then, as I bent over her to give her a hug, she kissed me fondly and wept again.

Mr Hardwick shook my hand when we got out of the dogcart at the station. I was going home for two days before reporting for duty.

"Take care, Abey. We shall miss you. When it's over, you come back to us. I shall need you."

I waved out of the train window as it slowly started puffing out of Remsditch. Mr Hardwick struck his hat hard against his trousers and I saw the last cloud of sawdust I was to see for a long time disappear into the wind as he waved his battered old hat until I had gone.

GLOSSARY

Adze	Tool with curved steel blade. The cutting edge at right angles to the wooden handle
Auger	A tool for boring large holes in wood
Bruzz or Buzz	A three-cornered chisel for trimming out the corners of mortices in a wheelstock
Betty (Saw)	Large bowsaw used vertically
Chamfer	A bevel cut on the corner where two surfaces meet
Coulter	The vertical blade of a plough which cuts the soil vertically in front of the share
Cutting gauge	Adjustable gauge with small knife for working across grain
Faggots	Bundles of sticks
Felloe, fellie	Curved section of the rim of a wheel
Frow	Brittle
Firmer chisel	General purpose square-sided chisel
Headland	The unploughed land round the edge of a field
Hovel	Open-fronted farm building
Jack plane	General purpose plane
Kerf	The slot or cut made by a saw
Linch pin	Pin for keeping the wheel on the axle
Marking gauge	Adjustable gauge with one scribing point
Maul	Heavy, large wooden mallet
Mortice	A slot cut in wood into which a tenon or another piece of wood fits
Mortice gauge	Gauge with one fixed and one adjustable scribing point for marking out mortices and tenons
Moulding plane	Plane with shaped cutting irons to produce section-shaped lengths of timber

Rave	Frame or ladder fitted at both ends of a waggon for carrying harvest and haywork
Ripsaw	Woodsaw for cutting along or down the grain
Scotch glue	Made from animal skins, bones etc., and used hot
Scribing gouge	A curved cutting tool with its cutting bevel on the inside of the curve
Seed fiddle	A simple hand device for broadcasting seeds
Shafts (Cart)	The long shaped pieces of timber between which the horse is harnessed
Share	Ploughshare. The front, pointed replaceable part of a plough that enters the earth
Skid-pan	Thick cast-iron shoe which could be let down on a chain in front of a cart or waggon wheel to check speed when descending a hill
Smoother or smoothing plane	Short plane for cleaning up wood surfaces
Spokeshave	A two-handled tool with blade set in the middle for planing and shaping spokes and other shaped pieces of wood
Stock	Wheelstock. The centre or hub of a wheel
Tenon	The cut part of a joint that slots into a mortice
Try, trying or truing plane	Long plane, sometimes called a jointer, for truing wood surfaces